Praise for *Beautiful Addictions*

"Tristan is a hottie, tattooed man who loves to read. Does it get any better than that?!"
—*Girls with Books*

"I never expected this book to grab a piece of my heart and not let go! I am still going through each of the characters and reliving this book over and over in my mind. Season Vining has found a fan in me!"
—*StarAngels' Reviews*

"Unique, gritty, and heartbreaking . . . you will not be disappointed. It was a fabulous read that kept me on the edge of my seat, and left me in tears."
—*Alison J's Book Blog*

"Sure to get your pulse racing . . . one hell of a ride."
—*Just Romantic Suspense*

"Dark, twisted, and full of surprises. It's completely engrossing. This is a fantastic debut from Season Vining and I'm very much looking forward to what she comes up with next."
—*Sinfully Sexy Book Reviews*

"I loved the dark, intense tone and the suspenseful plot. It stands out in its uniqueness, and I applaud Season for doing something different."
—*Lily Bloom Books*

"Oh my gosh, oh my gosh! All I can say is oh my gosh!!! *Beautiful Addictions* blew me the hell away. This is a love story that will take your breath away."
—*Nichole's Sizzling Pages Reviews*

"An entertaining read in which the characters' development and the arc of the story are deftly blended to create a wonderful unity.

Without a doubt I will be scouring the shelves for more works by Season Vining." —*New Adult Addiction*

"Both sweet and sensual, a new adult romance with a backdrop of darkness and heartbreak."

—*The Window Seat on a Rainy Day*

"This book completely sucked me in. I can't wait to see what this author has in store for her next book." —*Swoon Worthy Books*

"An amazing debut novel. I'll be watching Season Vining closely from now on." —MCG *Reviews and Rants*

ALSO BY SEASON VINING

BEAUTIFUL ADDICTIONS

HELD *against* YOU

SEASON VINING

ST. MARTIN'S GRIFFIN ☙ NEW YORK

This is a work of fiction. All of the characters, organizations, and events portrayed in this novel are either products of the author's imagination or are used fictitiously.

 Printed in the United States of America. For information, address St. Martin's Press, 175 Fifth Avenue, New York, N.Y. 10010.

www.stmartins.com

Designed by Anna Gorovoy

Library of Congress Cataloging-in-Publication Data

Vining, Season.
Held against you / Season Vining. — First edition.
pages ; cm

ISBN 978-1-250-04879-0 (trade paperback)
ISBN 978-1-4668-4986-0 (e-book)
1. Bounty hunters—Fiction. 2. Fugitives from justice—Fiction.
3. Man-woman relationships—Fiction. I. Title.
PS3622.I57H45 2015
813'.6—dc23

2014036968

St. Martin's Griffin books may be purchased for educational, business, or promotional use. For information on bulk purchases, please contact the Macmillan Corporate and Premium Sales Department at 1-800-221-7945, extension 5442, or write to specialmarkets@macmillan.com.

First Edition: January 2015

10 9 8 7 6 5 4 3 2 1

FOR MY MOTHER,
WHO PUT A BOOK IN MY HANDS
AND TOLD ME THAT ANYTHING WAS POSSIBLE,
WHO SPENT HOURS AT THE LIBRARY WHILE I SEARCHED
FOR BOOK TWO IN THE BABY-SITTERS CLUB SERIES,
CLAUDIA AND THE PHANTOM PHONE CALLS,
AND WHO TRAINED ME IN THE WAYS OF
THE MULTITASKING READING NINJA.

ACKNOWLEDGMENTS

Thank you to my friends in the BR Writers' Workshop, for always providing honest feedback and for telling me when my characters need to shut the hell up. Thanks to all my BETA readers, especially Kayla, Bridget, and Vanessa, who helped shape this wild ride into one that was believable. A grateful nod to the ladies in the NBC, who answered super-hard polls on what they found most attractive in book boyfriends. As always, much love to my Fuckery Book Club. They are dear friends, confidants, and provide my will to move forward when I have none. Big smooches to my street team, Vining's Vixens, who keep their pimp hand strong.

Shout out to all the wonderful authors I met this year at RT in New Orleans and RWA in San Antonio. You guys are the inspiration to keep telling stories and remembering to have fun while doing it. Thanks to the whole team at St. Martin's, who have been supportive and have answered 497 questions from me in the past year. There is a place in literary heaven for each of you. A special *merci beaucoup* to Rose and Rachel, who have each taught me so much and continue to do so every day.

Finally, to those who grew up in violent homes. Please know that your past does not define who you are today. The struggle is real, but there are always people who care. Speak up. Reach out. Be brave. Fight your way through that battlefield of memories and emerge victorious. We're all waiting for you on the other side. And we have cookies.

prologue: her

I drain the last of my coffee and slide to the edge of the booth. The bitter taste saturates my tongue or maybe it's nerves pushing my lunch back up. My bag, which holds all my possessions, is slung across my body. I look down at the handwritten bill. Tessy's Cafe. Seven dollars and fifty-three cents. I should have gotten pie, too. Then it would be an even ten. The waitress rounds the corner toward the kitchen, and for three seconds I wait to make sure she isn't coming back.

I take off, my sneakers squeaking against the wet floor like an alarm. My shoulder slams into a teenager loitering near the entrance before hitting the door. It swings open, getting caught in the wind, and whips against the building with a loud crash.

I keep my head down as raindrops pelt me like tiny rocks. I sprint past honking cars and parallel parkers, hurdling a small dog, whose incessant yapping sounds like "She's right here! She ran that way!" I run until I can't hear yelling anymore, until my lungs burn and my legs feel boneless. I find an alley and slide down against the wall, taking shelter from the rain. No one finds me here and I'm thankful. I wonder how—on top of everything else—I became a thief.

A couple hours later, my clothes are still damp and my shoes squish with every step. I pat down my bag and am thankful that most of the items inside are still dry. There's a pair of clean socks, some snacks, and a few trinkets I've collected on this impromptu trip from hell. No need to worry about a cell phone. It's probably right where I left it, restored to factory settings and sitting on top of my rarely used kitchen table. God, I miss technology. I miss my music and touch screens and chiming in on biased articles about Microsoft's latest launch.

Avoiding the highway, I walk through a field of high grass toward the truck stop ahead. My hands skim the top of the grass, each blade tickling my palm. The bright lights lure me in like the insects that buzz around me. There's a subtle eeriness to these places, especially after dark. The smell of diesel and the purr of generators add to the cold feel of machines and asphalt.

The big rigs are lined up neatly, tucked in for the night. I walk the maze of trucks and trailers, looking for any signs of life. I turn a corner and gasp when I catch a reflection of myself in a clean chrome bumper. Running my hands down my chest, I try to smooth out the damp and wrinkled clothes. Clothes I've been living in for weeks. It doesn't help. My dirty hair is pulled up into a ponytail with my overgrown bangs getting caught in my lashes. My mother would die if she saw me like this.

I focus on my reflection. No designer clothes, no makeup, and no manicures leave me feeling human again. It reminds me of where we came from, happier times and simpler dreams. My blue eyes look tired and dull reflected in the shiny metal. I'm a mess, and I can't help but wonder how much more of the unknown I can take.

A husky voice cuts through the night and I turn toward it. Three trucks ahead of me, I spot a bald man leaning against the front of his truck. He's got an overgrown white beard and rosy cheeks, Santa Claus of the open road. His T-shirt is two sizes too small, hugging his perfectly round belly. There's an old model cell phone pressed to his ear as he talks quietly. He's all warm smiles and I bet whoever's on the other end of that phone call can feel them. I make my approach as he ends his call and sighs into the cool air.

"Starry night," I say.

He startles a bit, but nods to agree. He doesn't give the usual what's-a-girl-like-you-doing-in-a-place-like-this look.

"It is."

"You here for the night?" I ask.

"Nope. About to get on the road north. Only got six hours between me and home."

"Could I get a ride?" My left foot rocks onto its outer edge and flattens again, a nervous habit from childhood.

"I'm not interested in lot lizards," he says.

"I'm not a prostitute. I just need a ride," I insist.

His eyebrows slide high on his forehead as he appraises me. "I don't know. You running from something?"

"Heading to Canada. My dad's up there."

Yes, I'm a liar, too. There's a long moment of silence. I wonder what he's debating.

"Are you legal? Over eighteen?"

"Why?"

He's leering at me and immediately, my defenses are up. I slide my bag behind me so that I can reach my knife, if needed. He quickly raises his hands in surrender and laughs.

"Don't get any ideas. I just don't want to be totin' juveniles around. I don't need no trouble."

"Oh," I say, relaxing my stance. "Yes, I'm well over eighteen."

"Alright. Get in. But, I'm only going as far as Tacoma. After that, you're on your own."

I bounce on my toes and clap my hands together.

"Thanks! I'll be no trouble at all. I promise. Quiet as a mouse. You won't even notice I'm there. The Silent Bob to your Jay."

"What on earth are you talking about?"

I shrug at him and paste on a charming smile. He nods toward the truck and climbs inside. I hop up into the passenger seat and watch as he presses buttons on a dashboard that could rival a space shuttle.

The inside of the truck is much cleaner than I expected. There's no smell of dirty socks or leftover food like some of the other trucks I've ridden in. A troll doll hangs from the rearview mirror. He's got blue hair and a gem in his bellybutton. There's a bobblehead stuck to the middle of the dash, a well-done likeness of the president. Lining the ceiling are various Seattle Seahawks pendants, rosters, and even a foam finger. Tucked next to the speedometer, and in a cup holder, are different photos of the same woman. She's beautiful, with black hair and kind eyes. There's something instantly comforting about her.

"She's pretty," I say.

He grins and taps the photo on his dash.

"That's my wife. My only reason for living."

I settle in, buckling my seatbelt. I ponder his only reason for living. Is it so bad to just float through life without a reason? Maybe I've already fulfilled my purpose. The way I see it, I had no choice. I did what had to be done and it led me down this path, one on the run.

When we're finally in motion, I unwind, kicking up my feet.

"Get your feet off my dash," he says, reaching over and tapping my shoes with his hand. I drop them to the floor. "Feel free to get some sleep. I'll wake you when we get there."

1. HIM

I sit in my parked car, sipping stale coffee and willing my tired eyes to stay open. I've been here all night, waiting for *her* to emerge. My eyes are glued to that innocent house with white siding and dark blue shutters. During the night, I watched the lights go on in one room, only to go off moments later. I wonder what she was up to in that house, and with whom. Had she charmed some middle-aged man into taking her in for the night?

The neighborhood finally wakes with the sun. I watch a van meander slowly down the street tossing newspapers at people's front doors. It makes one final throw to the house next to Katherine's hideout. The delivery joins a pile of three other plastic-wrapped papers on the front walk. Birds flit to an empty feeder and leave disappointed. The mailbox hangs open, envelopes and magazines jutting out of the cramped space. They've been gone a while.

A woman, in too much makeup and an outfit that belongs in the darkness of a dance club, struts by with a tiny dog on a leash. Her eyes scan a yellow house with an impeccably manicured front lawn. I chuckle when she trips over her dog, who has stopped to sniff an interesting spot of grass. She looks around, checks the yellow house again, and adjusts her cleavage. Five minutes later, she passes in front of the house again heading in the opposite direction. Three minutes after that, a shirtless man in pajama pants retrieves his paper from the sidewalk. She's missed her opportunity.

Kids ride their bikes up and down the quiet street, yawning mothers push strollers, and dutiful husbands walk dogs. The mailman comes and goes, but the front door I've been watching does not budge.

I bet she knows I'm getting closer. I hope she can feel me like a heavy breath down her neck. In the beginning, she would catch rides with truckers or anyone heading north. I assume she's running to Canada. I'm not sure how she's getting money to eat. My guess is that she's been relying on the kindness of strangers or she's turned to prostitution. I've seen it happen enough to know desperate times call for desperate thighs.

She's becoming impulsive and sloppy, sometimes even stealing meals and snatching purses. It never surprises me how people change along the way, letting self-preservation override any existing morals and values.

I don't know why there's a bounty on her head and I don't care. It's not part of my job to care. My job is to find her and bring her in. I never want to know the target's crime. It could influence my judgment and at this point in my career, I can't afford that. So here I wait, among the designer vehicles and white picket fences of suburbia, stalking like a black cloud.

I am beginning to resent the very idea of Katherine Percle, and clearly, in the past four weeks she's crawled beneath my skin. If I don't get to her soon, I feel like I'm going to snap. That's why I leave my gun in the car when I make stops. I am one smart remark or missing ketchup packet away from blowing someone's face off.

I've spoken to dozens of people while on her trail. Katherine has left a deep impression on all of them. Most couldn't or wouldn't believe *that* innocent, blue-eyed girl could have done anything worthy of arrest. Usually that meant they wouldn't help me track her. She seems to possess a certain charm that no one is immune to. It's only when I offer cash that they cave and provide information on her whereabouts. As much as it disgusts me, I rely on people's greed to get what I want.

All I need is to get her alone. It's then, when they have nowhere to run, that you see the truly primitive side of people. Fight or flight is instinctual and it resides in every human being. I assume Katherine will be no different.

I can admit my obsession with the girl is completely out of character. The one photo I have of her, now clipped to my visor, is worn and tattered. It shows an attractive young woman, her eyes full of hope for a future that will never come. I close my eyes and sigh, wondering what those eyes look like now. Will they guard her secrets or say everything out loud?

Slam.

My eyes shoot open just in time to see her skipping down the front steps. My pulse spikes as I lay eyes on Katherine, in the flesh, for the first time. She's wearing a conspicuous red hoodie with jeans and high-top tennis shoes. If I didn't know better, I'd say she was about eighteen years old. Her ponytail swings back and forth as she walks, flying wildly when the wind whips around her. I exit the car and tuck my pistol in my waistband.

I give her a wide berth as I follow down the sidewalk. Her brown hair and curvy body are not my type, yet I find myself staring at her ass. It's a great ass. The problem with skinny girls is they never have an ass like that.

She turns left at the end of the street and ducks into a convenience store. I follow her in and stay out of sight, just observing.

Katherine walks down the snack aisle as if she's browsing the items to make the best selection. Her eyes flick up to the cashier often. I stand at the end of the aisle and watch her through a large soda display. When she turns toward me, I'm struck by how pretty she is. Sure, I've been staring at her photo for a month, but in person there's an energy that seems to radiate from her. There's a natural kind of innocence and underlying sexiness to her beauty. I shake my head, pissed at my first reaction to the girl, and refocus on my objective.

She reaches for some individually wrapped Pop-Tarts while keeping her sights set on the cashier. She thinks he's preoccupied, watching television, but the reflection of light on his face doesn't change color. It's steady and unblinking, indicating that he's watching the store's closed circuit camera feed. The camera is directly behind me, so I know that I'm unseen. I can't afford to have her arrested for shoplifting and lose my opportunity, so I step into the aisle.

When I appear, Katherine replaces the Pop-Tarts on the shelf and blows her bangs from her eyes. She never looks at me, just turns and walks past with her head down. Everything about her looks guilty—her shifty eyes, her hunched posture, even the way her hands sink into the front pocket of her hoodie.

I grab a pack of gum and walk to the checkout. Katherine gets in line behind me. She smells like clean laundry with a hint of menthol cigarettes, though there's no other indication that she smokes. The nearness of her makes my chest tighten in anticipation. I can barely contain the smile that tugs at my lips. Victory pools in my mouth like venom. I pay for my purchase and exit the store, watching through the front window as she buys a pack of cigarettes and heads out again.

This time, I stay in front of her. She retraces her path, heading back toward the house, and I know this is my opportunity.

I slide between two parked cars and wait for her to come to me. No matter how many times I do this, the thrill never dulls. The hunt is one thing, but the actual capture, the reward for all your hard work and diligence, can't be put into words. Adrenaline surges through my veins and my fingers twitch while the rest of my body remains still. I am a sprinter waiting for the gun, a defensive lineman waiting for the snap. All I can hear are her soft footsteps and my pulse beating like a drum. When her shadow crosses, I lunge, wrapping one arm around her waist and clasping my other over her mouth. Katherine's body is warm against mine and for a second the shock of what's happening keeps her still. Then her feet kick at my shins and her muffled screams vibrate through my fingers.

I drag her into the shadows and press her against the side of an SUV.

"Please don't hurt me. Please," she begs after I remove my hand.

I force her hands behind her back and pull out my handcuffs. "I'm not here to hurt you. I'm here to bring you back to San Antonio."

She exhales a puff of air and slumps against the vehicle.

"Damn," she whispers as I click the cuffs closed over her wrists.

I turn her so that she faces me now and finally look into the eyes of Katherine Percle. They are relieved and swimming in tears. Her icy blue stare isn't bitter and hard as I thought it might be.

I pat her down, sliding my hands over her form and checking all her pockets. She's been in these same clothes for a while now. They're clean, but worn and stained. There's a hole in the thigh of her jeans, smooth skin peeking through the threads. I take her cigarettes and place them in my pocket. I pat down her right leg, then her left, finding a switchblade tucked into her tennis shoe. I slide that into my pocket as well and wonder what she had to do to get her hands on a knife like that.

She wears a silver chain. The charm attached looks like a tiny USB plug. I run my finger over it, pressing it into her chest.

"What's this?"

"Geek jewelry. I'm really into computers," she says, her voice surprisingly steady.

She blinks once and the tears finally fall. Her eyes follow the inked images covering my right arm. For a few seconds she looks scared, but it doesn't last. She wipes her cheek on her shoulder and shrugs at me.

"Don't you have to read me my rights or something?" Katherine asks.

"I'm not a cop."

Her eyes snap to mine and she squints as if that helps her think.

"So what are you?"

"A fugitive recovery agent."

"A bounty hunter," she says with a sharp breath that resembles a laugh. "Wow. Well, let's go."

There's no fear in her words, only resignation. I escort her back to the car and place her in the backseat, being sure the child locks are on. I slide into the driver's seat and remove my pistol, laying it on the passenger seat.

"Look here," I tell her.

With my phone, I take a picture of Katherine and send it, along with a text message, to my employer:

Target acquired.

"We'll be on the road for a few days. If you try to escape or cause any kind of disturbance in public, I will not hesitate to hand you over to local police, wherever we are. I guarantee *that* trip back to Texas won't be so pleasant."

My threat hits home as her eyes widen and she nods a few times. If only she knew that it is merely a threat. The payoff on this job is too high for me to turn her over and lose out on that.

"Four weeks. Four fucking weeks I've been chasing you." I watch her in the rearview mirror as she stares back. "It'll be good to get home again, sleep in my own bed, and not have to worry about where your ass is."

"Yeah, well, now that you've got my ass, what are you going to do with it?"

She hits me with a flirtatious smile in the mirror. I know her game.

"Don't start that. You and I both know how this trip ends, Katherine."

I watch as she slumps against the seat, letting her head roll back. Her eyes fix on the ceiling. I navigate my way through the city, finally reach the I-5, and head south. San Antonio is about 2,200 miles from here and I'm hoping to make it there in four days. I'll have to push myself, but the payout will be worth every missed hour of sleep.

My phone vibrates and I check the screen. It's Natasha again, the dreaded ex. Like I want to deal with that right now. I hit the button to silence the call and throw my phone into the cup holder.

My fingers tap against the steering wheel as I shift in my seat. Rain begins to dot the windshield and the sound creates its own pulse inside the car.

"Kat," I hear her say after almost thirty minutes of silence.

"What?"

"My name is Kat. Katherine was my grandmother."

I nod and return my eyes to the road, praying like hell that this drive will be uneventful.

2: her

It's dark now. This car smells like man and everything that implies. The interior is tan. It reminds me of human skin and makes me nauseated. I scoot forward on the seat trying to give my arms room to stretch, and the metal handcuffs bite at my wrists. My captor stares straight ahead, the red glow of taillights reflected on his face. White dashed lines slide by in a blurred trail of breadcrumbs leading home.

After being on the run for weeks, it's kind of nice to finally know my destination. I'm so tired of the unknown, the paranoia, the stealing, and the lying to survive. Even though this trip will deliver me to a life in prison—or worse, death row—I welcome it. That's what I keep telling myself, anyway.

As for this bounty hunter, I'm not sure what to make of him. He's immune to my weepy-girl crying act, so I'd say he probably tortured small animals as a child. With his stunning good looks, he's a far cry from Dog, the Bounty Hunter. I'm thankful for that, because who wants to spend days in a car with all that hair and pleather?

His hair is light brown and pushed back, just long enough so that the curled ends gather at the nape of his neck. It's messy and sexy in an unintentional way. The back of his neck is tan and beautifully contrasts the collar of his white T-shirt. I can see lines of black ink filled in with reds and blues beneath the thin material and I want to see more. I follow the path down his neck and over his wide shoulders. His arms are well-defined muscle, but not excessively so. They are covered in more tattoos. He looks strong, but not beefy. Long fingers drape over the steering wheel in a relaxed grip, a red rose decorates the back of his hand. There's no wedding band or any indication that one exists.

The stripe of face visible in the rearview mirror is handsome. Blue eyes, that earlier in the day reflected sky, now seem cold and gray in the shadows. He glances in the mirror and catches me staring. Tiny lines appear at the corners of his eyes when he squints. I don't look away.

"What would it take for you to just drop me off at the Canadian border?"

I keep my voice light and sweet, hoping to persuade him. He shakes his head.

"It would take a lot more than you've got," he says.

"Maybe I've got a lot more than you think." I wink and hope I'm coming off as seductive and not like a crackhead with a tic.

"I doubt that, princess." He returns his eyes to the road. "Besides, that's six hours in the opposite direction."

Deciding he must be unaffected by my powers of seduction, I watch him for a few minutes. His eyes start sliding closed and popping open again. He looks like me during my Information Theory classes. Professor Darcy's nasally and monotonous voice instantly fills my head. *"Kullback-Leibler divergence measures the difference between two distributions. It is sometimes called the relative entropy."* What a bore. I imagine this bounty hunter has sacrificed many nights of sleep to catch up with me. That thought makes me happier than it should. When his chin drops to his chest, I speak up.

"I'd appreciate it if you didn't sleep while driving. It can be hazardous to my health." He shrugs one shoulder and shifts in his seat. "My health is directly related to your paycheck, right? Can't get paid if I'm lying in pieces on the I-5."

I silently celebrate as he exits the highway and pulls into a motel. It's not the Ritz Carlton. Hell, it's not even the Holiday Inn, but after weeks on the road, it'll feel like a palace. While I did have the comfort of a bed last night, it wasn't without a price. The old lady made me scrub her house from top to bottom in exchange for a place to sleep. I was grateful though; it was better than sleeping outside.

"Where are we?" I ask.

"Eugene, Oregon, the anarchist capital of the U.S."

I whip my head toward him, surprised by his random side note. "What? I thought tree huggers were peaceful people."

He parks the car and turns in his seat. His blue eyes reflect the blinking vacancy sign and even through that, they are fierce.

"I'm going to go in and get a room. Do not fucking move."

"Not at all?" I ask.

"No."

"What if something itches? What if I sneeze?"

He doesn't say a word as he exits the car and sets the alarm.

When he's inside, I press my shoulders against the seat and lift my butt up. If I can just get my hands in front of my body, I'll have a better chance of escape. I stretch and tug and squeeze, but I just can't seem to get the right leverage in this cramped backseat. Now,

I'm regretting skipping those yoga classes my mom insisted on gifting me.

I place one foot on the front seat and try to lift again. My foot slides off and gets wedged between the seat and the door. I panic and try pulling it free, but it won't budge.

Suddenly, the car unlocks and the front door pops open.

"What are you doing?" he asks.

"I needed to stretch my leg."

"Just the one? Move it."

"I can't."

"What?"

"It's stuck," I admit.

He grabs my foot with both hands and jerks up. I pull it into the backseat as he sits down and starts the car.

"I guess flexibility is not one of your strong suits?" he asks.

"Wouldn't you like to know?"

With his stony face, it's hard to tell if he's teasing or serious. I would be willing to bet that's something he's practiced until it became a natural facade.

Soon we're driving around to the back of the building. There are more trees and less lights back here, the makings of a horror movie. He leaves me again, uses the keycard to enter the room and props the door open. Meanwhile, I check the nearby shrubs for killers in hockey masks wielding butcher knives. He retrieves a bag from the trunk, drops it inside, then returns for me. I slide over, eager to get out of this car.

He opens the door and bends down so that we're eye level. I'm caught off guard at how handsome he is up close. Of course, I've been staring at the back of his head for a while so anything is an improvement. There's a small jagged scar on his chin and a graveness to his eyes that hints of danger. His features are sharp and masculine, fixed in a solemn expression.

"Look, we both know it's useless for you to fight me. I have a gun and will use it if necessary. Are you going to be difficult?"

"Do I have a choice?" I ask with a bit of attitude. I hate being treated like a child and I know, from the tone of his voice, that's how he sees me.

"You always have a choice," he says.

"I won't be a problem."

His large hand wraps around my arm as he pulls me from the backseat and guides me into the room. When he sits me on the edge of the bed I stare into the large mirror there. My hair is even more of a mess now and there are dark circles under my eyes, the result of more than a few nights without sleep.

The walls are off-white with dollar-store art hung strategically over each piece of furniture. The toilet and shower are separate from the sink and mirror, reflecting mediocrity back at us. The carpet is dull, the pattern faded near the door and around the bed. An old television, sold before I was born, sits on a dresser. It reminds me of the TV my dad and I watched movies on in his office when my mom was busy catching up on her soaps. It was a big chunky thing with a VCR attached and a remote with only four buttons—a far cry from the sixty-inch flat screen I left behind, a Smart Television with Wi-Fi capabilities, HDMI connections, and a 450-hour DVR to record every episode of *Project Runway*, *Doctor Who*, and *The Golden Girls*.

The bedding in this place is a whole different story. It's soft and looks brand new. I secretly hope that it's new out of a desire to make patrons happy and not a necessity since the last guests were murdered in their sleep. It's a light green color with a swirling white pattern. There are four pillows stacked on the bed and I'm happy to see them. I miss pillows.

"There's only one bed," I point out.

"Nothing gets past you."

As much as I want to toy with him, my bladder has other ideas. "I need to pee," I announce.

He walks over and pulls the handcuff key from his pocket. He flips it over in his hand a few times before looking down at me.

"I'm going to take the cuffs off. Don't do anything stupid and they can stay off."

"Yeah, I got it."

When I'm free, I stand and shake my wrists out and roll my shoulders, all while glaring at my apathetic captor. I enter the bathroom and close the door behind me. The light is blinding and is amplified by the brilliant white surface of the tile, tub, and toilet. It feels sterile and cold, but at least it looks clean. I lean against the door and try to work out a plan, but I've got nothing. It's like being in his presence sucks all the smart from my brain. I pee and exit the room.

What I find makes me freeze. My feet are rooted to the sad carpet and my breath is stolen by the sight. He's in the middle of changing clothes, shirtless and standing in one leg of his jeans like some hot, decorated, muscled flamingo. His black boxer briefs act as a censor box blurring out the good bits. He's giving me lady wood.

"You're staring," he says.

I spin toward the sink to hide my face only to realize we can still see each other in the mirror. Like I said, all the smart is gone.

Removing my hoodie, I wash my face and pat it dry with a towel. I hide myself in the soft cotton cloth and inhale the fresh scent. It reminds me of laundry days with Mom—sitting on the washer and singing until the spin cycle hit, then racing around the Laundromat in rolling carts and switching people's clothes into different dryers. All of that was before Dennis came along, before his money and his rage destroyed what we had . . .

"Let me put the quarters in!" I shouted from across the room.

My mom nodded and motioned me over. I darted between the rows of machines and grabbed the bottle of liquid soap as I approached.

"I've already put the soap in, Katherine."

I didn't hide my disappointment as I slammed the lid closed and hopped up on top of it. My mom dropped the four quarters into my hand and moved to the next machine to start another load. Sliding each coin into a slot, I named them as I went.

"Jon. Richie. David. Tico."

I pushed the tray in and heard the machine come to life beneath me. My mom hit me with an annoyed look and poured soap into the next washer.

"Is your father letting you listen to Bon Jovi again? I told him you should make your own decisions about what kind of music you like."

"Mom, Bon Jovi was the voice of a generation, making music that moved people. 'Livin' on a Prayer' is like a motivational speech and 'You Give Love a Bad Name' is the quintessential ex-bashing. Great lyrics over catchy melodies and guitar riffs, all while sporting enormous hair. Not everyone could pull that off."

"Katherine, really. I've heard that same speech from your father for years. And every other band in the eighties had great lyrics, guitar riffs, and enormous hair. Don't you want to listen to Backstreet Boys or something current?"

" 'On a steel horse I ride,' " I sang.

I sometimes thought she resented that I was so much like my dad. Once her machine had started, she took a seat on the lid next to me.

"When are we getting a new washer?" I asked.

Mom sighed and stared across the aisle to the dryers spinning clothes around and around. It was a load of bright colors swirling and falling together.

"Soon. Your father is working overtime for another week and then we should have enough."

"I'll miss this place," I said. She looked at me like I'd grown a third

eye. "What? It smells like soap and sunshine. I like it. Remember when we made an obstacle course around the machines and raced to the front door?"

"I remember you cheating," she teased.

"I did not! I'm short. It was easier for me to go under that counter than over it!"

She frowned at me and we were silent. The swishing of the machines beneath our butts and the clank of loose change in one of the dryers was the only sound.

"Katherine Marie Percle, I challenge you to a rematch!"

By the time I lower the towel, he's dressed in cotton lounge pants. Still no shirt. I feign coolness, despite the spike in my pulse, and throw myself down on the bed. I stretch my arms over my head, arch my back, and then fold myself in half. My body is sore and aching everywhere. He walks to the door and slides all three locks closed. I roll my eyes and turn on the TV.

He takes a piss with the door open, while I flip through the channels until I find reruns of *The Cosby Show.* I grin and settle down into the pillows.

"Sweet. This is one of my favorite episodes. Theo wants an expensive shirt, but Denise says she can make him one that looks just like it."

"Sounds thrilling," he says as he smacks a button on the front and turns the television off.

I glare at him, flip the set back on, and watch as he leans into the mirror. He inspects himself and I wonder what he sees there. I get a better look at all his colorful tattoos and admire the way the images curve around the muscles of his chest and arms. The word UNFORGIVEN arcs across his chest in beautiful swirling script.

I see blue eyes like mine and eyelashes that would make drag queens weep. His jaw is covered in scruff and it makes him appear rugged and a bit dirty. He looks sleep-deprived, over-caffeinated, and sex-starved. He's the perfect combination of sexy and scary.

Unfortunately, the fact that he's holding me hostage is a total boner killer.

He catches me watching in the mirror. Unapologetically, my eyes travel down his chest and abs, settling on a tattoo right above his hip. It's a black-and-gray piece that disappears beneath his pants in the most tempting way.

"You sure are hot for an asshole," I say.

He smirks and begins brushing his teeth. My eyes never leave him as he spits into the sink and rinses out his mouth. "Why am I an asshole?" he asks.

"Seriously? You handcuffed me for hours probably causing irreversible nerve damage to my delicate wrists. Plus, you carry a gun."

"And that makes me an asshole?"

"Yep."

"But, a hot one?" he asks, raising an arrogant eyebrow.

"Whatever," I say, stunned by my sudden lack of verbal sparring skills.

He places his things back into his bag and I can't help but stare longingly.

"Do you have another one of those?"

"Another what?" he asks.

"Toothbrush. I'd kill for a toothbrush."

He shakes his head. I know I'm a little overdramatic about oral hygiene, but it's one of those things people take for granted, like valet parking and Prada boots.

"No, but if you behave I'll get you one in the morning."

"If I behave? I'm not a child," I insist, sitting up in bed.

He ignores me and sits on the opposite side of the mattress. He pulls the pack of cigarettes from his discarded shirt pocket and holds them out to me.

"You need to smoke?"

I laugh and grab the pack from his fingers.

"Ha! I forgot all about those. No, they're not mine. I don't smoke."

"You just buy cigarettes?"

"They were for the old lady I stayed with. Come on, they're Virginia Slim Menthols. Give me a little credit." He shrugs. "Poor woman never got her smokes. She probably thinks I stole her money and took off."

"I'm sure it's not the worst thing you've done."

I frown at him and place the cigarette pack on the nightstand. I hate that he's right.

"Now what?" I ask.

"Now, we sleep."

"I'm not sleeping in the same bed as a stranger," I say.

"Well, we've known each other for about five hours, so I say we're no longer strangers."

"Just because you say it, doesn't make it true. I don't even know your name."

"My name is insignificant," he replies.

"That's a cruel name. Were you an unwanted child? I'll just have to make one up for you." I pause and look him over. "Let's see, you look like a Robert, maybe a Steven. No, I knew a Steven in high school, he was so weird. Used to wear this black trench coat every day, even in the summer."

"Really, tell me more," he deadpans.

"Fine, I'll just keep trying names until one sticks."

"Can we go to sleep now?" he asks, exasperated.

"I told you. I'm not sleeping in this bed with you, oh nameless one."

He turns to face me and holds up the handcuffs, dangling them over the bed. "Not only are you sleeping in this bed, you'll be handcuffed to me."

"What? The cuffs again? My wrists are chafed."

"You'd prefer I tie you up?"

I close my eyes, letting those scenes play out behind my lids. I realize he means the bad tied up and hold out my arm willingly. He places one cuff around my right wrist and the other around his left. We pull back the covers and I crawl beneath.

We both stare at the television, although I'm not sure either one of us pay attention. My brain is reeling with the day's events and what they mean for my future. I roll onto my side to face him and notice the gun, his phone, and keys on the nightstand. I swallow down a joyful cheer as I formulate a plan. Once he's asleep, I can grab the keys, unlock myself, and be long gone before he even wakes up. Before I go, I'll make sure to change the language on his phone to Mongolian, delete all his contacts, and put a lock code on it, just for good measure.

Unfortunately, he turns to see what I'm staring at.

"Shit," he whispers.

He empties the bullets from the gun and slides it beneath the mattress. Then he takes the cuff key and tucks it into his underwear. We make eye contact, which is not awkward at all with his hand down his pants. He gives me a knowing grin, as if he can hear every thought in my head. I scowl at him and try to cross my arms, but the weight of his attached arm stops me mid-motion. My frustration grows and I slam our joined hands down onto the mattress.

"Something wrong, princess?"

"No. Everything is peachy, Frank."

"Go to sleep."

He turns the television off and rolls away from me, leaving our joined wrists in the neutral ground. I try to sleep, I do. I just can't seem to get comfortable. My jeans cut into my waist and the stiff denim scratches against my skin. The fact that the rest of my clothes are sitting at that old lady's house back in Tacoma pisses me off. After an hour of tossing and turning, he loses patience.

"What's the fucking problem now?"

His voice is deep and unnerving in the dark room.

"I can't sleep," I say.

"Well, take your jeans off, they can't be comfortable. I won't look."

"Ugh!" I grunt.

"I promise."

He leans over and turns the bedside lamp on. It creates a glowing amber halo of light behind him. My lips purse and slide to the left, not wanting to admit anything. The way he stares at me seems to unravel my confession.

"I can't take them off," I say.

"Why's that?"

"I'm not wearing panties."

His entire body stiffens as he looks at me. I don't miss his glance down to my jeans and back to my eyes.

"It's a funny story, actually . . ."

He leans over, pulls a pair of boxers from his bag and throws them at me.

"I don't care. Put those on."

"Fine. Can you turn around?" I ask while making a circling gesture with my index finger.

He turns away. I struggle to get my jeans off and his boxers on while handcuffed. I can't get much accomplished with one hand, so I use both. When I finally get my feet into his boxers and pull them up, the tips of his fingers drag all the way up my leg. A chill runs through me before he tucks them in, forming a fist.

"Would you hurry up? I'm exhausted," he growls.

"Aww. Poor widdle kidnapper is tiwerd."

"I'm not a kidnapper. I'm a fugitive recovery agent."

"You say po-tay-toe." A long slow sigh comes from him and I'm aware he may be at full-capacity annoyance. "Alright, I'm done."

He turns to find me kneeling with his boxers folded over enough times to rest on my hips. He stares at the exposed skin between my tank top and his underwear. Something stirs in my gut from the way he's looking at me.

"Like what you see, sexy kidnapper?"

He frowns and turns the lamp off. Within minutes I can hear his light snoring and let sleep take me under too.

3. HIM

"Theo!"

I groan and try to drag a pillow over my head.

"Theo, get up. I have to pee."

I sit, rub my eyes, and curse the tiny bladders of all women. Kat sits cross-legged on the bed, watching me closely. She swishes her lips back and forth across her face while she waits for me to respond. There's a sharp crescent-shaped line on her cheek from where the handcuff rested while she slept. Her left knee bounces slightly, an adult version of the potty dance.

"What are you looking at?" I ask.

"Oh nothing. Just ready to watch you retrieve that key."

I glance down to find my obvious morning wood pushing against the material of my sleep pants. Never one to be on the underside of an embarrassing situation, I grin at her.

"You want to fetch it?" I ask.

Her face contorts in horror and she quickly looks away. A pink tinge creeps into her cheeks and I like how it looks on her. I make a mental note to have it appear more often. I retrieve the key, ignoring my erection, and unlock the cuffs. Kat sprints to the bathroom, slamming the door behind her.

I try to will away my erection. I think of dead puppies, greasy truckers, and the fat guy at the front desk. That works like a charm. She emerges, washes her hands, and leans against the sink.

"About that toothbrush, Woody," Kat says before her eyes snap down to my crotch.

I grab the phone and dial zero for the front desk. The woman calls me honey and promises a quick delivery of the toothbrush in her sugary customer service voice.

Kat spins, eyeing herself in the mirror, and smooths down her hair. When she leans over the sink, the boxers ride up so high I can see the hint of her perfectly round ass peeking out.

"Can you stop staring at my ass? It's doing nothing for your little situation there," she says, turning and fluttering her hand toward my crotch.

I keep my eyes on her as I stand and drop my pants. Her gaze flickers down and back up again.

"Little?" I ask. We both know better.

Kat shakes her head and leans against the counter. "I swear, men and their size complexes. You've probably measured it, haven't you?"

"I'm done discussing my dick with you."

I reach for my jeans and slide them up.

Knock, knock.

"I'll get it!" she sings and heads for the door.

"Stay," I say, grabbing her elbow and turning her back toward the bathroom.

"Yes, master."

"Now, that name, I like."

When I open the door, I'm greeted by a guy holding a toothbrush out as if he couldn't be bothered. His shitty hotel uniform shirt is starched to death, every button fastened up to his skinny neck. His fingernails and eyebrows are too overworked for a straight man. I watch as he reaches over and straightens the brass number four on the front of the door so that it lines up perfectly with the others. He yawns and looks at his watch.

"Thanks," I say, taking the item from him. He finally looks at me and his eyes widen. His stiff posture relaxes as he leans against the doorframe and wets his thin lips.

"No problem at all. If you need *anything* else, be sure to ask for Matt."

He gives me a wink and taps his name tag twice.

"Will do," I say, nodding my head. It is too early to get eye fucked by the help.

Before I can close the door, Matt's hand shoots out and grabs my crotch. I'm surprised by his boldness, but I'm fast to react. My hand closes around his throat. I yank him inside and press him to the wall, my forearm leveraged against his chest. My other hand twists his wrist until he screams.

"Do not fucking touch me, fairy."

My anger multiplies until I've almost lost control. I recognize my desire to punish him and pull the rage back in. His gesture was a violation of my personal space and not one that I'll tolerate, but he doesn't deserve what I want to give him.

Matt's eyes are watery and scared. He claws at my hand trying to get air. Veins bulge in his forehead as his skin becomes a stippled purple color. When I think he's learned his lesson, I release him with one last shove. Matt coughs and sputters, bent at the waist gasping for air. His stiff shirt is now wrinkled and disheveled.

"Get out!" I yell.

He squeaks a reply before darting from the room. I take a deep breath to calm myself before snatching the toothbrush from the floor. Kat is standing in the corner, her arms wrapped tightly around her middle.

"What?" I snap.

My tone is too rough. She doesn't deserve my anger, but I don't care. She just shakes her head at me. I stomp across the room and notice the closer I get, the more she seems to shrink into the walls. She's scared. While I can use that to my advantage, I can't stand the look of terror on her face. It's too reminiscent of a past I'd rather forget.

"Thanks," she whispers as she takes the toothbrush from my hand, being sure not to touch me.

It's a silent standoff, both of us emotionally amped up, but for different reasons. Needing a distraction, I return to the bed and flip on the television. Kat scurries to the sink and brushes her teeth. Twice.

"Can I take a shower?" she asks. She stares down at her feet, her fingers fumbling with the hem of her shirt. One foot turns on its outer edge and her lips slide sideways on her face.

"We're leaving in twenty minutes, hurry."

She nods and quickly retreats to the bathroom, locking the door behind her.

While Kat's in the shower I reload my gun, throw on a clean shirt, and pack my bag. I'd love a shower, but there's no way to keep Kat from escaping. Unless I join her now. I stare into the dingy wall dividing us, almost able to construct the picture in my mind. I stop that train of thought before it gets away from me.

The bathroom door clicks open and I find Kat, in a small towel, backlit by fluorescent lights and steam. Her skin is covered in little droplets of water and I try to ignore the ones that slide down her tan legs, pooling onto the floor. I'm being tested.

"I don't have any clean clothes. Do you have something I can wear?" she asks.

I unzip my bag and pull out a pair of jersey shorts and a T-shirt.

"Here."

"Thanks, Johnny."

She gets dressed in the bathroom while I load my stuff into the car. I drop my bag in the trunk and slam it closed. The parking lot is empty except for three cars with out-of-state plates and a stray dog who trots up and down the sidewalk as if he's a registered guest. He sniffs every door and finally disappears around the corner of the building. Kat is still not out when I return so I bang on the bathroom door.

"Okay, okay," she mumbles.

She emerges, my shorts rolled at the waist and my T-shirt knotted behind her back, revealing her smooth stomach. She throws on her shoes and ties her hair up into a ponytail.

I open the door and grab her by the forearm, dragging her down the sidewalk to the lobby. When inside, I nod toward the tiny breakfast room.

"Grab something to eat."

I walk to the travel display in the lobby and randomly grab six different brochures, tucking them into my back pocket. The woman behind the desk offers a cheerful greeting and a forced smile. Her upside down name tag says her name is Melinda. She's wearing day-old makeup and her short curly hair is flat on one side. There's sweat at her hairline despite the cool temperature and she reeks of spiced rum. She knocks over a cup full of ink pens and hits her head on the counter while retrieving the ones from the floor. I'd say Melinda's had a fun night and a fairly rough morning. While I wait for her to print my receipt, I look for Kat.

She scampers through the small breakfast room, grabbing fruit, a muffin, a mini box of cereal, and a cup of coffee. She looks like a damn looter stuffing things under her arms and into her pockets. There aren't many people up at this hour—an elderly couple who have matching Styrofoam bowls of oatmeal before them and whose body language clearly demonstrates that they're not speaking, and a frazzled mother with mismatched socks and a toddler whose chubby fingers pluck out one piece of cereal from a pile and shove it into his mouth.

In the far corner sits a man who looks like his best days are behind him. By the cropped haircut and rigid posture I'd say he's former military. He's wearing a leather jacket and starched jeans. The black boots parked beneath the table almost shine except for the scuff on the top of the left foot from repeatedly shifting a motorcycle. His bagel sits untouched, the ice in his glass half melted. He's been here a while, but not eating. He watches Kat flit around, eyes glued to her ass. *Yeah buddy, I know.*

Still, the way he watches her gives me an uneasy feeling. His gaze is calculating, not casual. Something about the way he tracks her movements makes me question his motives. In this line of work, I've learned that when you have a bad feeling, it's usually for a good reason. I join Kat and fix my own cup of coffee for the road.

"Time to go."

She nods, stuffing the rest of a banana into her mouth, and

heads for the door. The biker's eyes never leave her and I make sure to get one last look at him before we exit. When we reach the car, Kat approaches the passenger side door.

"What are you doing?" I ask.

"I'm riding up front."

"Like hell you are."

"Seriously? This is like *Driving Miss Daisy*. Except I'm not a crabby old woman and you're not as charming as Morgan Freeman."

I stare at her like she's speaking a foreign language. "What are you talking about? Get in the back."

"And what if I don't?" She props one hand on her hip.

"Do you enjoy the handcuffs?"

"Damn," she mumbles and crawls into the backseat.

Within minutes we are back on I-5, heading south. Half an hour passes and I'm grateful for her silence. I need this time to clear my head and focus on my objective. Capture and deliver. Keep it professional. I stare out at the road ahead and repeat these words like a mantra.

"So, Duckie, do you have a radio in this thing? The silence sucks."

"I like silence."

"Yeah, well, I don't. So, give me some tunes or I'll start singing," she threatens.

I ignore her and finish off my tepid coffee. Moments later, the worst singing I've ever heard assaults my ears. It's the sound of cats in a dryer and howler monkeys.

"I'm Henry the Eighth, I am!"

I don't want to give in to her childish game, but when she starts on the third round, I break and turn on the radio.

"Fine. Just shut up. That's not even a real song," I argue.

"Yes, it is. Patrick Swayze sang it to Whoopi Goldberg."

"Huh?"

"The movie *Ghost*?" Kat says. I stare at her blankly. "Oh, come on! He's dead and she's a medium. Demi Moore has a gym teacher haircut. 'Unchained Melody' plays. You've never seen this?"

"No," I answer.

"You are a sheltered individual."

I can see her shaking her head in disapproval from the backseat. The radio commercial ends and a song starts playing that reminds me of neon spandex and big hair.

"Sweet. I love the music from the eighties. I mean, does it get better than Pat Benatar and side ponytails? Oh, and the movies! *Sixteen Candles* is the best movie, ever. I always wanted to have two kids and name them Jake Ryan and Samantha."

I shake my head and wonder how someone born in the nineties has such a fascination with the previous decade. Hell, I was a kid in the eighties and I cringe at the memories of parachute pants and mullet haircuts.

Kat pulls her feet up on the seat and wraps her arms around them. Her cheek rests on her bent knees while she stares out the window. A reflection of light hits my mirror and I notice a motorcycle following two cars behind us. I can't get a good look at the biker, but my gut tells me that it's the same one from Eugene. I change lanes as if I'm going to exit. He follows.

"Shit."

"What did I do now?" Kat asks.

"Nothing. Lay down on the seat."

"I'm not tired, but thanks. I slept rather well last night considering the circumstances."

"Just do it," I growl.

She complies and I get a better view of the bike. It looks like a Harley, chrome and clean lines. The rider wears a familiar black leather jacket.

Kat is distracting and making me get careless. No one gets

this close without me knowing. I move into the center lane of traffic and wait for the next exit to approach. At the last possible second I swerve to take the exit and watch as the motorcycle follows.

"Holy shit! Next time can a girl get some warning? I think I lost my pancreas on that last turn."

"Shut up and put your seatbelt on."

Kat undoubtedly recognizes the seriousness of my order. She sits up and clicks her seatbelt into place without another word.

I race through the streets, filled with people on their way to work and slow-moving school buses. I make turn after turn, avoiding collisions and trying to lose the biker. No matter what I do, I can't shake him. I approach a large intersection and see the light turn yellow, then red. A quick glance at the cross traffic finds one driver looking at his cell phone and the other applying lipstick in her visor's mirror. On the other side, the closest approaching car is almost stopped, so I know they don't have the momentum to clear the intersection before I do. I floor it, speeding through the light and barely missing their front end.

Kat screams and covers her eyes while the biker is left behind. After two more blocks, I turn and slide, tires screeching, into a parking garage. I round the first floor and return to the exit, parking off to the side. Kat's frightened eyes search the street in front of us.

"What are—" I cut her off by raising my hand.

I hear the approaching rumble of the hog's motor and exhale loudly when he drives past. Fuck me for thinking this was going to be easy. I thought the capture would be the hard part. I'm not prepared for competition.

I retrieve my phone and hit speed dial one. This girl is important to someone and I need to find out who.

"What's up, boss?" Brad answers.

"I need the record on Katherine Percle. Also, find out if there are any new competitors. Check with Dragon's men. Someone's tailing me."

"Sure thing. Sending the record now," he says.

"Thanks."

"Hey, boss? Natasha's been calling my line again."

I cringe and blow out a breath. She's a thorn in my side, constantly pushing to remind me she's there. I've had a few missed calls from her in the past few weeks after six months of no contact.

"What does she want?" I ask.

"She wouldn't say, but she kept asking me lots of questions about the job you're on now. She wanted to know where you are."

"Did you tell her anything?"

"Of course not."

"Good, keep it that way."

I hit the end call button and scroll to my e-mail, bringing up Kat's file. Seems princess here is wanted for the murder of one Dennis Brady. Funny, I never pegged her as a killer. There are no telltale signs, no detachment from society, not even an impression of guilt or pride. I glance back to find her staring over my shoulder.

"If you wanted to know, you could have just asked," she says.

I move the phone out of her sight. "Do you mind?"

Kat slumps back in her seat and crosses her arms. "Look, Maury, if that's information on me, I already know it. I just don't understand why anyone else needs to."

"Apparently, you're a very wanted woman. Any idea who might be following you?"

She shrugs and picks at her fingernails. "I thought he was following you."

I check the street and exit the garage, heading back toward the highway and keeping an eye out for our biker friend. There's no sign of him as I pull back onto the highway. I floor it, putting as much space between us as possible.

"So, not only do I have to worry about being delivered to prison or death row, but now I've got to deal with your moody ass and someone chasing us? I think I was better off on my own."

"You're probably right," I admit.

"Where are we anyway?"

"Medford, Oregon. Known for their pears."

"Too bad it's not their peas, because it would have given me the perfect segue," Kat says, giving me a guilty look. "Can we make a bathroom stop?"

"You're killing me."

"Not yet," she sings, a wicked smile gracing her lips.

"Is that a threat?" I ask.

She doesn't answer. This kid has no idea who she's dealing with. I've handled the hardest criminals, the most unsavory people. Though she's intriguing, she's just a target. I will not be outdone or intimidated by this girl.

I exit the highway and stop at the first gas station we come to. I pull in next to the pump and park.

"Stay in the car while I pump gas, then I'll take you to the bathroom."

Kat glares at me through the window while I watch the numbers count up. I ignore her pouting and scan the area. There's a teenager fueling up his truck. He stops pumping, checks the digital display on the pump, and starts pumping again. I watch it count up another ninety-seven cents and he stops again, landing exactly on thirty-two dollars. A balding, overweight man pumps gas into a metal can sitting on the tailgate of his truck. The bottom of his overalls are stained green and I'd bet he ran out of gas while mowing his lawn.

When finished, I open the car and let Kat out. She stretches her arms high above her head, making my knotted shirt ride up even more. I hold her by the forearm and drag her inside to the bathrooms.

"You've got five minutes."

"Then what? You coming in after me?" she asks, smirking and twirling a piece of hair.

"Four minutes, fifty-one seconds."

Kat sticks her tongue out at me and storms into the bathroom. *Great.* I'm dealing with a toddler. After three minutes, I push the door open and squat down to check for feet in each stall. Her black Converse are motionless in the middle stall. She underestimates me.

I enter the bathroom and lock the door behind me. Following the dirty green tile around the corner, I find Kat halfway out of a small window high up on the wall. There's a trashcan beneath her that she used to stand on. She went out head first, but her height is a disadvantage and she doesn't have the leverage to pull through. All I can see are her ass, dangling legs, and bare feet on this side of the wall.

She struggles for a whole minute, before I chuckle and walk over. "Nice try, Kat."

I see her body tense and then her legs drop, motionless. Slipping my body between her and the wall, I wrap my arms around her legs and walk forward. Kat falls out of the window and over my shoulder.

"Please, Carlton, I was just testing you."

"You need to test yourself for communicable diseases after walking on this disgusting floor with no shoes."

I shake my head and spin toward the door.

"As much as I enjoy the view of your ass, I'm getting dizzy," she says. "Put me down."

I bend over and plant Kat on her feet. A few pieces of hair have escaped from her ponytail. She blows them out of her eyes and scowls at me, a tiny line appearing between her eyebrows.

"I'm unaffected by little girls and their temper tantrums. Get in the car."

Kat grunts, fetches her shoes from the empty stall, and walks all the way back to the car, pouting. She crawls into the backseat and slumps down in defeat as I slide into the driver's seat.

"Give it up, Kat. You'll never get over on me. Just accept your fate and it'll make both of our lives easier."

Just as I'm about to take off, a middle-aged woman approaches my window. Her brown eyes shift from me to Kat in the backseat and back again. She leans over so that we're eye level and takes a deep breath. I slide down the window when she gestures to do so.

"Hi. I'm so sorry to bother you, but I've run out of gas and have a car full of kids." She turns and points to an old-model car with a dent in the front fender and three kids in the backseat. Two are rowdy and jumping around making the car rock, while the third sits calmly, face buried in a book. "In the rush to get out of the house, I forgot my wallet. Could you possibly spare some change or a few dollars? I just need to get back home."

Behind me, Kat coughs. "Scam."

I assess the woman before me. I can tell she's not usually a beggar. Her clothes are a decade old and worn, but they are clean. She wears tennis shoes that are at least five years old and an antique locket necklace that was probably inherited. Her eyes are hopeful while she struggles to hide her shame.

I nod and pull my wallet out, grabbing some cash. I hand it

over. The woman looks at it and her face screws up in confusion.

"No, sir. That's too much. I just need a few bucks," she says, trying to shove the money back at me. I place my hand over hers and curl it closed.

"Please take it," I insist.

Her mouth bobs open and closed. She's suspicious, but she nods.

"Thank you. God bless," she says before turning and walking back to her car.

I roll the window up and pull away from the pump.

"Did you just hand her a hundred bucks?" Kat asks from the backseat.

"Two."

"Two hundred dollars? Man, she played you, sucker."

"She needs it more than I do," I say.

"So, you can be nice to some people. Just not me?"

"You are a job. I don't get paid enough to be nice to you." The shrill ring of my phone cuts through the air. I answer immediately.

"You found something?"

"Jack said he heard about some new guy Dragon brought in from Alabama. He's ex-military and goes by the name Boots. He's into motorcycles and high-tech gadgets. Watch your ass."

"Boots? He sounds like a damned cartoon character. Keep me posted."

I hang up and head toward the highway.

"Who's Boots? Like Puss in Boots in the Shrek movies?" Kat says.

"Shrek?"

"Don't tell me you've never heard of Shrek."

It's then that I spot the motorcycle parked in the shade of

an overpass while Boots leans against it smoking a cigarette. We make eye contact as he gives a slight nod. It says everything that I wish I didn't recognize, *game on*.

"Shit," I say. "*That* is Boots."

"Oh," Kat answers. There's a few seconds of silence. "Wasn't he at the hotel this morning? He was that hot biker guy sitting alone, right?"

"Yes, he was."

Kat always seems to be in her own little world, so I'm surprised by her observation. I speed up though it doesn't seem to matter. He knew we were here. It can't be a coincidence. We travel for a few minutes with only the rhythmic sound of the highway beneath us.

"Who is he?" she asks.

I debate staying quiet, but the opportunity is too good to pass up. I can show her that it is to her advantage to stay with me and abandon all escape efforts.

"He's a contracted hit man."

"What?" Kat screeches. "A hit man? What does that mean?"

"That means he is hired to kill people for large sums of money—presumably you."

"Why? Who would do that?" She blows out a breath and leans her head back against the seat. Kat looks panicked and like she might be sick at any moment. "How is this my life? How did I go from graduating college to being a wanted woman with a price on my head?"

I switch lanes and keep quiet, letting Kat contemplate her own fate. I've got enough to deal with. The worried line between her brows lends a maturity to her expression. She puts on a brave face, but I can sense her struggling to make sense of every piece of this puzzle.

"It's a long way back to San Antonio and it'll go a lot faster if there's not dead silence for two thousand miles," Kat says.

She holds the charm on her necklace between her thumb and finger and mindlessly slides it back and forth. It makes a soft zipping sound as it moves along the chain. I realize she's right about the silence. I'm so used to existing in my own little bubble, that the idea of small talk makes me uneasy.

"Fine. What do you want to talk about, Kat?"

"We could play the ABC game," she says. "You know, you pick a subject and then we alternate back and forth through the alphabet trying to name things associated." I look at her blankly. "Okay, guess not. Well, movies and music are off the table. I'm a movie buff, especially eighties movies and you are clueless—which is another great movie, by the way. We could discuss your summer reading list or how you feel about China's supercomputer which has a total of 1.4 petabytes of RAM. I mean, that's big news. Or you could tell me your name."

"Next," I say shaking my head.

"Alright, but you'll tell me eventually," Kat says with too much confidence.

"I wouldn't count on it."

"How long have you been in the fugitive recovery business?" she asks.

"Fourteen years."

"Whoa," she says, looking at my reflection in the mirror, studying it. "How old are you?"

"Thirty-two."

"Oh. That's not too bad," she says, rubbing my shoulder as if consoling me.

"I appreciate your approval."

"Now it's your turn," she says.

"My turn for what?"

"To ask me a question."

Almost anything I want to know is in a file on my phone, but I decide to play her game. "Why did you kill Dennis Brady?"

Kat's face goes white and her eyes look haunted. "You don't beat around the bush, do you?"

"Not my style. So why did you do it?"

"I was accused of doing it. Aren't I supposed to be innocent until proven guilty?"

"So are you innocent then?"

"I believe it's my turn to ask a question." There's a couple seconds of silence before she asks, "Where do you live?"

"Under a rock," I answer.

"I have no trouble believing that, though it doesn't explain your golden tan. You've got to live somewhere."

"Some people don't have roots, Kat."

"You ever kill anybody?" she whispers while looking around as if there are other people in the car.

"Yes," I answer without thinking.

I cringe and wait for her reaction. Kat stares at the back of my head and I wonder if she's passing judgment. Does she see herself as a different kind of murderer than me? Or accused murderer, in her case. Though in my experience, it's always the guilty ones who run.

"So, why does this guy Boots want me?"

I shake my head and keep my eyes on the road. The thought of this biker sends me straight into a foul mood and now I'm pissed off again.

"How the fuck did he find us at the gas station?" I ask. It's a rhetorical question, but that doesn't stop Kat from answering.

"Well, for under $200 you can get a real-time GPS tracking device with magnetic mount and data logger. When coupled with the right software, it would allow someone to see a breadcrumb trail of where we've been and pinpoint our location."

I meet her know-it-all gaze in the mirror and she shrugs as

if this should be common knowledge. It's got to be GPS. I chastise myself for not thinking of it first.

I grit my teeth, annoyed that this fucker has bested me. That shit just doesn't happen. My fingers curl around the steering wheel and my knuckles turn white.

"Whoa, Hulk, calm down. You look like you're about to bust an artery. I can't deal with you stroking out on top of all this other stuff. Plus, I don't know CPR. You'd totally die."

"Do you *ever* shut up?"

Kat is silent then, and I wonder if I've hurt her feelings. Then I wonder what the hell's gotten into me, caring one way or another about a target's feelings.

A moment later she asks, "Is this really your car? Because it's kind of old lady looking. I bet you borrowed it from your mom, huh?"

The casual mention of my mother is like a lightning strike on the edge of a brewing storm.

"Kat, the less you know about me, the better."

She squints her eyes and tilts her head. I can almost see the gears turning, trying to figure me out, break me down into the simplest pieces. People have been trying to do that my whole life.

"I think you're scared," she says.

"There's not much I'm afraid of."

"I bet you're lonely. You probably have no friends. And I don't mean your favorite bartender down at the strip club you hit every Friday night, I mean people you trust. You go out to pick up chicks and never take them back to your place, right? What about family? Isn't there anyone out there wondering where you are?"

"No."

The air inside the car becomes thin and I feel strangled.

Anger eats away at me and it takes every bit of willpower to keep my eyes on the road.

"That's sad," she says.

"Not as sad as lethal injection for murder."

There's a beat of silence, disbelief on both our parts.

"Fuck you."

It's a low blow and I regret it as soon as it's out. But that's the thing about words, no take backs. I don't apologize. Kat is a job. I turn the radio up and watch as she closes her eyes, forcing the tears to slide down her cheeks.

She's right. I *am* an asshole.

4: her

"I'm hungry," I say, angry that I've been reduced to asking for food and permission to pee.

"We'll stop in Mt. Shasta."

"We're in California already?"

My pulse spikes. It's not a constant drumming, more like one big thump followed by absolute silence. I drop my chin to my chest and take in long pulls of air, so deep that my lungs protest. Time is my enemy, a rueful bitch. It doesn't tick by in small increments. Instead, it leaps past me in large fleeting blocks. Even if I were punished to a lifetime in the backseat of this car, it would be better than where I'm headed.

Reality wraps its clammy fingers around me, dragging me back to a life behind bars or sitting on death row. For now, I choose to ignore it and live my last free days on my own terms. Well, as much as possible when being held captive by the world's hottest bounty hunter in the back of a car most recently used to transport Rose, Blanche, and Dorothy to bingo.

We pull into a place called Black Bear Diner. Its sign is accompanied by a wooden bear statue near the road as if to wave customers in. A couple of teenagers take turns posing inappropriately with the bear and snapping pictures with their phones. No doubt, those pictures will be uploaded to some social media outlet for the world to see within minutes. I can barely remember a time when my own cares were so ordinary.

The outside of the building is rustic wood and windows surrounded by uniform hedges. After four weeks on the run and mostly eating what I could steal from convenience stores, I'd be happy if I never laid eyes on corn chips and beef jerky again. The absolute thrill of sitting down for a meal in the company of another person feels irrational, but I can't deny my excitement. This place looks like it has real food. The kind that you need utensils and napkins for.

I watch Mr. Cold As Steel get out and search around the car. I decide I need a name for him in my head, because not knowing is driving me crazy. Looking into his blue-gray eyes, I decide on Steel. Cold, hard, and unbending, it seems fitting in every way.

He kneels down behind the trunk and I wait to see if he finds anything. A family exits the diner and I'm distracted by their coordinating outfits of Hawaiian shirts and khaki shorts. I understand the mom and dad, but wonder how they got the kids to agree. There must be some kind of epic prize to endure that kind of humiliation.

"Come on guys. We've got to stick to our schedule. I want to make it into Reno before dark," the father says.

The teenage daughter walks past my window and drops her phone. It tumbles to the ground and slides past the cars into the parking lot. She walks past Steel, her eyes glued to that electronic wireless device that rules her life and connects her to the rest of the world. He jumps up and sticks his arm out, blocking her path just as a large truck barrels through.

The girl is dazed. She looks at her crushed phone and back to the towering man.

"That could have been you," Steel says, dropping his arm. "Pay attention."

"You just saved my life," she answers. There's a dreamy look in her eyes as she stares up at him, her mouth hanging open in awe. *Tell me about it, girl.*

"Be more careful," he says. His face is expressionless. The girl retrieves what's left of her phone and climbs into the minivan, throwing one more glance at him. When she's safely inside the vehicle, he slides over and sticks something beneath the minivan's bumper while giving me a pointed look through the glass.

He doesn't say a word as he escorts me inside. There is no physical contact, only an understanding that I do as I'm told. With his threat to turn me over to the police, I am all too willing to cooperate. It may only be a few more days of freedom, but I have a feeling they'll make all the difference.

As we wait for someone to seat us, I take a look around the place. The crowd is mostly men clad in work boots and plaid shirts. They all seem to be hot and sweaty, just clocked out from some grueling physical labor.

There's a long counter across the front of the diner. The swiveling chairs mounted along it resemble something from Fred Flintstone's car. They are pieced together Lincoln Logs that, frankly, look uncomfortable. We take a seat in one of the booths and wait for the waitress.

"So what did you find? Was I right?" I ask.

"Not that I owe you an explanation, but yes, there was a tracking device on the car. I moved it to the minivan."

"Was it from our friend Boots?" I ask. "Seems a bit advanced for him. He looks just one chromosome past caveman. What do you think he wants with me?"

Steel ignores my question as the waitress approaches and hands over the menus.

"Hi, my name is Mattie. I'll be serving you today," she says. Even though there's two of us at the table, Mattie keeps her eyes on my companion. "What can I get you to drink?"

"Water," he says.

I wait for Mattie to look at me, but she doesn't, just keeps unashamedly staring at Steel.

"I'll have a Diet Coke, thanks," I say too loudly.

She nods and heads off to the next table. I blow my bangs from my eyes and stare her down as if I have some claim to the man across from me. She's pretty, but this older woman with too much makeup doesn't stand a chance in her Black Bear suspenders and orthopedic shoes.

I finally tear my eyes away from Mattie and look over the selections. It's a big menu and my appetite is on overdrive. Like a dog, my mouth salivates just reading over each item and its description. Steel sits across from me tapping his fingers on the tabletop while watching the parking lot. I wonder if this guy ever relaxes.

A short time later, Mattie returns with our drinks.

"What can I get 'cha?" she asks Steel first.

I don't miss the way she looks at him and leans over to show off her freckled cleavage. I realize I'm giving this cougar a death look and quickly shift to a neutral expression.

"I'll take the Tri-Tip Dip with fries," he answers, ignoring her blatant flirting.

"Alrighty, and for you?"

"I'll take Bob's Big Bear Burger, add cheese, with potato salad, please."

Steel gawks at me, his eyebrows lifting toward his hairline. Mattie takes our menus and leaves to put our order in, shaking her ass so much I wonder if she's got a medical condition.

"You'll never be able to eat all that," he insists.

"Wanna bet?"

"What are the stakes?"

"If you win, I won't ask your name again. And if I win, you tell me."

"Why are you so interested in my name?" Steel asks.

"I just want to know who to curse while rotting away on death row," I answer half joking.

"Too bad."

"Ugh! You're such an asshole."

"But I'm a hot asshole, right?" he says. A tiny smirk pulls up the left side of his mouth and two dimples appear. It's sexy without trying.

"Wow, is that a sense of humor?" I ask, and his shoulders stiffen, a scowl pulling down on his face like a window shade. "I don't know. On a sliding scale, your asshole to hotness ratio is quickly ruining any small amount of appeal you may have had."

Steel rolls his eyes and leans back in the booth crossing his arms. Those arms look so strong and hard. I picture them restraining criminals and flexing as he carried me over his shoulder. This thought leads to a plethora of positions in my naughty girl mental bank before I refocus on the conversation. He looks uninterested, but I can tell he's still listening.

"You were an asshole to that guy at the hotel."

"He had it coming," he spits.

"It wasn't really fair, though. He was helpless. You're the one who answered the door half-hard, jeans hanging off, looking like a sexual invitation. That whole temper thing tipped the scale toward asshole. I thought you were going to come after me next."

He stares at me with an expression that is meant to be offended, but looks menacing.

"I don't hit girls. Ever." His voice is gruff and solemn. His eyes flick away and back toward me, a humorless lift to the corner of his mouth. "Though you love to tempt me."

My eyes widen and I swallow down the smart remark I had perched on the tip of my tongue. Instead, I try to appeal to his competitive nature.

"Well, there are things you could do to tip the scale back toward hot. I doubt you'd be up for the challenge."

"Like what?" he asks.

"Hotness points can be awarded for many things. Were you ever a firefighter?"

"No. I've never been one to risk my own life for perfect strangers."

"Too bad. That's major. Calendars are made of that kind of hotness. Have you ever poured a bottle of water over your head while shirtless?"

"Guys actually do that?"

"Hot ones do," I confirm. I picture him shirtless and wet. It's a thing of beauty.

"No, definitely not." Steel places his forearms on the table and leans forward. "Who sets the rules for this scale? These are ridiculous."

"You are completely out of touch with modern women's desires."

"No argument there," he says, rubbing the back of his neck. "I'm very . . . observant. I know how to look at a woman and assess her short-term needs, if you know what I'm saying."

I swallow and lean back in the booth. A floating kind of tension moves inside me at the thought of this man taking care of my short-term needs. "I doubt you have to work for it at all. I bet the ladies just fall into your lap, right?"

"I don't have time for the ladies."

"The dudes?" I ask.

He shakes his head and gives me a smirk. "I like being alone. No one to answer to. Plus, I work so much. I'm usually on the road."

"Do you enjoy what you do?" I ask.

"What do you mean?"

"Well, I mean, this is your profession, right?" He nods. "Do you get satisfaction out of delivering people to their deaths?"

"First, not all fugitives are being delivered to their deaths. I've found people who were wanted for unpaid child support and shit like that. Second, from where I started out in life, it's a cakewalk. I learned early on how to deal with unsavory people. Plus, it's not about satisfaction. It's about doing what you're good at. I have a certain set of skills that make me very good at this."

"If you're that good, why did it take you so long to find me? I'm not a professional criminal, no street smarts, no skills. Four weeks ago, the only weapon I knew how to use was my AmEx card."

"I don't really have an answer for that. I guess your pretty face got you further along than I planned."

I'm shocked at his statement and can feel the flaming heat in my cheeks. "You think I'm pretty? I bet you say that to all the fugitives."

Steel doesn't answer my question out loud, but his eyes stay on me and the heat in his gaze makes his answer perfectly clear.

I awkwardly pick at a jagged fingernail.

"Anyway," he continues. "I don't have the ability to see myself doing anything but this." He shrugs.

While his face is resigned, his words come from a sad, defeated place that gave up on dreams long ago. He doesn't elaborate, just stares out the window. His profile is lovely with a slight bump on the bridge of his nose, lips pursed. Light pours in through the blinds, painting his face in stripes of gold. His blue eyes look like glass.

His phone rings and he answers it quickly.

"What did you find?" I'm annoyed that I can only hear one side of this conversation. As much as I strain to listen, the noise in the diner keeps me from effectively eavesdropping. "Anything else?" A deep *v* appears between his eyebrows. His eyes become slits as if he's staring into the sun. "Thanks."

Steel ends the call just as our food arrives. The plates slide in front of us as if summoned by my growling stomach. I'd been impressed with the description of this burger, but to see it in person is something else entirely. It takes up most of the plate and the potato salad sits alongside. It's an afterthought, squished into a tiny space.

We both attack our meals, not pausing for conversation or table manners. A young couple takes a seat at the counter in front of us. They hold hands and look lovingly into each other's eyes like no one else exists. Their faces hold dumb smiles and I wonder if it's love or post-coital glow. Steel watches them, too.

"Wow. They're obviously in love," I say.

"Or they just had sex for the first time. Devirginized bliss."

"Ugh, I wouldn't have looked at anyone like that after my first time. It was awful, so awkward. I guess most first times are."

I roll my eyes and picture Jordan Webster's sweaty face above mine, his glasses sliding down his nose and falling into my hair. He's so into me, quite literally, that he doesn't notice. Thirty-seconds later, he's finished and I'm left wondering if what we did counts as sex. We have to work together to untangle his glasses from my hair. I sent him on his way with a kiss on the cheek and a turkey sandwich.

"Mine wasn't bad. When you're a sixteen-year-old boy, all sex is good sex. You are so excited you're getting laid, it doesn't matter what goes wrong. Anyway, they'll hate each other next week." He takes a bite of his sandwich and hums in satisfaction.

"You're a pessimist."

"I'm a realist," he argues after swallowing his mouthful of food.

"You've never had anyone look at you like that?" He ignores my question and takes another bite. "You've never been in love?"

"The only woman I ever loved was my mother."

I notice he uses past tense when speaking about his mother. The pain and anger in his eyes hints at a deeper story.

"And no girlfriends either?"

Steel shakes his head slightly and turns to the window again. "I had a girl. We were," he pauses, as if searching for the right word, "intense. She worked in my field, so we understood each other on that level. I trusted her. She was hot and the sex was good."

"Wow. Are those your only requirements for a relationship? Trust and great sex?"

"I didn't say it was great," Steel says, avoiding my question.

"But you didn't love her?" I ask.

"No."

"What was *her* name?"

He looks out of the window for a few seconds before turning back to me. I think he's going to ignore me again. "If I tell you, you can never ask my name again."

I don't like this bargaining, but my curiosity answers before I can mull it over. "Deal."

"Natasha," Steel says.

It's not the name I really want, but it's something. I celebrate the small victory in my head.

"I thought I was in love. I had a boyfriend before I left town. His name was Paul. I met him my sophomore year of college. He came from a wealthy family. My mother adored him. It wasn't fireworks and birds singing. It was comfortable and safe."

I stare down at my plate and think about the last time I saw him. It didn't go quite how I had expected. When I showed up at his condo at two o'clock in the morning, he was more than surprised.

"Katherine, what are you doing here?" he said. "When did you get out?"

Paul stood in the door and rubbed his eyes. He was only wearing a pair of boxers.

"I'm leaving, Paul. Marilyn is going to paint me as some kind of money-hungry trash after his money. I won't stand a chance against that family. I can't go to prison."

I had just made the decision an hour earlier. After a whirlwind of packing and saying good-bye to my old life, I stood on Paul's doorstep with tears in my eyes.

"Katherine, don't be an idiot. You can't run. You'll never make it out there without your afternoon lattes and Four Square check-ins. Go *turn yourself in."*

He scratched his stomach and started to close the door.

"I want you to come with me. I love you," I declared.

My hand shot out, pushing the door open. Paul looked down at his feet and tapped the doorframe just as a half-naked girl entered the room. She looked freshly fucked and a little drunk. While my mouth hung open in disbelief, he wore his defiance proudly.

"You know who my family is, Katherine. I can't be associated with a criminal. I'm sorry."

He closed the door in my face. It was one of many things that made leaving so easy.

"Hey, maybe you'll find a girlfriend in prison," Steel says, breaking me out of my memories. "You'll get matching tattoos or something."

"Asshole."

He forgets himself and smiles at me. My God, it's a gorgeous sight, all perfectly straight teeth and matching dimples on each side. I wish he smiled more. I pat my pockets, looking for a phone I don't have, just to capture the image.

"You guys doing okay?" Mattie asks, appearing beside Steel. "Can I refill that water for you, hun?"

He nods. As she pours water into his glass, she leans too far over, tucking her arms against her sides to push her boobs together. Smooth move, but it's amateur. Steel doesn't even look at her. I chuckle as Mattie stomps off.

"What?" he asks.

"Nothing," I answer, shaking my head. "You really are clueless."

After we clear our plates, Mattie appears and hands the check to Steel. He leaves cash on the table, and we head for the exit.

"You're going to pee before we leave," he announces, pulling me through the women's bathroom door and locking it.

I sit in the stall and listen as he empties his bladder next to me. I will my body to cooperate, but nothing happens.

"I can't pee with you listening," I whine.

"Well, I'm not leaving."

"Turn the faucet on." I hear the rush of water and soon I'm done. We wash our hands side by side and head outside.

"Surely I can ride in the front now?"

"Surely you are mistaken."

"What about our playful banter and sharing of personal information? We just peed together for Christ's sake!"

When we reach the car, Steel opens the back door and points. I grumble and crawl inside. Before we get back to the highway, I clap excitedly when one of my favorite songs comes on.

"This song is my jam. Michael Jackson was the best of the best."

The sound of *Smooth Criminal* has me singing along and bobbing my head to the beat. I slide the USB key along the chain around my neck and think about my own criminal status. Sitting in the back of this car, things seem more clear, more final. My destination ends at a murder trial. Though I've lived a full life, I try not to think about all the things I'll miss out on—like getting married, having kids, traveling the world, and growing old with someone by my side.

"Do you have a bucket list?" I ask.

"No."

"I guess you don't realize how important they are until you could be facing life behind bars. Mine's kind of long, because I've been working on it since I was twelve."

"That's kind of morbid for a twelve-year-old."

"Well, my dad died, so things were put into perspective back then. Some of the high points are cliff diving in Hawaii, seeing the Egyptian pyramids, walking the Great Wall of China, eating curry in India, visiting Grauman's Chinese Theater. . . ."

"Time out," he says, interrupting me. "All those world travels and then you group Grauman's Chinese Theater in with them?"

"I want to try my hands and feet in all the celebrity handprints and footprints."

"You'll need to change your list. It's not called Grauman's anymore."

"Doesn't really matter," I say, staring out the window. "I won't get to do any of that stuff."

There's a beat of silence and then, "Did you kill him?"

After a long while, I answer quietly. "Yes." I take a deep breath, close my eyes. "But I didn't mean to. No one has the right to take another person's life, no matter how vile of a person he was."

He nods his head and shifts his gaze to the road. "Did he deserve it?"

"Yes."

I can almost see the warring going on in his head. He wants to know more. He wants to know why. I toy with the idea of leaving it there, dangling in front of him. Finally, I put Steel out of his misery.

"Dennis was my stepfather. He used to beat my mom." There

is an instant change in Steel, a new stiffness to his shoulders, a worried line between his brows. A muscle on the side of his jaw twitches and it feels like a warning of some kind of fury lying just beneath his surface. "She'd been hospitalized so many times and she never would press charges. It was this huge secret that she kept hidden so well. Only me and my aunt Nora knew the truth. We both begged her to leave him, but she wouldn't do it. She said she loved him."

I take a deep breath and push it out slowly through my nose. My mother's bloodied face appears in my head. I can still see her broken fingers pointed in odd directions and the crisscrossed lines of purple bruises across her back.

"She ended up back in the hospital after he came home and beat her with his golf club. I vowed that would be the last time he touched her. It was an empty promise when I made it, but it came true."

Silence engulfs us but it doesn't feel confining. It's a needed break to absorb and process my confession. Steel takes a deep breath and opens his mouth to say something, but closes it again. He repeats this a few times until the words spill out like vomit.

"My father beat my mom too."

I reach out and place my hand on his shoulder, my fingers pressing in to the warm hard muscle there. Instantly, I understand the memories and the kind of childhood he must have had. I share his nightmares, his fears. It's like belonging to a club that you wish you didn't. *Hi, my name's Kat and I had an abusive parent.*

"I'm sorry," I say.

"Not as sorry as he was."

5. HIM

"Sacramento," Kat says reading the highway sign. "Isn't that the capital of California?"

"Yes."

"So, if I added 'Visit the capital of each state' to my bucket list, could we–"

"No." I interrupt her.

Kat crosses her arms and frowns at me. She looks out the window for a few minutes, taking in the city as we pass through.

"I don't see what's so special about this place. It looks kind of boring."

"It has more trees per capita than any other place in the U.S. And there's a huge network of tunnels that were built during the raising of the city to avoid flooding."

"You know all of that and you've never heard of the movie *Ghost*? Your priorities are seriously messed up."

I throw my shades on and stare out at the cars in front of us. Capture and deliver. Capture and deliver. I repeat my mantra a few times just to keep my hands around the steering wheel instead of her throat.

I exit onto Hwy 99 and decide we'll sleep in Bakersfield tonight. It's about four hours from here and I figure getting off the main highway will be a good idea. I know moving the GPS device to that minivan will only distract Boots for so long. He'll figure out what I've done and who knows what other tricks he has up his sleeve.

There's a loud pop and then a flapping sound. The car pulls hard to the left.

"Shit," I mumble as I pull over on the shoulder.

"What happened?" Kat asks.

"Flat tire."

I hop out and inspect the rear driver's side tire before opening the trunk in search of the spare. To my relief, I lift the bottom panel and find a tire tool and a full size spare. I pull them both out and set them on the ground. When I close the trunk, Kat is staring through the rear glass. Her face is a mask of worry, her bottom lip trapped between her teeth. I handcuff her, threaten her, we run from bikers and she's worried now? I don't understand women, especially this one.

The sun is setting fast and in the fading light I get started changing the tire. I remove my jacket and lay it on the roof of the car. Kat rolls down her window, stacking her forearms on the edge and placing her chin on top. She twists her lips to the side and looks on while tears hang on her eyelashes. It's the first time I've seen her this quiet. It's unnerving. I don't understand her tears and I don't have time to worry about whatever breakdown or revelation she's having at this very moment.

I use the tire tool to loosen the lug nuts and remove them. Then, I place the jack under the car and start to turn the crank.

Cars race past us, the force causing the car to rock. Kat looks to the highway and back to me often, like she's waiting for something.

I remove the tire and throw it to the side. It's then that I notice a matchbox-sized device attached to the backside of the tire. It looks homemade. I try to pull it off, but it's really stuck. I stand, place my foot on top of the tire, and pull on the box with all my might. It finally comes free and I go stumbling into the closest lane of traffic.

I hear Kat scream and turn to see a large van speeding toward me. Time doesn't slow down like you think it does in these situations. I'm on sensory overload. Kat's scream is only one note in the symphony of sounds surrounding me. Her voice is accompanied by the van's horn and screeching tires, the whir of cars flying by in every other lane and my furious pulse thundering. My feet remain still as I meet the van driver's eyes through the windshield, his confusion takes a backseat to the fear and anger displayed on his face. The van's left headlight is out and it feels like a one-eyed beast charging toward me. Finally my feet catch up with my brain and I throw myself back onto the shoulder just as the screeching van arrives.

He gives me the finger and speeds back up, leaving me in the dust. I lean over, resting my hands on my knees for a moment. The adrenaline racing through my body vibrates my insides. I take a few deep breaths to clear my head and look down at the contraption in my hand. There's a spike coming out of it that looks spring loaded. I push it inside the box and it pops right back out. On the outside, there are letters crudely scratched into the metal.

I hold it up at an angle and wait for the lights of the next car to pass over us. When they do, my eyes adjust and I read the words aloud.

"Too easy," it says. I wrap the box in my fist and throw it to the ground. "Fucking Boots!"

I smash it with my heel and though I don't do any real damage to it, I feel better. Staring down at the device, I realize that Boots means serious business. He's not like other competition I've had to deal with. He knows what I'm going to do before I even do it. I don't think it's a coincidence that he didn't make an appearance until I'd captured Kat. He's playing a game, manipulating the rules.

I get the spare on quickly, the lug nuts back in place, and lower the car down.

"Fuck!"

Kat sticks her head out of the window and wipes the wetness from her cheeks.

"What now?" she asks.

"The spare is flat."

I pull my bag out of the trunk, slip my jacket back on and grab my pistol and phone from the front seat.

"Are you going to call a tow truck?" Kat asks.

I dial my assistant.

"What's up?"

"I've got a flat tire right outside of Sacramento."

"Let me see what I can do," he says. I hear the click of a keyboard as Brad looks through his database. "I can get you a replacement. Let me make a call and get back with you."

I glance at the car and find the back door thrown open and Kat running down the shoulder of the highway. She stumbles and falls forward, landing hard on the concrete.

"Shit!"

I take off after her. She's back up on her feet, but moving slower now. My quick steps catch up to her soon enough. Kat turns when she hears me approaching. My arms are around her in no time and we tumble to the ground, with her body pinned beneath mine.

Our chests heave, pushing against each other as we fight to regain control of our breaths. My hands are trapped beneath us, gravel cutting into my skin. Her glassy eyes are inches away, her parted lips exhaling against mine. In any other situation, I would take time to relish this moment—this beautiful girl and her bare vulnerability—but I'm not a complete dick.

"Where are you running to?" I ask.

"I can't go to prison," she says as tears leak from the corners of her eyes and soak into her hairline.

Guilt stabs at my chest and I release her, sitting up. "And Boots? If he gets to you, you'll never see prison, Kat."

She swipes the wetness from her cheeks and drops her chin to her chest. "Maybe that's what I deserve."

I stand, dust off my hands and offer her one. "I can protect you if you stick with me."

Kat looks at my outstretched hand and back to my face. She nods, places her hand in mine and I help her up. I look at her tearstained face, watch her struggle not to cry.

"Why did you freak out back there?"

She doesn't let go of my hand. "Sorry."

"We don't have time for this, Kat. Seriously, what's the problem?" I ask.

She turns to look at me, her frightened eyes now enraged. "What's *the problem*? I'm being taken against my will to stand trial for murder. A murder I committed, and which I'll probably get the death penalty for. Oh, and there's a hit man trying to get the job done before my home state can do it. And you're asking me *what my problem is*? I understand you're a man with the emotional range of a rock, but I didn't think you were that dense."

I don't take offense to her words. There are worse labels for me than emotionless.

"No, what I mean is, why now? Why did a flat tire send you into a meltdown?"

She shakes her head. "I guess it's just getting to me, that's all. The reality of it."

I nod.

"And it reminded me . . ." More tears slide down her cheeks and she quickly wipes them away. "We were on a trip to Austin once—me, Mom, and Dennis. We got a flat tire and somehow Dennis blamed my mother for it. It was the first time he hit her in front of me."

"Gutless piece of shit." And there's another thing we have in common. Flashes of my mother's bruised face appear behind my closed eyes. I blink those images away and focus on Kat.

"They made me stay in the car and continued to fight outside. My mom wouldn't even look at me as I screamed and beat on the glass. I could read Dennis's body language, and I knew something bad was going to happen. I couldn't hear what my mom said, but it was Dennis's breaking point. He grabbed her by the throat and shoved her into oncoming traffic.

"Cars were speeding toward her and he watched with this evil indifferent smirk on his face. I tried to get out to help her, but he hit me with a look that warned I better not. Horns were honking, tires screeched, all while my mom crawled from the highway back onto the shoulder of the road. Right at his feet. Just like he wanted."

"If he wasn't dead already . . ." I said.

"My therapist says I have post-traumatic stress disorder because of that incident. He also says I use avoidance and humor to deflect dealing with stressful situations and real emotion. I'm sure you've noticed."

"Your therapist?"

"Two things that all rich kids have, Elliot: an AmEx card and a therapist. My mom thought it was a good idea after my dad died. I'm kind of fucked up."

I place the fingers of my free hand under her chin and lift her face. "We're all fucked up. Some of us are just better at pretending."

"Yeah."

"We can't stay here," I say.

"I know."

"Kat," I say leaning closer. "I've got you. We've just got to make it to that exit."

She nods, her gaze darts to the highway and back to our joined hands. The playful and smiling girl is a muted version of herself. I squeeze her hand and let go.

"Oh, no. If we're going to do this, you have to hold on to me," she says.

She leaps forward and slides her fingers between mine again. I'm shocked by her needy touch and want to pull away. This is different from talking her down from her escape attempt. That was on my terms and with my purpose. Kat's eyes check the highway again.

I grab my bag with my free hand. "Let's go."

As I start to walk, her quick nervous steps help her keep up. With the city behind us, there are large open plots of land in between businesses and warehouses. Across the highway there's a church with an empty parking lot. There aren't many cars on the highway, but each one that passes makes Kat press herself into my side.

"You've been on the run for a month. You should be used to this," I point out.

"I never hitchhiked on highways. I usually found rides in parking lots or truck stops."

I nod and pull her along.

"Distract me," she says.

I kick at a pebble and watch it hop and skip its way into the nearest traffic lane.

"Tell me about Dennis."

An asshole in a red Chevy blows his horn as he passes and Kat jumps. Her fingernails dig into the back of my hand. She loosens her grip, but doesn't let go. With the ducking of her head I can tell that she's annoyed and embarrassed by her reaction.

Even with all the women I've been with, holding hands was never part of the deal. Her soft, tiny hand in mine is strange, but not unpleasant. It makes me wonder what the rest of her skin feels like. I roll my eyes and curse myself for such weak thoughts.

"When he and my mom were dating it wasn't bad. Or, at least, I didn't see it. I was a kid then. So, some guy bringing me presents every time he came over was great. He could go from an endearing charmer to violence in seconds. It took nothing to set him off. He once destroyed a portrait of my dad because my mom brought him up at the dinner table. There were times when my mom would come home with bruises even back then. I confided in my Aunt Nora and she tried to persuade my mom to leave him. But she wouldn't do it. My mom chose Dennis over her sister and her own child."

"Once he saw what he could get away with, I'm sure it only got worse," I chime in, using my own memories for reference.

"I shot Dennis with his own gun. We were fighting and it went off. The look in his eyes as he bled out on the floor of his fancy office held no remorse for the kind of man he was. I stood over him, wanting to help, but wanting it all to be over. All I could think about was him living through this and my mother still being trapped. I just wanted to set her free. And the kicker is, my mom won't even talk to me now. She hates me for what happened. But, I didn't have a choice."

"You always have a choice," I reply.

While I'd love to have an excuse for some of the decisions I've made, I don't. The fact is we do always have a choice. In every situation there are options. With theoretical angels and demons sitting on each shoulder, it's common to talk yourself into the easy choice as if it's the only one. It may not be a simple decision or have the ideal outcome, but the alternatives are always there. It's something my mother drilled into me as a young child. I've always carried those words with me.

"I still think I made the right one. That bastard stole my mom from me. He beat her into someone else. Somebody I barely knew."

"Your mom holds some responsibility too."

"You're right."

I've met some despicable people in my line of work—deadbeat dads, murderers, thieves, and everything in between. None of it bothered me. I never passed judgment on these people. It was only the men who abused women and children that ever saw my wrath. There was an uncontrollable force inside me that wanted to punish them and make them accountable. It was a ghost that lived in my head and demanded that I ruin them like they ruined those they touched.

Anger fills my chest and an electric charge ignites my rage. It's a broken dam of memories as I compare Dennis to my own piece-of-shit father. He was a stranger to me. All I knew of him was the smell of his whiskey and the sound his boots made on the front porch. His authority didn't come from wealth, like Dennis's, but from the messages he delivered with closed fists and backhanded threats. He wasn't a rich man, but he held all the power.

"Men like him make me sick," I spit.

I don't know why I tell her that. I don't know why I say anything at all. Something in Kat pries these things from me.

"Once they were married, it got worse. Or maybe I just saw it more. We moved in with him and it was harder to hide their fights. I was getting older and eventually, I saw through the gifts he threw at me. They were bribes to keep quiet."

We walk a few more steps in silence. Kat's palm sweats against mine and her fingers squeeze tighter every few seconds. It's a Morse code S.O.S. in my hand. I feel a strange sense of irony as I keep my body between her and the highway. How can I be her protector and her captor?

"Your father had to be better than that," I say.

Kat smiles up at me and nods her head.

"He was amazing. Some of my earliest memories are of him reading stories to me in bed. No matter what book it was, he would do all these crazy voices to make me laugh. He was a great dad," she says, her voice softening. "He's the reason I love all things from the eighties. He never really left that decade behind. We used to have movie marathons and listen to his favorite bands on vinyl. It's a way to still feel connected to him."

I watch as she turns away from me and wipes at her cheek. I can't help but feel jealous that at least she had it good for a while. She had a normal father who adored her and fulfilled all the roles a father should. I had nothing.

"I'm sorry you got dealt a shit hand, Kat. But I'm just doing my job here. I've got to take you in. And now, on top of that, I've got to keep you safe from Boots. Maybe you'll get a decent defense attorney and get off on self-defense."

My phone rings and I'm quick to answer.

"What did you find?" I ask.

"I can get you a car in the next hour. Where are you?"

I look up at the exit sign ahead. "Exit 284, on Highway 99." I hear more typing.

"There's a place called Floor to Ceiling right off the highway. Wait on the northeast side of the parking lot."

"Got it."

Kat looks at me expectantly as I slip my phone back into my pocket.

"We'll have a new ride in less than an hour."

"What about your car?" she asks.

"Someone else will take care of it. It's not mine."

"I knew it!" Kat laughs and pumps her fist into the air. "I love being right!"

We exit the highway and cross the overpass, turning into the parking lot as instructed. I pick a spot between two buildings and drop my bag. I loosen my fingers from Kat's and pull my hand free, wiping it on my jeans. Kat's foot turns on its side as her gaze darts away from mine. She folds her arms across her chest.

"Now what?" she asks.

I take a seat and lean against the building, crossing my ankles in front of me.

"Now we wait."

6: her

“Isn’t that a car rental place next door?” I ask. Steel looks across the parking lot and shrugs. “Why wouldn’t you just rent a car?”

“I’d rather not.”

“Are you broke? Is the fugitive recovery business not what it used to be?” He shakes his head and checks his phone. “Seriously. You’ve been in a hurry this whole time and now we sit and wait?”

“Now we sit and wait.”

I huff and hold an imaginary microphone up to my lips, smiling into a nonexistent camera.

“Today in the news, Fugitive Recovery Agent with no name, from nowhere, gives another cryptic answer to an important question. More at 11 o’clock.”

Steel chuckles, although he turns away from me. My only proof are his shaking shoulders, the curve of his cheek in profile, and that elusive dimple.

"Deflective humor?" he asks.

"Deflective humor."

I lean my head against the building and roll it sideways. Behind us is another set of white cinderblock warehouses. The parking lot is dark back there, looks like the concrete just drops off. I imagine it's the end of the world and what it would be like to throw myself into the nothingness. Picturing concrete beneath my heels and my toes hanging over the blackness, it's easy to feel the adrenaline of teetering between life and death and wondering in which place I belong. Lifting my hands and tipping over, would I fall forever in my own personal hell, or just cease to exist, rightfully extinguished for my crime?

I look over to find Steel tapping away on his phone screen.

"Who did you call earlier?" I ask.

"My assistant."

"Oh! Fancy Recovery Agent has an assistant? I bet she's young, blonde, and calls you Big Daddy, huh?"

"Not exactly."

"Tell me," I insist.

"No."

"Come on. Tell me. I'll trade you something for it."

"What could you possibly bargain with?" he asks.

"I'll show you my party trick."

"Party trick?" he asks, looking at me sideways.

"Yeah. It's pretty epic. You know, that one quirky talent that you only pull out to entertain people at parties." Steel stares at me as if I've grown a second head. I return his stare and try to understand what he doesn't understand. "A party is a large group of people having fun, usually with the aid of alcohol." He rolls his eyes and pouts his pretty lips at me.

"Fine. His name is Brad. He's your age. Very good at his job. No social skills. He's got issues."

"Ha! Don't we all," I say. "Brad. That's a common name. Is he cute?"

Again, I get a strange look.

"How would I know?" Steel asks.

"Are you saying that because you're a heterosexual man, you couldn't possibly gauge the attractiveness of another man?"

Steel bends his knees and rests his forearms on them lazily. It's the first time I've seen him relax since we've met. He stares out at the vacant street.

"That's exactly what I'm saying."

A black car with dark tinted windows turns into the parking lot. Somehow Steel knows this is our ride. He stands, grabs his bag, and motions for me to get up. The car passes us and pulls near the edge of the lighted lot.

"Finally," I say. "Now this is how I'm meant to travel."

We walk toward the car, but Steel stops a few feet short. I bump into him and look up to see what's wrong. His eyes study the car so intently I feel like he's trying to penetrate the tint. Finally, the driver's door opens. One denim covered leg and motorcycle boot hit the ground.

"Run!" Steel yells.

I don't question him or look back at the car. For once, I simply follow instructions. I take off behind one of the buildings, disappearing into the dark. My eyes take too long to adjust to the dark and I'm running blind. I don't bother checking for Steel. I know he's close. I can hear his tandem footsteps echoing between the buildings. Finally his silhouette takes shape against the building and I follow it like Wendy after Peter Pan. We trail along the wall until we find a door. Steel tries the handle but it's locked.

"Where do we go?" I ask, folded over trying to catch my breath.

The alley we're in is flooded with light as the black car turns in. Both of us whip our heads toward the two leering headlights.

Steel grabs me by the wrist and pulls me farther down the row. I stumble, but manage to stay upright as we run. I hear the car's engine rev and the tires screech as it hurls toward us, but don't look back.

"In here!" Steel shouts. He drops to his stomach and slides under a large rolling door that is open about two feet. Steel disappears into the building and pulls his bag with him. I stand and stare at the empty space.

"Kat!"

I snap out of my daze and copy Steel's actions, rolling under the door and right into his feet. The light outside the door gets brighter as the car approaches. Steel steps to the door and slams it down, sliding a lock into place. We both stand with heaving chests and stare at the thin piece of metal separating good and evil. Though I have a hard time associating with either side of that coin.

Steel steps back and keeps his eyes on the door. There's a loud bang against the metal. I yelp and stumble back, tripping over Steel's bag and landing hard on my ass.

The handle on the bottom of the door rattles and I cover my mouth to hold my scream in. My chest feels like it's going to explode from the tension. I force myself to take slow, deep breaths and reign my fear back in.

"We're trapped," I say.

He spins in place, taking in our surroundings. It's a small office inside a larger warehouse. Steel goes over to the desk and grabs the phone. He pulls on the cord and sets the phone down right by the door. I stand and dust off as he dials a number and puts it on speaker phone.

A recorded voice comes over the phone. It recites the time, then weather and forecast. I look from the phone to Steel and back to the phone.

"What's that for?"

He points to the door. "He'll think it's one of us talking. It'll keep him back here while we try to find a way out." I nod, genuinely surprised at how good he is at this. "Let's move."

I follow Steel out of the office and across a warehouse with stacks of boxes and row after row of shiny cars. He pulls his phone from his pocket and dials.

"Change of plans. Boots is here," he says. "We're next door in the Hertz building. I think I can get to the front if your man can meet us there." There's silence and Steel shakes his head. "No. He'll have to come in through the front."

He slips his phone back into his pocket and keeps moving. We navigate through a maze of cars, our footsteps the only thing louder than our ragged breaths. I stop and lean against a small red sports car, leaving behind a handprint on its pristine driver's side window. Steel comes behind me and uses the bottom of his shirt to wipe it clean.

"No need to add to your list of crimes," he says walking past me.

"Isn't this breaking and entering? I just followed you! You're the one who's a man of the law, not me!" I whisper-shout.

Steel stops and spins to face me. I bump into his chest and crane my neck to look up at his murderous expression.

"You'd rather I leave you outside with him?" he asks pointing to the back door. His words are sharp and laced with more than anger. I pull away and shake my head. "Boots is the dangerous one here, Kat. I know who he works for, so I know how dangerous he is. While you may be his target, I'm the only thing standing between you. That puts me in his crosshairs too. I'm doing all this to save your ass."

"Don't pretend like you're doing me favors. We both know I'm just a job and a paycheck to you."

Steel runs his fingers through his hair, the tendons in his neck pull tight. "There are only two security cameras in this room. Keep your head down." He turns and takes off, all business again. I'm quick to follow.

"How do you know where we're going?" I ask.

"I don't. But our ride will be here," he looks at the watch on his wrist, "in approximately four minutes. We need to make it to the front door."

I follow Steel down a long hall, trying every door we come to. Most of them are open, but only lead to small storage rooms or offices. At the end of the hall, we turn right and see an exit sign. We jog over and push on the door. It doesn't budge.

"Damn," he says.

Steel scans the hall for another exit, but there's nothing. He leans forward and knocks his forehead against the wall a few times. I look at the ceiling and thank John Hughes for inspiration.

"Give me a boost," I say.

"What?"

"Up there. It's a drop ceiling. We'll go over the door." Steel stares at me, dumbfounded. Like it's so hard to believe that I have a good idea. "Time's ticking here," I remind him, tapping the face of his watch.

He bends his knees and laces his fingers together. I step into it and he lifts me easily. I push up on the panel and reach up, grabbing onto a bar. Steel lifts me higher and I pull myself through. It's dirty up here and smells like insulation. I cough a few times—more of a mental reaction than a physical one—and try not to think about the probability of hundreds of spiders surrounding me.

When I'm on my hands and knees, I stick my head back through the open panel and Steel hands me his bag. I pull it up and place it next to me. When I turn back around to see if he needs help getting in, he's already halfway up. I watch the muscles of his arms twist and flex as he pulls himself above the ceiling and lick my lips at the sight. They taste like dust.

"Stay on the metal grid," I tell him.

I carefully crawl in what I hope is the right direction. Counting six squares, I pull a panel up and drop my head down. It's the front office of Hertz. Freedom.

I get to a sitting position, grab onto the metal frame and swing my body through the hole. I hang there for a second before dropping to the floor. Smiling, I raise my arms in victory like gymnasts do after they stick the landing.

Steel's bag drops next to me and then he descends from the ceiling. His legs slide into view and then his stomach and that tattoo, revealed by his T-shirt riding up. I blink my eyes like a camera shutter and mentally bank this image for later. He drops to the floor, picks up his bag, and heads to the door. We each pull on the glass doors. Locked. We see a car come barreling into the parking lot, practically on two wheels. The headlights sweep across our faces as it turns in front of the building.

"Move!" Steel shouts.

I turn to see him grab a chair and hurl it at the glass door. It shatters into a spiderweb of tiny pieces. A deafening alarm sounds, it's wailing siren hurts my ears. Steel kicks out the glass and pulls me through just as the car pulls up. He opens the back door, throws me inside, then slides in next to me.

"Go!" he shouts. "Go! Go! Go!"

I look to the driver's seat to find a young blonde kid with spiky hair. He floors it, the screeching tires broadcasting our departure. As we turn the corner and speed onto the street I'm thrown across the backseat, landing in Steel's lap. He is all hard muscle and warm body beneath me. I realize too late that my hand is resting on his crotch. It's an instant reminder of what I've been missing the past few weeks, of what I'll be missing for the rest of my life.

"Sorry," I say, sliding off of him. "What about Boots?"

"I had a friend take care of that," the kid says.

I look back and find a big rig pulled sideways between the two buildings, blocking Boots in. I can just make out the black car stuck on the other side of the truck. I see Boots duck beneath the trailer and run into the road. I flip him off as we drive away, wearing a smile usually reserved for more casual situations.

"Holy shit, that was intense," I say, facing the front. "I've always wanted men to fight over me, but not like this."

Steel ignores me while the driver laughs. Finally, a normal human being.

"Hey, man. It's awesome to meet you. I've heard a lot about your work," the kid says glancing back at Steel. Steel nods and looks out the window. "So, who's this Boots character?"

"A pain in my ass," Steel answers as his fist taps against his knee. "He works for the system."

I turn to look at him, searching for a clue as to what "system" he's referring to. He doesn't meet my gaze.

"How long's he been on you?"

"Since I picked her up," he answers, gesturing toward me.

We drive along a road that runs next to the highway, turn into a lush green park, and pull to a stop.

"Well, at least she's worth it, right?" The kid meets my eyes in the mirror and smiles.

"A, can we stop talking about me like I'm not in the car? This feels like a family reunion where all the adults pretend you're deaf. And B, why are we stopping?"

"This is where I get out," the driver says.

Steel jumps out of the backseat, slides the child lock on, comes around to my side and repeats the process. I cross my arms and huff. At this point, I've decided I'm probably better off with him than without him. This Boots guy is crazy scary, while Steel is only sexy scary. I know he's driving me back to the authorities, back to a life in prison. But I'd rather be there than dead.

Steel opens the driver's door and waits.

I lean over the front seat. "You're leaving already? Thanks for the proper rescue. I suppose you won't tell me your name either?"

He gives me a strange look. "They call me Rich."

"Rich, as in Richard? Can I call you Dick?" I lower my eyes to his crotch.

Rich shifts his hips and offers me a grin. "You wouldn't be the first."

"If you're done flirting, we've got to go." Steel pulls him from the car by his shirt. "Shouldn't you be getting back to your parents' basement?"

He closes the door and we speed off, leaving the park and Rich behind.

"You're just going to leave him there?" I ask.

Steel doesn't answer me. The car speeds up as we merge onto the highway. His phone buzzes and he holds it to his ear.

"Yes. We're back on the highway now."

He plugs his phone into a charger and ends the call. Even in the dark I see his eyes slide to me in the mirror and back to the road.

"How did you know about the drop ceiling thing?" he asks.

"From that movie, *The Breakfast Club.*"

"With Audrey Hepburn, right?"

"No," I answer laughing. "That's *Breakfast at Tiffany's* from the sixties. *The Breakfast Club* is a John Hughes film from the eighties. Bender escapes a storage closet by crawling over the drop ceiling. Well, until he falls through."

Steel gives me that all too familiar blank look.

"Molly Ringwald? Anthony Michael Hall? Come on!"

"I've never heard of any of those people," he says.

"It's like you're from a different planet."

He frowns at me through the rearview mirror. I ignore his sour face and think about the letter they write at the end of the movie, a declaration refusing to wear labels. Wise beyond their years, they realize that individuals are not just one note. We are made of many pieces and combined in a unique way. I can easily identify with each one of the students' stereotypes—a brain, an athlete, a basket case, a princess, and a criminal. I'm an overachiever on that last one. I wonder if my father would be ashamed of that or proud of me for protecting mom.

I stared wide-eyed as the credits rolled and listened to the movie's anthem, "Don't You (Forget About Me)." My dad pressed Stop and Rewind on the VCR and the TV screen lit up blue. He leaned back and wrapped his arm around my shoulders.

"Well, kid, what did you think of that one?"

I closed my eyes and tried to choose the right words to explain how I felt. The honesty of those characters, the trials of being a teenager, the tragic and fantastic home lives of strangers you see every day—I was overwhelmed.

"Is high school really like that?" I asked.

He laughed and squeezed my shoulder before turning off the television.

"Sometimes. But don't be afraid to make your own rules, Kat."

I looked up into his smiling face and rested my head on his shoulder.

"The best part of that movie is that everyone started one way and ended another. They had all these theories on who they were and who the other kids were and they were all wrong."

"Even adults do that," he said. "We make snap judgments based on appearances, and most of the time we're missing the real person."

I looked at my reflection in the blank TV screen and wondered what people thought of me.

"Claire was such a brat. Even if I had all the money in the world, I'd never act like her. What a snob."

My dad tapped my knee twice and stood to leave.

"Well, that's not something you'll ever have to worry about, kid. We're tragically and forever middle-class."

We both laughed. When the VCR clicked, letting me know it was finished rewinding, I pressed Play and settled down to watch The Breakfast Club *one more time.*

I frown and stare at my lap. I had been wrong back then. When my dad died of an aneurism, we were suddenly and instantly left with a huge void in our lives. Though I kept his memories close to me, I was easily led astray by a captivating man with promises to fulfill all my dreams. When Dennis came into our lives, I was thrilled to have the best computers, the newest fashions, and highest expectations of everyone around me. And then it all collapsed into a nightmare.

I slide to the passenger side of the car and lean my head against the cool window trying to slow my racing thoughts. I focus on my breathing and how much more comfortable this new car is than the last one, letting myself sink into its plush seats and dark interior. My adrenaline is fading fast and with Steel's eyes on the road, the rhythmic passing of street lamps, and *thump thump thump* of the highway, I find it hard to stay awake.

7. HIM

I turn the radio on, but keep it low. There's nothing but darkness on each side of the highway. Staring out at the lone set of taillights ahead, I try to work out how Boots found us this time. If there was another device on the car, he could have located us that way, seen the flat tire and gone looking close by. It all seems a little too convenient.

I decide to leave those thoughts behind and focus on the present. Boots may know the direction we're heading, but I'm positive he can't be tracking us now. He's had no access to this vehicle.

In the backseat, Kat's head bobs up and down. When her chin drops, her eyes pop open and she resumes her battle. Watching her fight exhaustion, I find myself needing to comfort her. A piece of me wants to protect her from everything and get her to the Canadian border myself. I feel too connected to Kat. She's supposed to be a job and nothing more. Somehow, she's poking holes in my hard exterior and making me feel human again. It's foreign and makes me wary.

"Kat, you can sleep," I tell her.

"I know. I trust you."

I wince at her words. "Don't doubt what I am or what I do."

She shakes her head and frowns.

"I know you're delivering me to prison, or worse," she says, exhaling a shaky breath. "I know that this is your job. But, you don't have to be your job. I imagine in some alternate universe—which could actually exist and has been hypothesized, using constructive mathematics and non-halting computer programs, thank you very much—there's a guy who laughs at my stories, has a favorite football team, and wants more than some anonymous existence. You just don't see yourself clearly."

"And you only see what I let you."

"I don't want to sleep anyway," she says, effectively changing the subject. "I feel like these are my last full days of freedom. Well, I'm not exactly free, but you know what I mean." She sighs and starts again. "I don't want to waste a minute of it."

I can't argue with her. I've never known the physical confinements of prison walls, but I know what it is to be alone. In my career, I am a god. I'm who the amateurs want to be and the old pros want to crush. But, each night I sit alone in my small apartment, surrounded by four walls that hold nothing personal or meaningful. My neighbors are strangers and only my bank knows my real name. To most, I am an apparition, a thing they pass and when they look again, I'm gone. With no origin to speak of or family to claim, I barely exist by most standards.

We ride in silence for almost two hours, occasionally making eye contact in the mirror. Kat never looks away first, always questioning and challenging me with her gaze. We are more alike than I care to admit.

I check the car's gauges and exit to find a gas station. When I pull next to the pump, I throw the car in park and turn in my seat.

"We're getting close. I can feel it," Kat says. She plays with the charm on her necklace, sliding it back and forth.

"Just in Madera, the place dividing Northern and Southern California."

"Fascinating," she says absently.

"I want to trust you, but an open door may tempt a saint. I've seen it a million times. Wait here and I'll take you to the bathroom when I'm done."

"Yeah, okay," she answers.

The gas station is busy, a car parked next to almost every pump. I scan each car and its occupants for anything suspicious and find nothing out of the ordinary. Though, the couple across from us does offer an interesting tale. He stands outside the car, pumping gas. The buttons on his wrinkled oxford shirt are one off, giving his collar a lopsided shape. The woman reapplies lipstick in the visor mirror, rakes her fingers through her knotted hair and adjusts her tits. There are two distinctive handprints on the back glass, each angle hinting at a different position. She wears a wedding band, he does not.

After filling up, I open the door and let Kat exit the car. She stretches her arms to the sky and then bends at the waist, folding her body in half. I'm proud when I only ogle her ass for a few seconds before escorting her inside.

I give her a few moments alone in the bathroom, then step inside and lock the door. She wipes her hands on one of the rough paper towels.

"God, I look like shit." She smooths down her bangs and tucks stray pieces of hair behind her ear. "I need a haircut," she pauses and looks at her hands, "and a manicure. In my old life, that's something I actually cared about. It seems so stupid now, manicures. Now all I see, is a man's blood on my hands. It never goes away, stained into my skin permanently like your tattoos."

I watch as her bottom lip trembles and her eyes become glassy. Before the dirty mirrors of that gas station bathroom, Katherine Percle finally breaks down. Her loud sobs echo off the tiled walls and pound into my head. Her hands grip the edge of the counter and her shoulders slump in defeat.

"Kat," I whisper.

Her red eyes are framed by dark, wet lashes and she questions me silently. I nod, not knowing what I'm agreeing to, just knowing that I should. Kat throws herself at me, wrapping her arms tight around my waist and burying her face in my chest. I stand motionless at first, unsure of what she needs from me or what I'm willing to give. I hate the helpless feeling that scratches at my brain and my body's instinctual reaction to her. My mind battles between what I shouldn't do and what I must. Eventually, I wrap my arms around her while she sobs.

I hold Kat close and rub circles on her back. It's the only thing I know to do. My mom used to use the same sweeping motion when I was upset. Kat's fingers claw at my back as she pulls in tighter, muffling her sobs against my chest. It's overwhelming, the feel of her body pressed against mine, along with the smell of her hair and the push and pull of her breaths. I'm not sure what I'm doing.

I want to force her away and tell her to suck it up. I want that familiar detachment I'm used to. For some reason, with this girl, I don't have the strength to deny her.

We stand there ignoring the voices outside the door and the incessant knocking. We stay until her eyes run dry and all that is left are her stuttered sighs and whimpers. I pick her up, unlock the door, and bypass all the gawking on the way to the car. I lay her in the backseat and cover her with my jacket.

She makes no move to acknowledge my actions, she just stares ahead. By the time I pull back onto the highway, she's asleep. We have a little under two hours until we reach Bakersfield.

I chastise myself for getting tangled up with Kat. I've never let a case get to me like this. I've never allowed anyone to get past my anonymous existence. I shared my past with her, a past that I haven't thought about in years. The thought of her coaxing me into confessions makes me angry. I have to regain control and remind her and myself of what I'm here to do.

With my professional barricade back in place, I drive the dark highway and enjoy the silence. It's past eleven when we reach Bakersfield. I pull into a hotel, get a room, and make it back into the car without Kat stirring.

I park the car near our room and scrub at my face. I'm exhausted and frustrated and need to be done with this trip and this girl. When I drop my hands I find Kat staring at me through the mirror. Her eyes are still red, but her face holds no other signs of the breakdown.

In our room, Kat emerges from the bathroom, her face freshly washed. She pulls her hair free from the ponytail and I watch as she shakes the long brown waves down her back. I flip on the television, trade my jeans for sleep pants, and slide into bed. The air around us is uneasy and too quiet to be comfortable.

She removes her shoes and eyes me from her side of the bed.

"Can I borrow your boxers again?"

I dig through my bag and toss them at her without a word.

"Thanks," she murmurs.

Kat returns to the bathroom to change and I exhale into the empty room. I don't want to be a dick, but it'll be easier this way. It's as if I'm a divided man, half of me wanting to set her free and the other half needing to hold on tighter. Whether those thoughts are professional or emotional, I'm not sure. And I don't want to explore them to find out. If I can't hold on to my indifference, then I'll let anger lead.

Anger is familiar and I am comfortable in it. This girl is making me question everything I know and everything I think I am. She's making me consider bailing on the biggest payout of my career. She's forcing her pretty smile and shining blue eyes into my every waking thought. And that, is what makes me angry. While I want to blame Kat, I know it's myself I'm furious with.

I empty the bullets from my gun and remove the cuffs from my bag. Kat enters the room with my boxers in place and my shorts folded over her arm. She avoids eye contact as she settles into bed.

I slide one cuff around my wrist, motioning for her to give me her hand. I secure her wrist and lie back down, tucking the key into the waistband of my boxer briefs again. Kat's eyes stare blankly at the television, but there's no indication that she's really watching or listening. Our joined hands lay side by side on the mattress. Her pinky sweeps back and forth, sliding closer to mine and retreating again.

"Thank you," she says into the dark room.

"For what?"

"Earlier, at the gas station."

I don't answer her, but return my attention to the television. What am I supposed to say? You're welcome? Anytime? Everything that crosses my mind seems inappropriate and weak, so

I don't say anything. I simply hand over the remote and watch as she flips through the channels.

"Mom! No!"

Her bruised face forces a reassuring smile before I hear him coming. Heavy footsteps count off like a ticking bomb. The floor shakes beneath my feet or maybe it's just my legs. She tells me to hide and turns to face him. He is only a large black shadow bearing down on us. His voice is ice cold. The words are lost on me. She screams, but it's cut short by the sound of fist meeting flesh. Her body hits the ground with a thunderous finality. Red creeps along the floor, soaking into my white socks. I step away, but it persists. His words come again. I've learned that they are a prequel to his violence. I run. And then, he comes for me.

My own screaming wakes me. My eyes shoot open in the dark to find Kat's worried expression above me. The warmth of her palms on my face only adds to the heat of my flushed cheeks. I try to fully wake as my chest heaves with stuttered breaths and my blurred eyes work to focus. She runs her fingers through my hair and places her lips near my ear, whispering, "Shhhhhh."

I close my eyes again and struggle against her, not wanting this comfort. Every muscle in my body is taut and she winces when my grip on her shoulder becomes too tight. I release her and try to push away.

"Don't let go," she whispers. "Please." Her body shifts above me, pleading with prayers on her lips. "Please," she begs again, sliding her lips against my neck before biting down.

I lay frozen and undecided. The feel of Kat against me makes me dizzy. Her desperation is tangible. It recognizes its counterpart in me and pulls it to the surface. Before I can clear the dark dreams from my brain, Kat gently presses her lips to mine. With one kiss, I am lost.

We taste each other, slowly at first, nibbling and sucking on tongue and lips. My hand slides up her body, loving every inch of soft skin and curve I come across. I pull roughly at her hair. I'm rewarded with a deep, throaty moan.

She trails her lips down my neck to my chest where she places kisses in a sweeping arc over my UNFORGIVEN tattoo. I roll away, trying to regain control, but it's no use. Kat straddles my body now and shifts backward until I can feel her heat above my hardness. There is no denying I want her. She leans down to capture my lips again.

"I *need* this. Just one last time," she begs. Her breaths are fast and heavy, her hair falls like a curtain around us.

Her plea destroys me. I am defeated and hungry for her. We work together to push my pants and boxer briefs down. I tug at her tank top, slipping it over her head and down her arm where it hangs from our joined wrists. I lick my lips just to taste her and try to remember when I've ever been so desperate for something.

"Kat," I say.

I reach up with my free hand and trail my fingers down her neck, across her collarbone and around the swell of her breast. She shimmies free from the boxers and now we are both bared flesh and desire.

Something inside me fractures. My raw and desperate need for her is now the only thought in my head. I sit up and kiss her again, for once dominating this. I nudge Kat backward until my body covers hers. Our cuffed hands grip each other and hold my weight while I align myself with her. Her other hand slides from my hair down to where my neck meets my shoulder. Her thumb sweeps across my hurried pulse. I pause and look into Kat's eyes. I'm silently asking questions that I don't dare say out loud.

"Yes," she breathes.

Our bodies come together and it's pins and needles on my skin, enveloping warmth and dancing lights behind my lids. Kat cries out and her body arches toward me like a bow pulled tight. Her face, a perfect portrait of pleasure, turns to the side and she pulls her bottom lip between her teeth. After a minute, I begin to rock my hips against her. Our rhythm matches each panting breath that escapes my lips. She claws and scrapes at my back, unable to use her words. This is heaven and hell and everything in between.

I don't think of consequences or tomorrow morning. All I focus on is her needy mouth kissing mine, my fingers holding hers, her body owning me. I bury my face in her tits and place hard, sucking kisses there. Kat slides her hand into my hair and pulls, bringing my mouth to hers again.

"More," she pleads against my lips.

I quicken the pace, as we connect in the most primal way. It's wild and erratic. Kat wraps her legs around me, her knees digging into my ribs and creating an almost painful bliss. Each breath is carried on a pleasured gasp. The sound is pure sex and it sends a new pang of desire through me. She slides her hand down to my shoulder and digs her nails in. The heat and light inside her finally breaks free. Kat cries out before biting down on her lip. It is a violent and beautiful thing to witness. It's only now that I wish I had given her my name. To hear that word from her at this moment, with her flushed cheeks and satisfied smile, would be amazing. My entire body quakes as my own orgasm knocks the air from my lungs.

We both lay sweaty and exhausted, drifting off to a blissful sleep.

8: her

It's still early when I wake. I turn to find my bounty hunter deep asleep. His naked body lays on top of the sheets and I want to touch him again. I roll onto my side and feel something cold against my skin. Sliding my free hand between my hip and the bed, I pull out the handcuff key. My eyes adjust in the dark room as I stare at liberty in the palm of my hand.

I debate staying. Do I really want a life on the run? I'll always be checking over my shoulder, never able to trust anyone. And then there is Boots, a dangerous hit man who seems to have limitless resources. I weigh my options—freedom, prison, possibly death—and decide that freedom is worth the risk. Maybe what I'd shared with Steel last night was a vivid reminder of what it feels like to be truly alive. Whatever the reason, I wasn't ready to give it up for a cold, empty existence behind bars.

I push the key into the lock and turn it. The tiny click sounds like a gunshot in the quiet room. Steel does not stir. Gently, I remove my wrist from the cuff and roll out of bed. I am silent and stealthy as I find my old jeans and hoodie in his bag and redress. I check the rest of the contents for anything helpful. Littering the bottom of the bag is a stack of travel brochures highlighting attractions in cities spanning several states. I thumb through them quickly and glance at Steel wondering why he has these. In his wallet I only find a worn photo of myself and eighty bucks.

The picture was taken at my mom's birthday dinner last year. I'm smiling at the camera while holding a glass of wine. I remember how my mom had to wear long sleeves in the middle of the summer because of the bruises. Dennis's controlling arm stayed around her waist all night. There was hurt and anger that sat heavy at that table between me and the rest of the party. I wondered if all those people were ignorant or indifferent to my mother's suffering.

The air was sickeningly sweet with Chanel perfume and aged wine. I made my way around the private dining room, sticking to the shadows as much as possible. I stopped and exchanged pleasantries with my mother's closest friends while avoiding the birthday girl completely. My usual saving grace, Aunt Nora, was absent, no longer able to face my mom and her abusive husband.

My boyfriend, Paul, stood beside Dennis, each of them perched like voyeurs at the highest point in the room. I approached them and placed a kiss on Paul's cheek.

"Hey, baby," he said. "Sorry I'm late. It's quite a good turnout though, right?"

I nodded and sipped my wine. Dennis did not acknowledge me.

"There's Patrick," Dennis said to Paul. "We should go ask for a rematch on that last golf game."

Paul followed Dennis across the room like a puppy after its master. The admiration he had for that man made me sick.

"I don't even know half these people." I turned to find my mom beside me. She looked beautiful and wore her pretend smile perfectly. The thick makeup on her cheek covered a bruise that I knew was still there.

"Then why invite them?"

"Dennis says it's good for business, socializing with his high-end clients."

"All about appearances, right?" I asked, shooting her an angry glance. "What's your story this time, huh? You fall down a flight of stairs?"

She unconsciously touched her cheek and then folded her arms across her chest. This was her defensive move. I had seen it too many times.

"Don't start, Katherine. Not tonight."

"Why do you stay with him?"

Her gaze drifted across the room and landed on Dennis. "I love him."

"Love shouldn't leave you black and blue. When you've had enough, let me know. I'll do anything to help you. Happy birthday, Mom."

I walked away, knowing the battle wouldn't be won that night. I caught Paul's eye and waved toward the bathroom, letting him know where I'd be. Once inside the posh sitting room, I set my clutch on the counter and leaned into the large gilded mirror. My makeup was fine, but I searched out my lipstick and reapplied just to kill some time. Just as I traced the curve of my bottom lip, Marilyn appeared in the mirror beside me.

Her appearance was flawless—designer clothes, impeccable hair, and permanent sneer firmly in place. Like her brother Dennis, she maintained an immaculate façade to hide the ugliness underneath.

"Katherine," she greeted without meeting my eyes.

"Marilyn," I responded, mocking her tone.

"I see your mother has somehow wrangled the Warby sisters into her social circle."

I shrug. "Sad you didn't get your raggedy claws into them first?"

Her face remained expressionless and I assumed all the Botox had done some permanent damage.

"I've always heard they're a bunch of bleeding hearts, so I'm sure they're just thrilled to tackle a case like your mother."

I turned to face her, but she continued to face her reflection. I curled my hands into fists and wondered at what angle I'd have to punch her to knock the feeling back into her forehead.

"Maybe they'll keep her occupied," she continued. "Heaven knows I'm tired of seeing her hanging around the office like a goddammed groupie, decorating the lobby with her tacky taste. She needs a hobby or something. Don't you think?"

"I think you should worry less about what she's doing and more about those telling age spots and crow's feet decorating your face."

I left her there and rejoined the party, taking my place among all the other fakes and forgeries in the room. Every time my mother moved, she was tugging at her long sleeves, making sure to hide beneath the silk charmeuse.

When the photographer approached, I turned away, only to meet my mother's pleading eyes. She silently begged me to play along. To make her happy, I raised my glass to the camera and pasted on my most convincing smile.

I run my fingers over the photo version of me and wonder how Steel got this photo. It could have only come from someone in the family. That stings and sets thoughts in motion that I don't have time to dwell on. I leave the photo in his wallet and take the money.

Each lock on the door seems to be louder than the one before. I cringe when the deadbolt finally slides free. Steel doesn't move. He still lays on his side peacefully sleeping. I take one last long look at him. I memorize this moment, his face and exactly how I feel. Whispering good-bye, I squeeze out the door and into the dark.

Before I realize it, I'm sprinting. My feet feel like lead as they carry me away from that building, away from him. Tears build and spill over and I'm not sure why.

I run until I physically can't anymore. I stop on a street corner and struggle for air while my hands rest on my thighs to keep me from collapsing. Spotting a park across the street, I walk over and tuck myself inside a playground structure.

I lean back and let the cool metal press against my sweaty back. It sends a chill down my spine, goose bumps breaking over my skin. The feeling reminds me of Steel's hands on my body, his breath on my neck. I pound my fist against my leg, angry that he's who he is and I'm who I am.

I despise that I have to transform myself back into Kat on the run instead of just Kat. Her alias is Lisa. She's charming and sickeningly sweet. She flirts to get what she wants. She steals to get what she needs. She's a lie and I hate her.

I can't even identify with the girl that I was six months ago. When my dad died, I somehow let all the good things about me get buried with him. I forgot about getting joy from simple things—like chasing after the ice cream truck or finding a ladybug crawling on you. I kept my distance from people as Dennis and my mother groomed me to fit in with their high-society friends.

Though I feel awful about Dennis' death, I can't help but give credit to that event for unearthing the old me. It's as if the sound of a single gunshot snapped me out of the role I'd been playing and brought me back to life.

With Steel, I could be myself. There was no pressure to behave a certain way or impress him. Even being from two different worlds, we shared a common history. He didn't care about my past or my money or my education. He was a man that lived only in the present. That, along with his handsome face and inviting mystery, is what made him so desirable. I don't know if I'm better off without him, or safer with him, but in that pivotal moment, I knew I had to take the chance.

From here I watch the sun rise over the trees. The pink and orange hues paint my face with warmth and freedom. When I'm rested, I go in search of provisions. I ask a jogging woman where I can find the nearest store. She points me a couple of miles down the road. I start that way and as I walk, I wonder if Steel has woken up yet. Is he mad or relieved that I'm gone?

I imagine his temper gets the best of him and he takes it out on some helpless piece of furniture that won't survive his wrath. He'll be angrier at himself than at me. He didn't want me the way I wanted him. I could feel his resistance. I took advantage of him, using our mutual attraction—his only vulnerability—to get what I needed. The thing is, after only two days, there was more than physical desire there. There was a frightening underlying need to open him up and heal him, to pardon his past and give him new life. I convince myself that I can't be that for him, or anyone else for that matter.

The bright lights and shiny floors of the big box store welcome me in. I grab a cart with a wobbly wheel, shaky and spinning around like it refuses to follow the other three. It makes a little sharp sound and then a thump. It's kind of a funky beat, so instead of switching it out, I keep this cart. We have a kinship.

We squeak and rattle our way to the clothing section, where I'm instantly drawn to vintage looking T-shirts with movie quotes on them. I watch as a young girl and her friend browse the aisle, making flippant remarks about everything.

"Whoa. Gina, look at this," the blonde girl says with mockery in her voice. "I think my grandma wore this in the seventies."

"What does that even mean? 'Wax on, wax off'," Gina replies, laughing while she pokes at the shirt.

I run over and grab the shirt from the rack, cradling it to my chest like a protective mother.

"It's not from the seventies. It's from the eighties. The fact that you don't even know what it refers to speaks volumes about your OMG LOL skinny jeans generation."

I scowl at them and know that I'm not really angry at these girls. They represent my past and everything I did wrong. Still, I want to rip them down until they are bare bones and innocence. They need to appreciate their futures, because nothing is guaranteed. I hold the shirt out and swing it back and forth on the hanger, realizing I'm just the one to make them see. A woman passes by, eyeing our standoff and I'm suddenly aware that I'm causing a scene. Regardless, I can't seem to tear myself away from the fight.

"Whatever. You're totes cray-cray," Gina says. "And what? You're like three years older than us?"

Both girls giggle as their thumbs scramble over the keys on their phones. They have dismissed me.

"Cray-cray? That's not even a word! Neither is totes. Okay, it is, but not how you used it. Have you completely abandoned the English language in favor of some text message code? You sound like idiots," I say quietly, but firmly.

Both girls stare at me, stunned. I spin around and stomp back to my cart, throwing the T-shirt inside.

"For the record, 'Wax on, Wax off' is in reference to the original *Karate Kid*. Do yourselves a favor and watch it. And not that crappy remake!"

Though I know I've made no headway with these girls, I feel better getting it off my chest. Hell, I've educated them. Once they see put-him-in-a-body-bag-Johnny and Daniel-san go at it, they'll be thanking me.

I spend most of Steel's money buying myself a new pair of jeans, underwear, deodorant, some snacks, and a bag to carry it all in. I change in the bathroom with only a few side-glances from other customers.

When I'm done, I feel human again. I stare at myself in the

bathroom mirror and realize that I'm still young, and even if it's a life on the run, I've still got a lot of life to live. And it's then I decide where I need to go next. Just like that, I have a destination. I tuck myself into a shady spot in the parking lot and try to work out a plan. I've got to get to another truck stop or find someone traveling.

"Mommy, Mommy! Look at my new doll!" a little girl shouts as she pulls a toy from a shiny plastic box.

"I know dear, I bought it for you." The mother barely glances at the girl as they cross the parking lot.

"She has blonde hair like you, Mommy! She's beautiful like you, too," the girl says.

She holds the doll up high in the air, barely reaching her mother's shoulder, and smiling a gap-toothed smile as she waves the doll around. The woman never notices that she's being admired, worshipped.

I feel heartbroken for that little girl and angry at the mother. I long for the days of my childhood, back when my dad was still alive and my mom made me feel loved. Before Dennis and his money, we had been happy. I wonder what my mom is doing now. Is she concerned about my safety? Will she ever forgive me? No, what I did was unforgivable. I know that and I accept the penalty of losing everything in my life that mattered. At the time, it felt like I didn't have a choice. But Steel is right, you always have a choice.

I shove the last of a granola bar into my mouth and stand. I set my sights and dart out from between two cars, running right into the blonde's shopping cart, almost knocking her over.

"Oh! I'm so sorry," I say.

The woman humphs and bends down to pick up her purse and all of its contents. The little girl chases a rolling tube of lip gloss across the asphalt while I bend down to help.

"Really, I'm sorry. I didn't even see you there."

"I'm sure you didn't," the woman replies, painting me with her disdain.

I'm holding a handful of receipts, her phone, a pack of gum, and a compact in my hands. She holds out her purse and I drop them inside. The little girl returns with the lip gloss and drops it in as well.

"I helped," she says, smiling up at her mother, begging for approval.

"You did a great job," I say, ruffling her blonde curls.

The woman says nothing and drags the girl away to their car.

"Sorry again," I say. When she's out of earshot, "Bitch."

I return to my spot and pull the woman's wallet from my pocket. If she hadn't been such a terrible mother, I might feel guilty for ripping her off, but as it stands, I'm kind of proud.

I slide her license from its plastic window and read over her information. Theresa Ann Morris of State Street is five feet five inches tall and definitely lies about her weight. I open the wallet and discover around eighty dollars in cash. I slide the cash into my pocket and hide the wallet in a shrub.

I've got to get out of this town, so I stand to survey the parking lot. There are parents with kids in tow. An elderly man drives in and backs out of a space three times before finally parking. Way in the back of the lot, an old RV pulls in. It's covered in layers of dust and red mud.

I watch as three guys and two girls pour out the side door. They are all tan and lean, wearing what looks like homemade clothes and sandals. The girls' hair is in braids with various beads and feathers clipped in. One guy is bald while the other two have dreadlocks. They look tired and dirty, but content. The group enters the store and I'm quick to follow them in.

I slink around, staying out of sight and listening to their conversations. I need some kind of intel that will help me get my foot in the door, literally, with this group. I follow them through the sporting goods section, shoes, bedding, and finally to the food.

"I want some of those veggie chips," one guy says. The group moans unanimously. "What? You guys know those are my favorite."

"No, Ryan," a blonde girl says. "Those were Hannah's favorites. You've got to let her go, man. It's over."

"Yeah," the other girl of the group says, "she dumped you when she got her first gig. That's so lame. She was using you. You know you can't trust actresses."

"She's going to be a star. I just know it."

The tall bald guy throws his arm around Ryan's shoulders and nudges him.

"Well, she'll be a star without you, buddy. You should date a waitress. They're totally reliable, always have cash, and smell like gravy. My kind of girl."

The group laughs and pulls their friend down the aisle. The veggie chips stay on the shelf.

I head outside when they get in line and make my way across the lot. Smoothing down my hair, I apply my new fruity lip balm and park myself under a tree. When the group approaches, arms loaded down with plastic bags, I stand and make my approach.

"Hey," I say, giving a small wave and looking down at my feet. The group stops, but no one answers my greeting. "Are you guys heading south? I was wondering if I could get a ride to LA."

"I don't see why not. We've got the space, right Dave?" the blonde asks.

"Yeah, man. The more the merrier," Dave answers. He comes over and lays his arm across my shoulders.

"I'd love to share some space with you. I'm Amber," the taller girl says, giving me a flirtatious smile.

"It's just that, my boyfriend stranded me here. He left me in this parking lot. I'm trying to get to LA so I can get my stuff before he destroys it all. I've been here two hours already. I don't have much money. I spent most of my tips on food."

"So he's your ex-boyfriend now, huh?" Amber asks, hopeful.

"Looks that way," I answer, shrugging.

"Tips? Are you a dancer? You know, an exotic engineer? Pole slider?" Dave asks.

"No, I'm a waitress at the House of Blues. I'd really appreciate a ride. I'll make it up to you guys sometime. Get you into a show or something?"

"Sold!" Dave exclaims. The girls chuckle and climb into the RV along with the driver. "What's your name?" Dave asks.

"Lisa."

"Lisa, this is my very good friend, Ryan. Ryan, this is Lisa, the waitress."

He wiggles his eyebrows and escorts me into the RV. Ryan follows and sits next to me on the bench. Amber looks put out, but takes a seat across from me. It's not a new RV, but I can tell the group has made their own improvements. I can barely make out the flowered wallpaper behind a painted mural of peace signs and birds. There are glow-in-the-dark stars affixed to the ceiling and the tabletop has been covered in comic book pages. It smells like dirt and sweat, but not in a bad way, in a way that has been earned.

I'm relieved when we get moving. Though the air becomes stifling when I realize all eyes are on me. Dave is the first one to speak.

"What are you doing up here?" he asks.

This is the part that comes easy. My time on the road has made me a liar, a vandal, a thief. I'm ashamed to be an expert at these things.

"We were visiting my boyfriend's parents. We stopped at the store for snacks and got into this huge fight when he admits he's been cheating on me for like four months!"

I wave my hands around and shake my head to be convincing.

"No," Ryan says.

"You can't share the love without permission, man," Amber chimes in.

"I know! With his ex, too. I just couldn't get back into the car with him. I told him to leave me. Imagine my surprise when he actually did."

"What a dick move," Dave says.

"Yeah, if I had a girl like you, I'd never leave her alone," Ryan says as he gives me a goofy grin.

He's got that starry-eyed, smell your hair, steal your underwear kind of look and it makes me understand why Ryan may have lost his last girlfriend. Still, I see my opportunity.

"Hey, I left my phone in my boyfriend's car, could I borrow yours?" I ask him.

He hands it over. I walk to the back of the RV and seclude myself behind a folding door. Holding the smartphone in my hand is like being home again. After dialing one of the six phone numbers banked in my memory, I take a seat on the small bed.

"Hello?"

"Aunt Nora?"

"Katherine? Is that you? Katherine where are you?"

"That's not important," I say.

"It is very important, Katherine. You've skipped bail. You're a wanted criminal for Christ's sake! Your poor mother is worried sick. You're all over the local news."

"I know, I know. I just called to tell you something."

"Okay, out with it," she says cautiously. "Though, I have to say, I don't want to hear any confessions from you, sweetheart. I prayed every day for that man to disappear. I'm so sorry it had to be you that made that happen. So, please don't tell me anything that they'll force out of me in a courtroom."

"This is the last time you'll hear from me. I'm going to disappear. I love you and Mom, so much. I hope that one day she can forgive me."

The line is silent. I can't hear her breathing or any background noise. Then there is some murmured whispering and shuffling of the phone.

"Hello?" I ask. "Aunt Nora?"

"It's me, dear." My mother's voice fills me with relief and overwhelming feelings of loneliness. Instinctually, I straighten my posture and take a deep, calming breath before speaking.

"Mom?"

"Do you still have the key?" she asks.

"What?" My hand seeks out the charm on my necklace and I press it into my skin.

"The key, Katherine. Do you still have it? Marilyn says that she'll—"

"The key? That's all you care about, right? Well, you can tell Marilyn that it's gone."

"You don't mean that, baby." The word *baby* stabs at me like a terrible lie. "Just come home and we'll get you the best lawyers. All you have to do is give up the key."

I pull the phone away from my face and press the end call button. I stare at the lifeless device and wonder when money became more important than her own daughter. When did my own mother trade me in for high-end cars and Botox? I delete my mother's number from the recent calls list, swipe the tears from my eyes, and rejoin the others. The group's conversation stalls when I sit down.

"He's going to put my stuff in the front yard. Jerk," I say.

My comment breaks the ice as the girls begin to bash my nonexistent boyfriend, suddenly warming up to me as the victimized girlfriend. After that, it's easy conversation all the way back to LA, until they ask for my address.

"Oh, I hate to be trouble. Just get to where you guys are going and I'll call someone to pick me up," I say.

"No can do," the driver says, "We're heading down to San Diego."

"Oh." I pause, frantically searching my brain for something that won't destroy my cover story. "You guys could just drop me off at work. I need to pick up my paycheck anyway."

The scenery changes quickly as we approach Los Angeles. The highway splits into five lanes, a wide path leading toward a murky skyline of bar graph buildings against a blue sky. I'm wide-eyed at the window, loving the palm trees that line the streets and the colorful graffiti along the way. I search every hill for the Hollywood sign and every corner for celebrities. The RV navigates its path through the city and soon we're parked in front of the House of Blues on Sunset Boulevard.

The girls offer a tight smile and Ryan looks nervous. Dave gives me a big thumbs up as I step to the door.

"Umm, Lisa? Would it be okay if I call you sometime?" Ryan asks. "You know, so I can let you know when we're back in town?"

"Sure," I say, holding my hand out for his phone.

I suppress the giggle that wants to erupt from my throat as I enter the numbers 867-5309 into his phone. Meanwhile, the song supplying my fake number keeps playing in my head. *Jenny I got your number.* I slide the phone into his waiting hand and I'm out the door before he can check it.

The RV rumbles down the street and I give a wave as I watch them go.

9. HIM

I wake to absolute quiet and a bar of golden light peeking through the gap in the curtains. Details come to me like still photographs in a slide show—the floral-printed wallpaper, the blank television, my bare chest, and sheets around my hips. Still tired and reeling from the previous night's events, I bring my hands up to rub my face only to get smacked in the forehead with the attached and empty handcuff.

"No, no, no, no," I mumble.

Panicking, I look to the other side of the bed to find it empty. Cool sheets and her pillow's indention are all that's left of Katherine Percle. I jump up and throw on my jeans while searching the room. My head spins as I check the bathroom and closet, making sure she's gone. I feel dizzy and nauseated. I lean over the sink, sucking in deep breaths. My pulse thunders in my ears and I can't calm the rage building inside.

"Fuck!"

My scream does nothing to calm me. With no thought, I raise my fist and throw it forward. The mirror shatters, jagged pieces pointing in toward the center. Blood paints my knuckles and the pain finally brings me down.

Once I clean my wounds, I throw everything into my bag and slip into my shoes. I check the room one last time, making sure she's left no clue, nothing of herself. I throw the door open and find Boots there. He drops his cigarette and crushes it with the heel of his boot before pulling a pistol and pointing it at my chest. I slide my shades down over my eyes and feign indifference.

"Give me the girl," he says. His voice is a deep rasp with a heavy Southern twang.

He's leaned against his bike, all shiny chrome and leather, wearing a smirk that just asks to be knocked off. He looks dirty and worn out, wearing the same clothes from three days ago. Besides his cold grin, his face is hard and lifeless. He looks like he's been in the business too long. He's me in fifteen years.

"She's gone," I say.

I walk to the trunk and throw my bag inside. I can feel his cold gaze and the gun's barrel following my every move.

"Well, shit. This bitch is turning out to be a worthy opponent. I just love the thrill of the chase. Though, I can't imagine how she could have gotten out on *you*."

His accent is thick. It makes him sound slow and dumb. His words insinuate that he knows exactly how Kat escaped. I'm furious at myself and at him for pointing out my failure.

"You're Boots, right?" I ask, leaning against the car. I try to appear relaxed, though inside I'm on red alert. The feel of my own gun presses into my back and I know I can reach it if needed. Boots must know I'm carrying, but he doesn't ask for my piece. That alone shows his arrogance. He doesn't consider me a threat.

"The one and only," he answers.

"What the fuck kind of name is that?"

He ignores me. "I know exactly who you are." Boots sneers. "Your reputation precedes you."

"Well, I *am* the best."

"Were," he corrects, hitting himself in the chest. "You're also known for your out-of-control temper and your mysterious past. Though I don't think you're such a mystery. I think you're a punk kid who's just about outworn his usefulness."

Boots pulls the back the hammer and the click sends a chill down my spine. One squeeze of that trigger and I'm a goner. Behind the dark lenses of my sunglasses, I hold his gaze and stand my ground. He may not be able to see it, but I know he feels it.

"How'd you find us?"

"I followed the yellow brick road," he answers.

"You work for Dragon, right?" I ask, stepping toward him.

"I work for justice."

I laugh at his implied superhero status. "How noble of you," I spit. I take another step toward him.

"I like to think so."

I jump out of his line of fire and swing to hit him but he steps forward and blocks my arm. His gun goes clattering to the ground. He lands a fist to my ribs and all the air leaves my body. I'm a little surprised that the old man can pack a punch like that. I double over and he knees me in the stomach. Still reeling from the pain I spin and stand, throwing my elbow at his face. It lands on his nose with a crack. Rivers of blood pour over his mouth. I pull my own pistol and point it at his head. He only gives me an evil smile, white teeth painted crimson.

"Get off the bike," I say. He follows my instructions with his hands up, seeming amused at my demand. When he's on the sidewalk, I step to his bike and pull off the fuel line, tearing it in half and watching the gasoline leak onto the asphalt. "That should hold you up for a while."

"I wouldn't count on it. I always have a backup strategy," Boots says, spitting blood onto the sidewalk.

"Stop fucking following me. I found her first."

"I can't do that," he says. His smug expression tempts me to just put a bullet between his eyes right now. "I know that *you* don't work for Dragon. So who hired you?"

I shift my weight and readjust the grip on my pistol.

"She doesn't know, does she? Katherine?"

I push my piece into his throat. "I'll end you right now."

"When were you going to tell her?" My silence gives him the only answer he needs. "Oh, you weren't."

My anger boils over and I hit him in the temple with the butt of the gun. He slumps and falls to the ground, out cold.

"More like Puss in Boots," I mumble before jumping in the car and speeding out of the parking lot. I check my mirrors to make sure I'm not being followed and speed toward the highway. Weaving in and out of traffic, I ignore the honking horns and middle finger gestures, only thinking of Kat and her whereabouts.

"Damn!" I shout. The sound of my own desperate voice hits me like a blow to the chest. "Fuck! Fuck! Fuck!"

I'm off track. Kat did this to me. She slipped past every wall I built and brought me down like a house of cards. I won't be outplayed. Not by this girl.

I instinctually drive south and decide not to tell my employer about this little problem. I'm confident I can find Kat again. As the mile markers tick by, I mentally scroll through every conversation with her. I revisit the inappropriate comments, all the random chatter, and every annoying admission until I remember her ridiculous bucket list.

I press the pedal down further, speeding toward the City of Angels.

My phone buzzes for the fourth time in the past two hours and I can't ignore it anymore.

"What?" I say.

"Is that anyway to greet me, darling?"

"Natasha."

"That's better. I've been trying to get at you for two weeks now. Have you been avoiding my calls?"

"Isn't that what exes do?"

Natasha was my only serious relationship in the past ten years. We started out strictly professional, a mentor and student. I'm not sure when things changed, when she got her claws into me, but she did. Soon, her training took a backseat to our fast and fiery relationship. She filled a void in my life. I craved her day and night.

It never went further than that physical desire for me. I wanted her body. I was never attached.

So, I took her under my wing and taught her everything I know. She's a natural. Tall and blonde, an innocent face that gets her anything she wants. Anything, except me.

Our breakup was ugly. There were tears and threats on her end, empty nothingness on mine. She took a tire iron to my car before I could restrain her. It didn't matter to me, material things are expendable, replaceable. She told me she loved me, that it couldn't be over. It was the first time that I wished I could feel something back.

We went our separate ways, but still cross paths professionally. She likes to pretend we're still friends. Because I'm a lonesome bastard, I like to let her.

"I hear you're working a new case, darling. A girl?" I don't answer. It's never good to give Natasha ammunition. "Is she pretty?"

"She's a target."

"She can still be pretty even though she's a target, no?" she asks while laughing.

Her laughter is soft and flirty. It's exactly the same every time, like it's been rehearsed to the point of becoming a natural response.

"You've been trying to get in touch with me for weeks and you want to talk about my job? What do you really want?"

She says something just as someone cuts me off on the freeway. I slam on the brakes and barely avoid the collision.

"You dick!" I shout.

"Did you hear me?" Natasha asks. "I said, I'm offering my help. I hear it's a big payout and I want in."

My stomach churns as I picture Natasha and Kat in the same room. It's the scene of a predator toying with its dinner. I can't stomach the outcome.

"No. I've got it under control," I answer.

"That's not what I hear."

"How? What did you hear?" I yell.

"Just that you found her, fucked her, and lost her." Natasha laughs again, but this time it's at my expense.

"Who told you?" I growl.

My fingers slide around the steering wheel, squeezing until my knuckles pop and crack from the pressure.

"You know the boys talk like a bunch of old ladies. It's not every day that *The Great and Powerful Oz* loses a target. It's kind of a big deal."

"Like I said, I've got it."

"Alright, darling. But if you need me, I'll come running."

There was a time when I thought her use of the word *darling* was endearing. Now, it feels like nails through my flesh.

I end the call and throw my phone onto the passenger seat. Things are spinning away from me and even worse, my reputation is at stake. I've got to find Kat and finish this job. At this point, it's the only thing that matters.

When I get to LA, I realize that Kat's stolen the last of my cash. I find an ATM and restock my wallet, cursing her the whole time. I check into a shitty hotel. The red door's paint is chipped and peeling, revealing a mint green color beneath it. There are scratches around the keyhole on the doorknob. It could be from years of drunk guests fumbling with the key or from people trying to break in. My gut says it's a combination of both.

When I enter the room, I find the brown carpet stained and matted down in places. The air smells like pine-scented cleaner on top of cigarette smoke. I shove all worries of the room out of my head. It provides all that I need, just somewhere to regroup.

I take a quick shower, finally washing away Katherine Percle and my feelings of regret. I breathe in the steam and lean my forehead against the tile, staying there until the water turns cold.

When I'm dressed, I head out into the city. I walk down Hollywood Boulevard and take in the sights. In all my travels and all my jobs, I've never had a reason to come here before. I can say that I'm not impressed. At the very least, I thought it would be clean. Litter and trash accompany celebrity stars along the sidewalk. I read each name as I pass them and can only think of Kat when I don't recognize most of them.

On the corner of Hollywood and Vine, I run into some kids asking for change. I give them a few dollars and show them the photo of Kat. They say they haven't seen her. I believe them.

I grab a bite to eat and keep moving. As I finish off the hot dog, I make a mental note to get back to the gym when this is over. A month of eating convenience food is making me feel like shit. Fast meals, hotels, and endless hours in a car were not what I pictured when I got into this career. My mentor made it sound glamorous, like I'd be a hero. When I graduated high school, I knew I wasn't heading to college. I'm not the brainiac type. I needed some way to prove my life wasn't wasted.

After I left my foster home, I got into some trouble. Small robberies and stealing cars left me reaching for something bigger. I needed a purpose. Mickey van Sant gave me that.

He was big time. He drove fancy cars and always had a hot woman on his arm. He threw elaborate parties at his house with endless supplies of drugs and alcohol. I never understood why he hung out with us trashy kids, why he let us into his world.

One night he took me aside into his private office. I sat in a leather chair while he perched on the end of his massive desk.

"Hey, kid. How ya doin'?" he said.

"Good, Mickey. Good. Thanks for that loan. I promise I'll get it back to you as soon as possible."

"Forget it. Look, I been watchin' you. You got somethin' special about you. Some kind of charm that these other kids ain't got."

"I don't know about that."

He tipped his head down at me. His look told me to shut my mouth.

"Close your eyes," he instructed. I did as I was told. "Now tell me how many books are on the second shelf behind you."

"Seven," I answered, surprising myself.

"And what color is my tie?"

"Maroon with white diagonal stripes."

"What objects are on my desk?" he asked.

I squeezed my eyes closed tighter and made a mental picture of the top of his desk.

"There's a crystal paperweight, two pens—one black, one red, a notebook, and an antique lamp with a crack in the porcelain base."

"And?" he hedged.

I tilted my head and checked my mental catalog of items before blindly smiling up at him.

"Your ass."

Mickey laughed and slapped me on the shoulder. My eyes opened and I checked the desk, finding exactly what I'd said. I'd been looking at details my whole life, never before realizing that I retained the information.

"I say you got somethin' special, then you got it." I nodded absently. "I been looking for an assistant, someone to help when cases get too much, ya know? So many jobs and only one me."

"Yeah, I'd love to," I agreed. At the time, I didn't even know what he did. I just knew that I wanted his life or something farther away from what I had.

He leaned over and took my chin in his hand, pulling me forward roughly.

"You got a thick skin, kid? It ain't no easy ride out there. You gotta be quick and smarter than them. You gotta check your emotions at the door. Can you do that?" He pulled my face up and down, nodding for me. "Good. Come back here tomorrow and we'll get started. There's some stuff we got to cover first. I trust you kid, but an open door may tempt a saint."

For a year, I was his shadow. He taught me how to track people using my skills of observation and my persuasive nature.

He said my good looks were nothing but an advantage. I learned how to manipulate conversations to get what I wanted. I knew when people were lying or telling half-truths. I could identify a certain gesture or nervous laugh and let it lead me to a better line of questioning. I was able to detach myself from the job, to become this heartless machine.

I was good at it, too. Soon I left Mickey and started out on my own. Jobs were hard to come by in this business, but my reputation grew quickly. I never failed to get my target. Word spread and then I couldn't keep up with the requests. It was job after job. So much money that I didn't know what to do.

Eventually, I matured and grew into my career. It became all that I lived for, all that I am. I stay in a small apartment, with elderly neighbors who I never see. I've stashed all my money away, besides a couple of real estate investments. After ten years, I sit on a large nest egg and a desire to leave the business. Kat was right. I sleep with random women and never commit to more than one or two nights. I only have two friends. I trust no one, besides them. It is a lonely existence.

Still, after four weeks on the road, I long for that pathetic life. Kat has turned me upside down. She's got me twisted and I hate feeling out of control. I can't wait to get back to my place and back to my schedule. I want to be on my own time, not driven by money, employers, or targets.

Maybe I'll give it all up and head down to my house in Cabo San Lucas. That place is my sanctuary. Nameless senoritas and time with my surfboard sounds amazing. My footsteps quicken as I picture retiring on the beach with a cold beer in hand and the ocean breeze washing over me.

The tourists seem to multiply the closer I get to the theater. There are vacationing families and couples, everyone taking pictures with their phones. A dollar store version of Spider-Man poses with two boys as the dad makes faces at them. The kids strike a fierce pose and then fall out with the giggles. Captain America walks about aimlessly, no damsels in distress or dollar bills to save. Catwoman purrs when I pass. She looks hot in that suit, but there's something crazy about her eyes. What I don't need is another crazy woman in my life.

I make my way to the corner of the building and sit in the shade. I watch people put their feet in celebrity footprints and trace the names of movie stars. The sun sets over the hills and the streetlights come on. I don't leave my post.

10: her

I choose a direction and walk. Los Angeles is much different from what I imagined. I've walked for an hour and haven't seen one celebrity yet. I love wandering aimlessly, exploring the city. I came here for a specific reason, but there's no way I can pass up seeing more of West Hollywood.

It's a warm day, so I take my hoodie off and tie it around my waist. There's too much traffic here and the air smells different from anywhere I've been before. Billboards and advertisements cover entire buildings trying to sell the latest movie or designer perfume. I stand in front of a bus shelter and mimic the model in the poster. She's beautiful, but awkwardly posed.

An old man watches me from his bench, disapproving that I'd mock such beauty. When I've finally got the pose down, legs crossed and mouth hanging open, a kid slides in front of me. He's about sixteen years old. His hair is in braids and piercing sepia eyes stare back at me. He's much taller than me, sporting a dirty blue jean jacket and shoes with holes. His sharp jaw is peppered with pubescent stubble and his smile is purposely crooked.

"No, you've got to put your hand here," he says. He grabs my hand and places it on my hip. "Perfect."

"I've got it? I look like her?" I suck in my cheeks and try to imitate the hollow, lifeless eyes of the model.

"Hell no, shortie. You look way better." I release my pose, shaking out my legs and relaxing against the brick building.

"I doubt that, but thanks."

"No really, she's got nothin' on you. Look, she's too skinny. She needs to eat a cheeseburger or something."

I laugh and stare down at our shoes. We have matching black Converse—both worn in—but his are much worse than mine.

"Hey, I'm looking for Grauman's Theater. Could you point me in that direction?" I ask.

"You're not from here, are you?" He leans on his shoulder next to me. We're closer than strangers should be. I get the feeling that this guy has no issues with personal space.

"Is it that obvious?" I ask.

"Yeah, it is. I won't hold it against you. You new to the streets too?"

"The streets?"

"Yeah. I don't wanna make assumptions, but you look residentially challenged," he says.

"Oh, you mean homeless? I guess so. I'm more of a wanderer."

"Well, wanderer, I can take you to Grauman's if you want."

"You don't have to do that, really. Just point me in the right direction."

"Nah, I ain't got nothin' to do," he interrupts. "It's no problem."

I debate the pros and cons in my head. In my travels, I've been lucky so far. It creates a false feeling of invincibility that I embrace. I imagine what Dennis would think about him. All he would see is a homeless black kid, worthless trash. I decide Dennis was the kind of judgmental asshole who didn't know shit about people. So, I decide to trust this guy.

"I'm Lisa," I say, holding out my hand.

"Gregory. Don't worry, I'll take good care of you." He takes my hand and brings it to his lips. His kiss is soft, but his eyes look up at me to seal the gesture. It's cheesy and strange, but I go with it.

"So, Gregory. How are we traveling?"

"I got a bike. You get the handlebars."

I laugh and shake my head. "No shit? I haven't done that since I was like ten. Hey, I'm down."

"Good. Let's roll."

Gregory walks me a block over and unchains an old beach cruiser from a parking meter. I slide my bag in front of my body and climb onto the handlebars. My ass is a bit heavier since the last time I did this, I hope this kid's upper body strength is enough to keep us straight.

Gregory points out things as we pass them, great views of the city and extravagant houses up in the hills. The metal bar is digging into my ass, but I'm too scared of toppling over to readjust.

Two police cruisers zoom past us and my entire body tenses up. It saddens me that my gut reaction is fear. Will it always be this way? Yes, I realize. Whether I suffer a life on the run or one in prison, I will always be paying for my actions that night in Dennis' office. And I accept that. I took a man's life and will have to live with the consequences for the rest of my days—however numbered they may be.

I try not to dwell on the fact that I'm sightseeing while being on the run from the law, a hit man, and one gorgeous bounty hunter. This is my life now. Freedom is the only thing I have left, and I want to take advantage of every minute.

"Is this the way to the theater?" I ask when I notice the neighborhood changing.

"It's just a shortcut," Gregory says. "Don't worry, I know this city like the back of my hand."

"Okay," I say.

Gregory turns into an alley that even in the afternoon is really dark. The buildings here are all boarded up and abandoned. They're covered in illegible graffiti. Two men lean against a Dumpster, counting out money.

"Aww shit," Gregory says.

One of the men, an enormous bald beast of a guy, steps in front of us blocking the way. He crosses his arms and nods his chin to the other man who disappears without a word. Gregory slows to a stop. Losing my balance, I hop off the bike and stretch my legs. My hands knead my ass unapologetically.

"Man, that is not a great seat," I say.

"It was good for me," Gregory answers and winks at me. I can tell he's uncomfortable and trying to make light of the situation.

"Greg," the big guys offers a greeting. "Who's this?"

"This is Lisa. She's with me."

"Maybe she is, maybe she isn't. Sweetheart, are you with him?"

All eyes are on me and I shove my shaking hands into my pockets to hide them.

"He's my tour guide. I rode on his handlebars," I blurt out.

"I bet you did," the big guy says. "Don't you got somewhere to be, Greg?"

Gregory snaps to attention and grabs me by the elbow. "Uh, yeah. We'll go. Hop back on, shortie."

"Leave her."

Those two words pull the breath from my lungs. My legs feel

weak, like they may collapse on me. I look to Gregory, begging him. *Please don't leave me here.*

"Come on, Damon. She got people waiting on her. We don't want no trouble."

He walks slowly toward me. My feet are glued to the spot. As much as my brain screams to flee, I don't move. I wonder what's happened to my sense of self-preservation now. I wonder what Steel would do in this situation and am now regretting my decision to run from him.

When Damon stands in front of me, I realize he's even bigger than I thought. He has a huge scar running down his cheek and I try not to stare at it. He stands close to me. So close that I can smell cigarette smoke and beer on him.

"I don't want no trouble either," Damon says. "Just some company."

He reaches out with mitt-sized hands and runs them along my shoulders. I flex my fingers, making a plan to bend down and grab my knife when I realize it's not there. I mentally call Steel every name I can think of before refocusing on the man in front of me. Though I don't want to appear weak, my eyes sting with tears.

"I've really got to go. My boyfriend is waiting for me."

"Don't worry about him," he says. He closes the last bit of distance. "All you need to worry about is me."

Damon's arms surround me and I'm helpless. So, I do the only thing I can think of. I scream. Finally, my brain catches up with the gravity of the situation and I start to fight him.

"Let her go, man!" Gregory yells, jumping onto Damon's back.

I stomp my feet and swing my arms frantically. Though I land several blows against Damon, he doesn't even flinch. I'm no match for him, but I don't give up. He shrugs Gregory off like he's swatting away a bug.

"Please don't do this," I whimper as Damon presses me to the dirty brick wall.

When he leans down, I see an opportunity and take it. I lift my foot and kick forward with all my might. Both of his hands grab his crotch and he goes down. I try to scramble away from him, but he catches me by the ankle. I scream and hit the ground hard, knocking my face on the bike on my way down.

There's a loud thud and his grip on my leg goes limp. I turn to see Gregory standing over Damon's motionless body wielding a large brick. His expression is murderous, but relaxes when he meets my eyes.

"Is he dead?" I ask.

"I don't think so. But let's not wait around to find out."

Gregory grabs his bike and we take off down the alley. On the next street, we turn left and keep running for a couple of blocks. I lean against a mailbox, trying to catch my breath. I feel like my heart is going to explode.

"Come on, shortie! We can't stop now. Damon runs this neighborhood. We got to move!"

I jump up on his handlebars again and we're off. I can tell he's tired, but Gregory keeps pedaling us to safety. We make so many twists and turns through warehouses and neighborhoods it feels like we'll never break free. Finally, we come to a well-lit street with lots of people milling about.

I hop off the bike as he locks it to a streetlamp. Leaning on a coffee shop window, I try and calm my racing pulse. Gregory stands on the corner, asking people for change. I can tell that he's been on the streets a while. He's got an honest face that puts you at ease and eyes that look guarded, always aware of his surroundings. I watch as couples pass him by without a second glance. They walk their dogs and fetch their dinners like I wasn't just attacked, like this brave kid doesn't exist. They live in their safe little bubble and they are untouchable. I cringe when I remember that used to be me.

I catch my reflection in the window and sigh. My hair's knotted, my clothes are dirty, and my cheek is bruising. I'm a mess, but I don't feel like a victim. I feel alive and thankful for it.

"Here, I only got a couple of bucks," Gregory says, pouring a handful of coins into my palm. "It won't get you far."

"Thanks, Greg, for saving me from that ogre." I give him the change back and another twenty dollars from my bag. "I don't need it. You take it."

"Looks like you don't need my help no more. And my name is Gregory. I only let Damon call me Greg because he's crazy and dangerous. Nobody else gets away with that shit." He winks at me and I smile back.

"Ow!" The ache in my face surprises me and hits me like another blow. "Damn, your bike pedal got me good."

"You had some good moves of your own. Sure surprised the hell outta me. You look all soft and you bringin' down street thugs, girl."

"I surprised myself too," I admit.

"You ever been in a fight before?"

"Once," I say. Images of a violent Dennis, hands around my throat, flash through my head.

"Well, you're a natural then. I got to be moving along. Damon will be looking for me. Where you headed?"

"Grauman's," I answer.

"I'm headed that way anyway. Let me walk you there. Teach you a few things on the way." He starts off down the sidewalk and I fall in step next to him. "First, don't go off with strangers."

"You're a stranger."

"Exactly. It's like you learned nothin' today. You lucky I got a soft spot for older ladies."

I shake my head at him. "I don't feel lucky."

"Believe me, that situation could have been much worse." I nod in agreement. "Alright, next. If you're asking for change, you want to target the middle people. The rich won't give and the poor don't have it. When in doubt, check out people's shoes."

"No strangers. Look at shoes. Got it."

"In this city, don't wear red or blue. Don't throw gang signs. Don't tell anyone where you're from or where you're going."

"No primary colors. No sign language. Mum's the word." He rolls his eyes at me as we cross the street. "How did it get so cold? It was warm a few hours ago."

"Welcome to LA," he says.

He stops, removes his denim jacket and unbuttons his green-and-white plaid shirt before sliding it off his arms. He wears a dirty white T-shirt underneath.

"Is this where you're from?"

"I'm from nowhere, going nowhere." His voice isn't dismal, just reciting the facts. "Here," he says, holding the shirt up for me. "You lost your hoodie back in the alley."

I slide my arms inside and pull it tight around me. I expect it to smell bad, but it doesn't. I feel like a presumptuous ass for even thinking it.

"Thanks. Aren't you the charming gentleman," I tease. He puts his jacket back on and we continue our journey.

"Nah. A gentleman would have given you his jacket. But, I don't part with this. A friend gave it to me."

"A girlfriend?" I ask, poking his ribs.

He grunts and shakes his head. "No. Just a friend. She died a couple of years ago. It's all I got left."

"I'm sorry," I offer.

"No worries, shortie. That's life. Sometimes people come in to help you along and leave just as quick. She was good people. Like you."

"And you," I say.

He grins and pulls me along the star-lined sidewalk.

11. HIM

Yawning, I stretch my arms wide and push out my chest. I'm so wound up, my muscles and head ache. I rub my temples and stare out over the courtyard, ignoring the possibility that Kat has already come and gone from this place. I refuse to believe that she could have done so with no resources.

So, I continue to sit and wait. I wait for the girl who's had me on the road for over four weeks, making me laugh when I don't want to, and confess things I never have before. I wait for the girl who tears down my walls like they're made of paper. She makes me crazy and yet, I want to see her again.

I stand up and walk to the gift shop just to get the feeling back in my ass. There's a short line at the register that seems to be moving slowly. The employee behind the counter is distracted and barely present. I follow her gaze as it moves across the store and finds a guy in matching uniform pretending to fold T-shirts. He works on the same one three times before moving on to the next. The two clerks give each other secret smiles, their unresolved sexual tension palpable. I ignore them and look through some postcards while keeping an eye on the theater.

"You look like Superman," says a tiny voice.

I look down to find a little girl smiling up at me. She's got brown ringlets and a black shirt that sparkles with a cartoon cat on it. There's a stamp on her hand that says Madame Tussauds. Her lips and cheeks are pink against her innocent porcelain face. I check the immediate area for parents and find none.

"Who me?" I ask.

"Yep. And I know 'cause my brudder watches dat movie all the time. I know it real good. There's a fake Superman out dere," she whispers pointing to the sidewalk.

I squat down so that we're eye level now. With my long sleeve shirt and most of my tattoos covered, I can understand how she doesn't find me threatening. Still, she moves closer and I'm put off at how comfortable she seems to be with me.

"Can you keep a secret?" I ask. She nods. Her brown eyes shine. "You're right."

I smile at her and she covers her mouth with both hands, giggling. She steps forward now, her pink shoes between mine.

"I won't tell," she says. "Are you here to stop a cwiminal?"

"Something like that."

"What did they do?"

"They hurt someone," I answer in the simplest way possible.

"Sounds like a vewy bad cwiminal."

I cringe at the little girl's words. Kat is not the criminal, not really. She's so much more than her crime. Something deep inside me breaks as I realize how much more she is and how much more I want.

Just then, a frazzled woman appears above us. She's got shopping bags, a purse, and a diaper bag thrown over her shoulder, a baby on her hip.

"Maggie! There you are!"

She frowns at me and grabs the little girl by the hand, yanking her away protectively. Maggie wraps her arms around her mother's leg, but still smiles at me. I stand up and hold the woman's accusatory gaze. She doesn't back down until they're halfway out of the store.

"I would never," I say to no one.

I shake my head and turn toward a display on the wall. Just as I'm about to flip through celebrity photos, I spot Kat.

My stomach drops and I can do nothing but stare. She walks with a tall black kid to the center of the courtyard and spins around. His tattered shoes and the way his clothes are dirtier on one side tells me he's homeless. Kat throws her arms out and bounces on her toes. I can feel her excitement and wonder from here. The kid laughs at her and so do I. There's something about seeing her again that makes me anxious.

I debate leaving her here. No one would ever know. My reputation would be ruined, but it might save me from doing something stupid later on. That thought leaves my head and I shake free of it. I can't do it. I'm not sure if it's because I need to complete this job or because I'm not willing to give up my time with her.

I step out of the shop as the two of them hug. He pats her on the head like an obedient child and leaves. I could easily grab her now and get back on the road, but I won't deny her this. My heart drums against my chest as I watch her dance around from square to square. She places her feet in the cement imprints of celebrity footprints, sometimes bending over to do the same with her hands. Her hair is down and wild, hiding most of her face. Still, I can see that she grins at some squares and frowns at others. Her lips move and I know she's making comments about each one, as if anyone is listening. Finally, Kat takes a seat on the ground, wraps her hands around her knees, and closes her eyes.

My steps are silent as I approach. I want to be angry with her, but I'm not. I can't blame her for running.

Tourists navigate around Kat as she sits in her square, blissfully ignorant to their gawking. My shadow falls over her and she doesn't move or indicate that she knows it's me.

"What are you doing?" I ask.

Kat's shoulders jump, undoubtedly recognizing my voice. She drops her face down, curling in on herself.

"You're ruining my moment."

I sigh and cross my arms. "What moment would that be?"

"Johnny Depp's hands are on my ass."

I look down at the square and sure enough, she's sitting on his handprints. I bend down and try to persuade her to make this easy.

"Kat, we've got to go."

"I don't want to go to prison," she says. "Can't you just leave me here? Let me disappear and you'll never have to think of me again."

I shake my head and refuse to tell her how impossible that would be. Kat opens her eyes and lifts her head. There's a red mark across her cheek and I'm filled with instant fury. The same bruises across my mother's face flash in my head. I reach out, but stop myself before I touch her.

"What happened?"

She ignores my question, stands and takes off toward the sidewalk.

"Kat! What happened?" I ask again, chasing after her.

Her footsteps quicken. I know she's not running from me, but from my questioning. When she gets to the street, she looks left, then right. I wrap my hands around her shoulders and turn her around too roughly.

"What the fuck happened to you?" My voice is loud and several people look on with concern. I release her, cross my arms tight across my chest, and wait for an answer.

"Why do you care? This is nothing compared to what you're taking away from me!"

Something about the tone of her voice, the way it breaks, slices through me. "Kat, you made your decisions. Don't put that on me. You broke the law. I'm just doing my job. You want to be out on the streets alone with Boots and whoever did that to your face?"

"You're right," she says. "You're right. Let's go."

I tuck my hands into my pockets and nod my head in the direction of the hotel. We walk two blocks until I can't stand the silence.

"So, you're just going to come with me? No fight? No running?" I ask.

"What good would it do?" she asks. "We played that game and I lost, remember?" Kat turns to me, a look of fascination on her face. "I guess I'm kind of impressed that you were paying attention enough to know where I'd go. I bet you knew I was coming here before I did."

"Maybe," I say. "We're a whole day off schedule now."

"I'm sorry ruining my life is putting you behind schedule."

I exhale roughly into the night sky and continue on. After a few steps, I notice Kat's not by my side. I turn to find her rooted in place. She stares ahead at something past me.

"Why'd you stop?" I ask.

"Uh, maybe we should go another way."

"What? The hotel is this way," I say, pointing over my shoulder.

She takes a step back and then another. I turn to look behind me and find a bald guy stalking toward us. He's huge and menacing, an ugly scar down his face. He wears a plaid button down shirt buttoned all the way to his thick neck and heavily starched khaki pants. His military boots clomp loudly against the road and his sights are set on Kat. A smaller man follows wearing almost the same outfit as if it's some kind of street uniform.

"Let's go!" she finally yells at me.

"Who is that?" I ask.

She shakes her head and looks down at the sidewalk.

"His name is Damon," her soft voice replies.

I stand between them now, squaring my shoulders and facing Damon. He tries to duck around me, but I step into his path. It's only then that he takes his eyes off Kat and sees me.

"Move, boy," he growls.

I don't say a word and stand firm. His goon comes at me, but Damon raises his hand, silently stopping him.

"So, you're the boyfriend, huh?" I don't answer. I assume Kat has told this guy some story and I intend to stick to it. "Shit, I ain't mad at ya. That's a sweet piece right there. She's mine tonight. You can have her back when I'm done."

Rage builds inside me and I can't explain it away. I want to knock his teeth in and blind him for the way he's looking at her. I don't turn to see Kat, but the fact that she's quiet means she's scared.

"Did you do that to her face?" I ask, my teeth clamped down tight as I try to control my rage.

He steps to me, our chests almost touching, and looks down. "That ain't all I'm gonna do to her."

The last thread holding me back snaps. I cock my arm, feeling the burn in my already sore ribs, and hit him in the eye. There's a crunching sound and I'm not sure if it's his skull or my knuckles. He stumbles away from me. Pain radiates through my hand, but I fight through it.

The smaller guy comes forward. There's a recognizable determination in his face, a need to prove himself. Before he can get closer, I step up, grab the side of his head and slam it into a nearby light post. The metal clang is loud, like the bell in a boxing ring as he goes down and stays there.

"Look out!" Kat shouts.

I turn to find Damon in my face. From this close, I can see that his pupils are dilated and he's sweating profusely. He's high and therefore, unpredictable. He hits me in the ribs, the same damn place that Boots had. I cough out all my air and stumble backward. Damon comes forward again and hits me in the jaw. My head snaps sideways and I taste blood where my teeth cut the inside of my cheek. Kat screams as I go down on all fours.

I hit the sidewalk hard, but her voice gives me the strength to get up again. I shake my head and try to clear my vision. When I'm standing, I slide my piece out of my waistband and point it right between Damon's eyes.

"One more step and you're fucking dead," I say.

Damon grunts, his chest heaves from the fight and he points his finger at Kat.

"Fine, bitch. You win this time. But I'll find your lil' pal, Greg."

He jogs past us and out of sight, leaving his friend behind. Kat runs over to me.

"Oh, God! Are you okay?"

"Yeah, I just . . ." I take a deep breath and stand up fully, placing a hand over my ribs. "That's the second time today I got punched in the ribs."

"What?" Kat asks, her voice high and nervous.

"Never mind," I say and point down the block. Tucking my gun back into my jeans, I start for the hotel. She takes my hand, helping me along. I ignore the memories of her touch from last night and focus on putting one foot in front of the other.

When we're in the room, Kat grabs the ice bucket and leaves me there. I grunt and wince as I pull my shirt off. There's bruising on my ribcage, but I don't think anything is broken. I'm standing in front of the mirror when Kat returns. She pours some ice into a towel and wraps it up.

"Lay down," she says, sweeping a pile of travel brochures from the bed onto the floor.

I obey her without thought. Kat kneels next to me and places the towel of ice on my jaw.

"My ribs hurt more," I protest.

"Your jaw is swelling already. This will help."

I nod and try to look anywhere but at her face. With no distractions, I return there quickly. Her eyes hold mine and a crackling energy flows between us. I don't protest when she removes the ice and runs her fingers along my face. The moment is earnest, both of us fighting something bigger than ourselves.

"I bet you didn't know what you were in for when you took this job, huh?" Kat asks.

"I'm certainly earning my payout."

"How much am I worth to you?" she asks.

That's a loaded question and my brain stumbles through a million different answers.

"Five hundred thousand dollars." The number slips from my lips before I can stop it.

"That's a lot of money. Glad I made you work for it," she says, half-serious.

"You should put that ice on your face," I offer.

Kat shakes her head and turns to look in the mirror. She lifts her fingers to her cheek and sweeps over the bruise there.

"We're quite a pair, huh?"

I sit up next to her and stare at our reflection. We are a pair, a pair of battered misfits.

She reaches up and slides the small charm around her necklace. I notice she does it often. Like it's a habit now, to touch it, to make sure it's there. Security.

"That's not just jewelry is it?" I ask.

Her fist wraps around the charm before tucking into her shirt. She chews on her bottom lip and shakes her head ever so slightly.

"It's a key."

"Okay," I say, hoping she'll explain. I lie back on the bed and wait.

"I have a degree in Computer Science. Dennis and his sister, Marilyn ran an investment firm in San Antonio. I worked for him after college, in the I.T. department."

"You really are good with computers, huh?"

"Yeah. Too good. I found out they were stealing money from their clients. It was kind of genius. This key is the only way to access the money and the proof." She pulls at the charm on her necklace and shows it to me. "It's all on this USB drive that takes two keys to access the information."

"So, why do you still have it? He's dead," I point out.

She pats her necklace and looks down at the floor.

"Because, Marilyn can't access it without having this key."

"I'm impressed," I admit. She gives me a shy smile and looks away.

"That night, with Dennis, it was never about this key or the money. I wanted to blackmail him into letting my mom go, letting her leave. Things just . . . got out of hand."

Kat closes her eyes and takes a deep breath. When she opens them again, I can see everything there—all her guilt, pain, and regret. Her trembling fingers mindlessly trace the rose tattoo on the back of my right hand.

"You want to tell me what happened with that guy?"

She shakes her head and presses the ice back to my jaw. "Can you hold the ice here? I'm going to take a shower."

I bring my hand up and cover hers. The comfort of her touch makes me crave more before she slips away. Having her here with me again fills me with relief and fear. I don't know how to act or who I am. For the first time in a decade, I don't know what my next move will be.

Kat grabs her bag and disappears into the bathroom. It's quiet for a long time, no water running, nothing. I get up and stand outside that door for a while. I tell myself it's just to make sure she's not trying to escape. The truth is I need to know she's okay.

When the water turns on I relax a bit. I lean my forehead against the wall and close my eyes. Then, the sound of Kat's crying seeps through the door. My fingers grip the doorframe and the anger builds in me. The cheap wood cracks under my fingers, the sound is my resolve breaking.

I tamp down all the scenarios that spin through my head. Something terrible happened to her and I can't do anything about it. Everything that I imagine sends me further into my spiraling rage. This emotion expands in me until I can't fight it anymore.

I push away from the door and grab the dusty lamp. I hurl it across the room and feel satisfied when it shatters against the wall. My face is throbbing, my ribs ache, but none of that matters. I hate feeling out of control and it seems to only happen when Kat's around.

Slumping down onto the bed, I pull out my phone and send a message to my employer.

Delayed. San Antonio ETA two days.

Moments later, my phone buzzes. I stare at the screen, the dreaded word framed by a rectangle of light in the dark room.

Excellent.

An hour later, Kat lies in bed next to me. Her hair is damp and she smells like soap. She wears a tiny tank that exposes her arms and a small band of skin just below her navel. My mind and hands remember exactly what that skin feels like and the sight before me is a torturous temptation. We both keep our eyes on the television, which is playing local news. There's a story about a wanted rapist who may be part of a gang.

"I wanted you to kill him," Kat says.

"Who?"

"Damon." I look at her and nod. "I wanted you to squeeze that trigger and end him right there."

"We've already got enough trouble, don't you think?"

She gives a hollow laugh and turns on her side to face me. Kat's relaxed and comfortable here with me and I try to comprehend it.

"I don't want to have those kinds of thoughts. I mean, yeah, I've killed someone, but I don't want that to change who I am."

"I understand," I say. I don't tell her that it's too late. The moment you're responsible for ending someone's life, it marks you, scarring you in ways that last a lifetime.

"Do you? Because I feel like we just let a monster out into

the world. He's free to do whatever he wants to the next girl and that's our fault. We could have stopped him."

"You can't save everyone, Kat."

"I know," she says, playing with the edge of the sheet. "You ever been in trouble with the law?"

I contemplate keeping quiet on this one, but the way she looks at me makes my ability to stay silent ineffective. Maybe I tell her as a warning. *This is the kind of person I am.* Or maybe I tell her simply because she asked.

"I was into some bad shit when I was younger. I had a partner once who screwed up. We were caught and interrogated in this tiny town's police station. He was useless, telling them anything they wanted to know. I decided I had to get out before they started asking questions about me.

"I asked for something to drink, complaining about how hot it was. One cop left and returned with a cup of water. I took it from him, gulped it down and pretended to choke. When he came to check on me, I grabbed his gun, held it against my partner's head, and used him as a hostage until we escaped."

"How did you know it would work?" she asks, wide-eyed.

"I didn't."

"And you were willing to risk both of your lives to find out?"

"Yes."

"Wow. I don't know if that's brave or stupid."

"A little bit of A, a little bit of B," I answer.

Kat gives a sad laugh and lays her head on her bent arm.

"When I was little, my dad used to take me to the park near our house," she says. "It had this slide that seemed enormous. Every time we'd go, I'd stand next to the slide and just look up the ladder. Sometimes, I'd get one or two steps up before chickening out and coming back down.

"My dad watched, but he never judged me for being scared.

Every time we got in the car to leave, he'd tell me 'Take chances, Kat. That's how you grow. Being brave is finding a way through fear. You'll do it one day.' "

"Did you ever go down the slide?" I ask.

She blinks and a single tear slides over her cheek and soaks into the cotton pillowcase.

"I did. But he never got to see it."

12: her

It's strange lying in bed and talking with Steel. Even after exploring every part of his body, this feels far more intimate than anything we've done. There's such a personal connection to memories and confessions. They hold so much weight inside, but once freed, they seem to float away into vapor. At least, that's how it feels with him.

With the lamp broken, the only light comes from the muted television. His skin is highlighted in flickering blue and silver light. He lies on his back on top of the sheets, his ankles crossed leisurely. That calm and cool exterior gives no clue to the complicated creature inside.

I can't explain why I'm drawn to him, but it's undeniable. At first, it was just physical, because let's face it, he's gorgeous. There's the ruggedly handsome face, anchored by ice blue eyes that seem to see every piece of me, no matter how hidden away. His body is lean with golden skin molding around the curves and valleys of muscle. Though his arms and chest are covered with tattoos, the black-and-gray piece on his hip taunts me, always. It disappears beneath the waistband of his pants, just begging me to explore.

Now, after all the danger we've been through, there's something else. Something lying just below his surface, something he guards with his life.

"No handcuffs tonight?" I say, wiggling my eyebrows at him.

"No handcuffs," Steel answers. "I figure you're telling the truth when you say you're done running."

"Sorry I've been such a pain in the ass," I say, fluffing my deflated pillow. "Nothing like one last grand adventure before being locked up indefinitely. Kat and Ted's Excellent Adventure, dude. Wyld Stallyns!"

"I feel like I need a translator to have a conversation with you sometimes," he says, frowning up at the ceiling.

"Tell me why you don't know any of the things I talk about."

He sighs and stares at the television. "We didn't have a TV when I was growing up. We were poor, so no movies or anything. There was a radio, but it was downstairs. I liked to hide out in my room most of the time. What money we did have went to my father's whiskey and cigarettes. He put food on the table and that was the extent of his providing."

"I'm sorry you had to go through that. We were on the low end of middle class, before Dennis, that is. But at least we were happy."

Steel nods and turns to face me. We mirror each other on our separate sides of the bed. My eyes follow the art of his muscled chest, down to my favorite tattoo. Without thinking, I reach out and run my fingers over the black circle and the elaborate design around it. His stomach muscles contract and he holds in a breath.

"What is it?" I ask.

"A compass."

It's then I can make out the N, E, S, W within the circle. It's exquisite, such detail in the swirling pattern surrounding the compass and thick masculine lines carving through. It's truly a work of art.

"A reference to your travels?"

He shakes his head and I pull my hand back, tucking it under my cheek to keep from touching him again.

"Not just that. It's more about choices, something my mom always told me."

"You always have a choice," I say.

He gives me a surprised smile. "Yeah." Steel hooks his thumb on his pants and pulls them down a little so I can see the entire design. "It has no needle. No direction. Limitless choices."

"Tell me about her."

His brow dips and his mouth turns down into a severe scowl. He shakes his head and turns onto his back again.

"She's dead."

The pain in his voice is unbearable. I want to hold him and comfort him, but I won't cross that line again. I have a feeling he'll just break my heart.

"Do you believe in God?"

"No," he answers quickly.

"Me and my mom used to say our prayers every night. I had this super long list of people I'd ask God to protect." I replay the memory of night-lights and Disney Princess PJ's. "My mom would stick around for a while, but eventually she would get tired of waiting on me to finish."

I close my eyes and picture her kneeling next to my twin-size bed. She always smelled like vanilla. I think it was her perfume. Her hair would be pulled up into a bun and she'd clasp her hands together in her lap. She'd run her hand along my head and place a kiss on my forehead before heading off to bed. I wonder if she still prays. I wonder if she prays for me.

"I guess now that I'm a bad person, it would be easier to believe that there isn't someone waiting to pass judgment on me."

"You're not a bad person, Kat."

"If I'm not bad, then neither are you."

"We are not the same," he insists.

"My grandmother always told me that I'd grow up to be successful and loved. She thought that I'd marry a rich doctor and have two point five kids. Of course, she also thought the VCR was trying to kill her. She'd be so disappointed now. She's buried in Paradise Memorial in Avondale, Arizona. That's where my dad's family is from. I got lost last time I went to visit her grave. I remember finally finding her, staring out over the lake and telling her about my life."

"When was that?"

"When I was eighteen. Seems like so long ago. My problems of prom dresses and college majors seem lame compared to the tales I could tell her now." I glance at the television and back to his face. "I was named after her. You know, I didn't even realize that until she died. She'd always been Mimi to me. It wasn't until the funeral that I realized her name was Katherine."

"I'm named after my grandfather," he says.

I pop up in bed and try to maintain my casual expression. "Oh yeah? What was *his* name?"

"Nice try." Steel shakes his head and smirks in my direction, one dimple appears. I should have known it wouldn't be that easy.

"Damn. I don't know why it's such a big deal. It's not like I'll ever see you again. You'll be rid of me in two days and then you won't ever have to worry about Katherine the Terrible."

"If it's not a big deal, why do you want to know?" he asks.

I shrug my shoulders and look down at him. The way he looks, lying beneath me, reminds me of last night. I close my eyes for a moment and envision our bodies tangled together, exchanging breaths and moans of pleasure. When I open my eyes, he's still waiting on an answer.

"I suppose a person's name is very personal and revealing. I understand why you won't tell me. I just wish you would."

He reaches over and turns off the television, blanketing the room in complete darkness. I drop back down onto my pillow, pull the sheet over me, and close my eyes.

"I wish I could tell you too."

My eyes pop open in the dark. I stare at the black space that holds him. My breathing picks up as I process his words. After a minute, my eyes adjust to the light and I can make out the rise and fall of his chest as he sleeps. It's then that I realize, maybe under all that anger and armor, is just a man.

I'm startled awake as Steel clamps his hand over my mouth. I sit up in a panic and he motions wildly for me to keep quiet. He points to the door. I glance over and see the handle moving back and forth. I pull my lips in and bite down to keep from screaming. My heart is hammering, my pulse so loud it echoes in my head. It's all I can hear in the quiet room, like an eerie soundtrack in a horror film.

I look back to Steel and he motions for me to get out of bed. I follow him through the dark room to the closet where he pushes me inside. I watch as he grabs the handcuffs and snaps one side around the bathroom door handle. He then turns the shower on, closes the curtain, and closes the bathroom door.

I move over and make room for him. He slides in behind me and closes the closet door, leaving only a slight crack. I lean against Steel, my back to his chest in the small space. He wraps his arm around my chest. I'm not sure if it's to keep me still or comfort me and I don't care. Our erratic pulses beat together in one frenetic rhythm. I'm mindful of my breathing, forcing myself to take slow controlled breaths. My fingers grip onto his forearm just to have something to hold on to.

After a minute, I hear a click, then a snap, and the sound of the cut metal chain clinking against the doorframe. The door swings open and my whole body stiffens, every muscle rigid and ready—but for what, I don't know.

I hear footsteps around the room and then I see a leather jacket through the crack. I hold my breath. Boots pays no attention to the handcuffs and slowly opens the bathroom door. Steam pours out and engulfs him. He takes two steps across the small room and grabs hold of the shower curtain. I feel like I'm going to vomit or pass out, but I keep my eyes on his back.

Boots pulls the curtain back and sees no one there.

"What the hell?"

In a flash, we're out of the closet and running. Steel pulls the bathroom door closed and cuffs the other side to a towel rack next to the sink. I grab my bag and head for the door.

"Go! Go!" he says. He throws his bag over his shoulder and we hightail it out of the room. "It won't hold him long."

I run to the car and try to get in, but it's locked. I look to Steel.

"Hurry up!" I say.

"Not there, in case he's tracking the car again."

"Then what?" I ask, panic lining my voice.

He runs his hand through his hair and searches the parking lot. There's a linen delivery truck parked near the front office. The driver throws bags of laundry inside and closes the door before heading into the office.

"This way."

Steel pulls me along and we hop into the back of the van closing the door behind us. There are windows on the van, but they're covered with sticky graphic ads. We can see out, but you can't see in. The only sound is our ragged breathing.

"What if he . . ." I start, but can't bear to finish the sentence.

Boots plows out of our room, gun drawn. I whimper as Steel pulls his gun. The driver comes out of the office and Boots quickly tucks his weapon away. He runs to the van, waving at the driver.

"Hey!" he yells. "Hey!" The driver opens his door. "You seen a young couple running around here this morning? Probably still in their drawers?"

"No, man. Sorry," the driver says.

This is the first good look I've gotten of Boots. He's a big guy, beefy and tall. He wears jeans and a black T-shirt covered by a very worn leather jacket. His face is tan and freckled, made up of hard masculine angles. His short black hair is greasy and pushed back from his face, the result of wearing a helmet. He's appealing in a bad-boy kind of way, but he's gone too far toward dangerous to be attractive.

"You sure? You better not be lying, boy," Boots says. He holds the driver's door open and glares into the truck.

"I swear," the driver says. "I haven't seen anyone."

As the driver starts the van, we see Boots pull out his phone and place a call.

"I lost them again. I don't fucking know. This bitch is getting to be more trouble than she's worth. Call me back when you have a location or it's your ass on the line."

The van pulls out of the lot and we can do nothing but watch as Boots and the hotel disappear. With a metal wall between us and the driver, we feel it's safe to move around, though it's difficult on the mounds of laundry bags.

"Who do you think he was talking to?" I ask softly.

Steel drops his cotton pants and opens his bag. I stare as he awkwardly slides into his jeans while balancing on the bags. Sitting there, surrounded by clouds of white, he is almost naked and so sexy. He turns and catches me staring.

"I don't know. Get dressed," he says.

I nod and get busy changing into my jeans and Gregory's shirt since I left my other one in the bathroom. I don't miss that Steel sneaks glances at me in various states of undress as well. I make sure to bend and stretch, giving him a show. When I peel off my tank top and sit there topless, Steel chokes on his own saliva. Mr. Professional is slipping.

I start buttoning Gregory's shirt up from the bottom. "You okay?"

"Was that necessary?" he whispers.

"Yes," I answer while shaking my head "no."

He silently flips me off wearing a tiny smile. Definitely slipping.

A few minutes later, we pull into another hotel and the driver backs up to the office. I sling my bag across my body and Steel carries his. There are no door handles inside, so we have to wait for the driver to open the doors. When he does, we hop down.

"Whoa!" he yells and drops his clipboard. "Where'd you come from?"

"Thanks for the ride, man. It was good for me," I tease. Steel rolls his eyes and we walk away quickly, crossing the parking lot and around the side of the building. "Oh my God, I think we gave him a heart attack."

It's still early and a bit cool out. There's not many people awake yet and no one in the parking lot. Steel starts trying the handles of every car we pass.

"What are you doing?"

"We need a new car," he says as if it should have been obvious.

"We're going to steal one? You're going to end up in prison with me. What kind of bounty hunter are you?"

"Borrow," he says, correcting me. "Desperate times and all that. Now, help me."

I shrug and start checking door handles. The third one I try is open. It's a green, late model minivan with peeling paint and the distinct smell of weed inside.

"Hey! I got one," I say.

Steel comes over and hops into the driver's seat. In a matter of minutes, he's pulled part of the dash away and is sparking two wires together. After a few attempts, the thing starts.

"Are you kidding me? Where'd you learn that, MacGyver?"

"From my misspent youth," he says, backing out of the space and pulling onto the street.

As we tear down the road, I click my seatbelt into place. "He almost got us," I say. "I can't believe we escaped again. Thanks for that. I don't want to die at the hands of some shady guy after getting this far."

Steel frowns, his hands slide around the steering wheel until it creaks from his grip. By the time we make it to the freeway, he seems distracted and back to his old self. He doesn't answer my questions and just stares blankly at the road. The man who laid in bed with me and exchanged childhood stories is gone. It's like he flips a switch and all of that is forgotten. His walls are in place. He is detached. I guess it's better this way. It'll be easier when he turns me in.

13. HIM

The traffic in Los Angeles is a nightmare. We sit in one spot for almost thirty minutes without moving. The smog surrounding us and the endless sea of cars makes me feel on edge. Kat has me floundering. It's like her chatter and know-it-all smile unravel me to my core. I can't allow it.

"Come on, move," I growl at no one in particular.

"I'm not sure why you wanted to leave during morning rush hour traffic. This is your own fault," Kat says.

It's not my fault we're on the run. Boots isn't after me. But I don't say anything. I don't even look at her. The sound of her voice, the sight of her face infuriates me. It's not her fault. It's mine. I let her in. I allowed this.

"I always wanted to live in LA," she says.

I focus on the brake lights in front of us.

"I don't know what's so desirable about this." I glance over to see a woman on the phone, shiny trails of tears down her face. "I mean, look at this lady next to us. She's got her power suit on, cell phone attached to her ear, two empty child seats in the back, and she's crying."

"When I was a kid, I would make up stories for people in their cars," Kat says. "Let's say she pretended to go to work like any other day. But really she called in sick, so that she could meet her lover. He blew her off and now she's stuck in traffic, halfway between her suburban home where she lives with her husband and kids, and her lover's apartment. She's got no place to go and she's wondering how she can have so much and still feel so empty."

I stare at the woman as she covers her mouth with the back of her hand and shakes her head. More tears fall and it's easy to believe Kat's story.

"Or look at this guy on the other side. He's smiling and checking his watch constantly. Maybe he's on his way to the airport to pick up his daughter who's been backpacking through Europe for the last two months. He missed her and is sad that she'll be leaving for college soon. She'll be happy to see him, but will wonder if he's still dating that snooty bitch from Orange County. They'll argue about the girlfriend and she'll end up leaving for college early. He'll miss her every day, but he won't call, so she'll never know."

I turn and stare at her.

"What?" she asks.

"Jesus, Kat. Do any of your stories have happy endings?"

"Not anymore." She searches each car as we pass, assessing the occupants and telling their invented tales. "Ooooh, look at this one. This is a good one. You do this one, Montel."

I shake my head and keep my eyes on the bumper in front of me.

"Of course. You couldn't possibly lower yourself."

Her disgusted tone goads me. "Fine, you want a story? Let's see. She's a bottle blonde, great rack, fake fingernails. I say she's one of those tramps from *The Price Is Right*. She just got finished blowing Bob Barker for her weekly bonus."

"You suck at this game," Kat says, huffing and crossing her arms.

"My story isn't any worse than yours. And I threw in some TV details I thought you'd appreciate. I'm not completely ignorant of television shows. The woman in my first foster home was obsessed with Plinko."

"I appreciate the effort, but your facts are all wrong. Bob Barker retired. Drew Carey is the host of *The Price Is Right* now."

"The ugly guy with the buzz cut and glasses?"

"The very one. And he's not ugly. His personality and sense of humor make him adorable." I frown at her. Kat sighs. "Not everyone can pull off the whole 'beautiful tortured' look, like you."

She reaches over, pinches my cheek and gives it a light slap. I force myself away from her touch.

"What's our story?" I ask, trying to distract her.

"Let's see, we're a couple who've only been dating for three months. We met in the seafood department of Whole Foods. You were trying to pick out tilapia filets when I offered help. Of course, you swept me off my feet." She pauses, smiling off into the distance, as if envisioning our meeting. Her face turns hard and she stares down at her lap. "Two days ago, I found out I was pregnant. We just left the clinic, where it was terminated. You're bringing me back to my place, where you'll tuck me in and place supportive kisses on my forehead. I'll never see you again."

I look over. Kat leans her head back and kicks her feet up

on the dash. She ignores my blatant staring. The traffic finally starts moving as we make our way onto I-10. I turn up the radio to dispel the tension.

When we finally get past Palm Springs, I exit to grab some food.

"Oh, thank god! I'm starving," Kat says as I pull into a fast food joint.

"What do you want?"

"Oh, I get to choose?" she asks.

"You always have a choice."

Kat rolls her eyes. "I should have known you would say that. Umm, I want a hamburger kid's meal with a Coke." I raise an eyebrow at her. "I know, it's not the most glamorous meal, but it'll do."

After getting our food, I hand Kat her meal box, toy included, and hop back on the freeway. The traffic is lighter now and I'll easily be able to make up our lost time from LA. The van is quiet as we eat, the only sound comes from the radio. A commercial for College of the Desert tells us that we can all be college graduates in just two years.

"Guess I won't be needing my college degree where I'm going," Kat says. "Hey, they probably have computers in prison, right?" I shrug. "I'll just spend my time there, hacking government websites and writing algorithms to send millions of spam emails to Marilyn."

"Whatever that means."

"An algorithm is a set of detailed instructions that results in a predictable end-state from a known beginning. It's used in computer programming, among other things. Each program is a series of instructions, and is listed in a specific order, designed to perform a task. It's also used to solve math equations and define behaviors of our brains."

"You're that smart and you want to use it to send spam emails to your aunt?"

She nods and brings her feet up on the seat.

"Technically, she's my step-aunt. Marilyn always hated me and my mom. She thought we were poor trash. Well, payback is a bitch." Kat shoves a few fries into her mouth and chews. "Marilyn said Dennis was lowering his standards by marrying my mom, said my mom was a gold digger. We used to go to her house for Christmas. She was all rainbows and sunshine when Dennis was around, but when he left the room she would treat me and my mother like we were dirt."

I nod at her and keep quiet. I never had an extended family, so I can't fathom big Christmas dinners around a table. It's all very surreal in my head.

"I remember going there after the birth of her first kid. I thought that her becoming a mother would maybe soften her up, but she only got worse. I was playing with the baby while everyone else sat eating dinner. When she noticed, she stormed over, snatched him from my arms, and told me to keep my filthy hands off of him. So yeah, it was a pretty awesome Christmas."

Growing up, I always imagined people with money having perfect holidays. Perfect lives. Kat was proof of how wrong I'd been.

"What do you think my chances are of getting a decent public defense attorney?" she asks after a few moments of silence.

"I don't know, Kat. You don't think your mom will buy you a big fancy lawyer?"

"No," she says, chewing her lip. "I wouldn't accept it if she did. You can't shun me one minute and offer help the next. Come on, you're around this all the time. You have no opinion?"

"I don't stick around for the trials," I insist.

"So what's the plan? You just drive by the prison and push me out on your way to the bank?"

I don't like her attitude or the direction of this conversation.

"Not exactly."

"Well?" she asks.

"It's different for each case, Kat."

"Tell me about it." I shake my head at her. "Come on, I told you about my Mimi, shared my traffic game with you, confessed my crime, and kissed away your nightmares."

I choke on her last words.

"You don't want to know," I say, punctuating each word with my fist against the steering wheel.

"Yes, I do," she says, her frustrated voice growing louder. She turns in her seat and points her finger at me. "You won't tell me your name, you keep this hard mask in place and I can't stand it! I've never met anyone so infuriating in my life. One minute you're open and honest and the next you're closed off again. What the hell made you this way?"

I slam on the brakes and pull to the side of the freeway. My seat belt locks and cuts into my shoulder as I lurch forward. Rocks crunch under the sliding tires and then all is quiet.

"Fine! You want to know me?" I pick up my gun and point it at her. "This gun is the only thing I trust. I wasn't strong enough to save my mother. My father took her life and it was my fault. Her death is on me. I have lied, cheated, and stolen in order to capture hundreds of targets, delivering them to whoever paid the highest fee. I've tortured truths out of friends. I've betrayed my employers and I've used women for sex. I don't regret any of it. I don't want your sympathy or your judgment. My conscience, along with my humanity, died long ago."

In twenty-seconds I confessed more to Kat than I've ever even admitted to myself. I face forward and tuck my gun away.

Slamming my fist against the dashboard, I feel satisfied when she jumps. The silence surrounds us, draining the fight from my head.

Checking my mirrors, I merge back onto the road. I press the accelerator down, asking too much from this piece of shit van. I feel trapped and anxious in here, so I crack the window and let the fresh air calm me.

"It's not true," she says softly. I ignore her, keeping my eyes on the horizon. "Your humanity is not dead. The will to change is dead. You've lost the belief that there is good left in you. You've accepted your title as a monster when you don't have to be one. You're not a monster."

For the next hour, we drive in silence. The scenery flies by at a blur, never anchoring us to any place. I feel the weight of Kat's words in my head and try to shake free of them. She's wrong. I can't change who I am.

Kat presses the buttons on the radio and searches until she finds something clear. She begins to sing along, her voice soft and noncommittal to the lyrics. I chance a look in her direction and find her arms wrapped around her knees. She stares out the front of the van. Kat's fidgeting hands play with the frayed edge of her shirtsleeve, wrapping a long string around her finger and then unwinding it again.

It's moments like this when it's easy to see her innocence. Her life has been unfairly stolen by an abusive stepfather. As much as she sees the monster in herself for taking his life, she fails to see one in me. I want her to have an easy life, free from hurt and guilt. But, she won't have any of those things. In twenty-four hours, she won't have anything at all.

As we creep toward Texas, I notice Kat's fidgeting get worse. There's no singing now. She just hugs her legs tight and rocks back and forth.

My phone rings.

"Yeah."

"Boss, you in town yet?" Brad asks.

"No, had a delay. We'll be in town tomorrow night."

"I checked the account and they've transferred half the money already, the rest will be transferred when the job's done."

"Good."

"Also, I spoke to Jack this morning. He said Dragon's pissed because this Boots guy hasn't checked in with him in the last two days."

"Okay. Let me know if Boots contacts any of Dragon's people," I say glancing over to Kat. She returns my gaze.

"Will do. Did you need assistance for the delivery?" Brad asks hopefully. The answer has never been yes.

"No, I'll be finishing this alone." Kat glares down at her shoes.

"Right. Well, I'll let you know if I hear anything."

I hang up and I try to get my head around this job and what it means to complete it. I know exactly what it means for her, but not for me. I mentally scroll through everything I read in her file. Facts, names, and numbers jump out at me, but nothing in that file explains the inner workings of the girl that has inexplicably wrapped herself around me.

"Oh God! Pull over! I'm gonna be sick," Kat shouts. I slam on the brakes and change lanes, sliding onto the shoulder quickly. I throw the van in park as Kat hurls herself out of the door.

She empties her stomach onto the ground. I jump out and run around to her side. When she's finished, I hand her napkins from our food bag and the rest of my water. She kneels in the dirt, continuing to dry heave.

"Kat," I say, dropping to my knees in front of her. "Kat." When her eyes meet mine, I feel crippled by the fear there. "What is it?"

I watch as her hand raises straight out behind me. I follow

the extension of her arm, leading to her pointing finger. There it stands, not twenty feet from us, glaring with its reflective letters. WELCOME TO ARIZONA. It's a blatant sign of her time left, each state line counting down to her grim future. Each mile steals a bit of her carefree attitude, replacing it with fear.

She kneels on the ground, staring off into the distance, her arms wrapped around her middle. I'm at a loss. So, I do the only thing I can. I pick her up, dust her off, and place her in the back of the van.

Kat eventually falls asleep. The silence is comforting, but being alone with my thoughts is proving to be difficult. I wonder if this will truly be the end of Katherine Percle. If I can get through the delivery, then I'll be done. She'll be out of my hair and I'll never see her again. *Is that what I truly want?*

While crossing the state line brought to light just how close she is to her unavoidable future, she has no idea what really lays waiting for her in San Antonio. Am I a bastard for keeping her in the dark? Maybe, but it's easier for everyone this way.

Still, I feel like I owe her something. I feel like she deserves more after everything she's been through. At the very least, somewhere to clear her head. When I see the freeway sign, I know I've found that place. I search the directions on my phone and take the next exit.

I can't give her my name or even my word, but I can give her this.

14: her

"Kat, wake up." My eyes shoot open and I snap up, gasping for air. Dread fills my body and I feel like this is the end. "Don't worry, we're not there yet."

My hand covers my heart, where I try to rub away the furious pounding. "I thought—" I start, but can't bring myself to finish.

"Still about fourteen hours out. We took a detour. Come on," Steel says.

He exits the van and comes around to open my door. I stand and stretch before righting my clothes and smoothing down my hair. There is a funky taste in my mouth, so I dig out the mouthwash from my bag, swish it around until it burns and spit it on the ground. I finish off the water bottle and wipe my face with the bottom of my shirt.

"Feel better?" Steel asks.

I nod and look around. This place is green, something out of place in the desert. There are trees and flowers everywhere, even a lake. The floral scent flits around me and I inhale deeply to get more. It's like I fell asleep in Kansas and woke up in Oz. Steel nods to a sign behind me and when I turn to read it, I can't believe my eyes.

"Paradise Memorial Gardens? We're in Avondale?" I cover my mouth with the back of my hand.

"Do you remember where she is?" he asks.

I stare at him in awe. I'm trying to piece together the cold, hard man with the one who brings me to visit my grandmother's grave. Steel doesn't make eye contact. Instead, his eyes scan the grounds. I start down the road and he quietly follows.

"She's buried near the lake. The family thought it would be best since Mimi loved the water so much."

As we walk, I can't help but steal glances at him. I wonder what his motivation is for bringing me here. Is it just an act of kindness or is it guilt? I can't imagine he's feeling guilty about anything. I'm only a job to him, a girl who's made his life hell for the past month. There's something in the way he avoids my gaze, some kind of warning.

I leave the road and turn toward the lake. We walk through the thick, green grass to the edge of the water. The air is warm as a gentle breeze blows like a whisper. Ducks that were settled in the grass hop into the water as we approach. They swim off quacking softly, the ripples creating an animated arrow in the water. I turn and read the name printed on Mimi's headstone, running my fingers over the embossed letters.

"Katherine Marie Percle," I say aloud. "It's strange seeing your own name on a headstone."

I take a seat in front of the headstone and sit with my legs crossed. I pat the ground next to me, indicating that Steel should sit, but he shakes his head and keeps his distance. I look around and only find a couple of parked cars, no other people. It's quiet and peaceful here.

"Mimi, I miss you so much. I'm not sure if you can hear me or not, but I'm going to talk." I stare at the lifeless stone half expecting her to answer me. She doesn't. "I'm sorry I didn't turn out the way you wanted me to. I tried, I did. I was a good girl, most of the time. I mean college was kind of a blur, but that doesn't count, right?"

I give a little laugh and blink away the tears swimming in my eyes. The drops of saltwater carve a path over my cheeks and drop from my chin. When the breeze blows across my face I can feel the cool wetness even more. I pretend it's a kiss from Mimi.

"I've lost everything. With Dad gone and Mom becoming Cruella, I've got no one. I did something bad and now I've got to pay the price. You know what? I think you would have done the same thing if you'd been in my shoes.

"Anyway, I love you and miss you so much. My friend, Pedro, brought me to see you." I turn to Steel and he shakes his head at my newest name for him. The setting sun casts a golden blanket over everything and he looks like a bronze statue beside the water. "He's a decent guy and not too bad to look at, if you know what I mean. If you can hear me, please watch over Mom and tell Daddy that I miss him so much. Every day."

I run my fingers along the curve of her headstone, then stand and dust off the seat of my jeans. I use the bottom of my shirt to dab the last tears from my eyes and turn to face the inevitable. A huge gust of wind blows through, rustling the leaves on the trees. A nearby flag waves and snaps at us.

"Well, that was touching," a deep voice says. Steel pulls his gun and points it as Boots appears. My stomach flips and I gasp for air as he leans against a tree and lights a cigarette. "Katherine, dear, it's time to go now."

I shake my head and tuck my trembling hands into fists. "No."

"She's not going anywhere with you," Steel says.

"We'll see about that," Boots answers. His voice is calm and annoyingly sure.

I stand halfway between the two men. My head turning back and forth as if I'm watching a tennis match. The tension is thick and pulls me back and forth like a tug of war. Steel looks rattled. I can tell it's unusual for him to be taken by surprise.

"Kat, let's go," Steel says, backing away. I take a step with him.

"Not so fast, Katherine." Something about the tone of his voice or the way he says my name makes me stop. Boots takes a long drag and blows out the smoke. It swirls around his face before disappearing. "I don't suppose in the time that you've spent together, your captor has told you who he works for, has he?"

I look at Steel then back to this stranger. "No," I answer, confused. "I don't know."

"While I intend to deliver you to the proper authorities, *he* is privately funded. Did he tell you how much your bounty is?"

"Five hundred thousand dollars," I whisper.

Confusion swirls around my head, making me dizzy as I try to define the words privately funded. Boots laughs and pushes off the tree, exhaling another puff of smoke. He seems to not be fazed by Steel's gun at all. When he faces me I can clearly see that he has two black eyes and his nose is swollen.

"No public office would pay that much for one person," he says.

I try to process his words as I glance back and forth between the two men. I turn to Steel and for the first time since I met him, he looks guilty. His blue eyes shine as he readjusts the grip on his gun and squares his shoulders.

"Who hired you?" I ask. He says nothing, only shakes his head back and forth. His motions are mechanical, as if he's a puppet with someone else at the controls. "Who hired you?" I ask again.

"When a private party hires this guy to find someone before I do, it can only mean one thing. You'll never see the inside of a courtroom or look into the eyes of a jury. You're already dead. The moment he found you, you were dead."

"Is that true? Were you hired to kill me? Who hired you?" Steel remains silent, his gun still pointed at Boots. "Answer me, you coward!"

"Yes," he says. "It's true." In the fading light, I can barely see his mouth move, but I hear those words loud and clear.

"What? I don't . . ." My voice abandons me as I fight the shock and panic. I'm shaking and shattered, my insides crumple in on themselves. I fight for each breath, not wanting to process anything. I lean onto a nearby headstone to keep myself steady.

"But, I wasn't going to do it," Steel yells. "I can't."

"He's lying," Boots says. He lifts his hand and waves me over. "Come with me, Katherine. I'll make sure you get to where you're supposed to be."

I move toward Boots, feeling my chances are better with him. The lies and betrayal eat away at me and I can't make myself face Steel.

"Kat!" he yells. "We can run! We'll go to Mexico and disappear!" He sounds desperate, only I'm not sure of his motivation anymore.

"Stop it! You're just lying again!" I tell him. "All that time you had me believing that he was the hit man! It was you!"

"Kat," he says again, softer, pleading. My name sounds like a lie from his lips and I take another step away.

"You were going to *kill* me," I cry, my hands trembling as I clasp them together. I take one last look at him. He stands alone, breathless and waiting. I'm not sure how I feel, but I know what to do. I turn my back and join Boots.

He grins in Steel's direction. It's a sign of victory and I hate it.

The place is so quiet that all I hear are our soft footsteps in the grass. We take a few steps before I hear Steel again.

"Samuel!" he shouts. This time his voice is clear. It seems to float on the wind and filter through the trees. Every other sound falls away and all I hear is his voice. I turn to see him standing near Mimi's headstone, his gun lowered and chest heaving. He looks absolutely vulnerable.

"What?" I ask. My eyes squint to make out his shape against the water.

"My name," he says, his voice strains from the confession. "My name is Samuel. I was born and raised in Las Vegas. I've never been in love and I fucking hate eighties music. I am *not* a monster, but I have been a hired thug since I was seventeen. This was going to be the biggest job of my career. I just had to bring you to San Antonio to finish the job, then I was going to retire to Mexico. But I couldn't do it, Kat. I can't hurt you. If you don't believe anything else I've ever said, please believe that."

My body responds to his declaration before I can make sense of it. My feet move in his direction as if he's finally given me what I need. Samuel's eyes stay trained on mine, pulling me in with their complete honesty.

"Stop!" Boots yells. His deep voice booms around us. I obey without thought. I spin and see that he now has a gun pointed at me. Samuel raises his weapon again and I'm caught between them.

"Come on, Kat. He won't shoot you. He needs you alive."

"I guarantee that's not true," Boots says. "Maybe she had a weapon. She *is* a dangerous, wanted killer after all. It would be self-defense." His hard stare slides over me and I don't doubt his threat. "Whether willingly or in a body bag, you're coming with me, Katherine."

I look to Samuel, but his gaze moves past me to Boots. I turn back to Boots just in time to watch him lower his aim to my chest.

I lose my breath, squeeze my eyes closed, and wait for the pain. A single shot is fired, but nothing hits me. I scream and drop to the ground, covering my head with my hands. I open my eyes just in time to watch Boots' body hit the grass with a soft thud.

Samuel runs to me and pulls my fingers from my face. His eyes meet mine and I see so many things there—things that I want to shake free from. I jerk my hand from his grip and slap him across the face. His head turns from the force and the sting burns my hand. I get no relief from the hit, so I try it again. This time he catches my hand.

"I'm sorry. I know I deserve it, but there's no time," he says. He pulls me to my feet and turns to Boots. "We've got to go."

"Samuel," I say, testing out his name. It's satisfying, like honey on my tongue. I want to say it again. "Samuel."

He spins to face me. It's as if the sound of his name has transformed him into something else, something softer. He pulls me to his body and plants his lips on mine. The kiss leaves me breathless and desperate for more. The force behind that kiss, the sheer joy and pain of it surrounds us and binds us to each other.

When he releases me, I stumble back, fighting to catch my breath. I press my fingers to my lips, still tingling with his taste. Samuel steps to Boots' body, takes his gun, and tucks it into his waistband. He digs his wallet and keys out and takes those, too.

"You killed him," I say.

"It was him or you, Kat," he says holding his hand out for me.

I take it without thinking and climb into the van as Samuel slides into the driver's seat. He starts it and we're off, speeding through the cemetery and exiting onto the street.

"What now?" I ask.

"They're expecting us tomorrow evening, so that's a small window of time to get ahead."

15. HIM

As I tear through the streets of Avondale, I pick up my phone and dial the only person that can help. It doesn't even ring once before he picks up.

"Hello, you absentee mother fucker."

"Jack, I'm sending you a photo. I need a new identity. Social, passport, everything. Code ADAM for both of us."

"Good to hear from you, too. Yeah, we're doing great, thanks for asking. The kids are growing like weeds."

"You don't even have kids. No time for this, Jack."

"So, this isn't a social call. Alright, man. You know I got you," he says. "Where should I send it?"

"I need it tonight," I say and wait for his protest.

"What? Are you crazy? There's a Ninja Turtle marathon on Cartoon Network."

I roll my eyes and huff into the phone. “You know I wouldn’t ask if it wasn’t important.”

“Guess you’re in the area? I’ll get it done, but you owe me big for this one,” Jack says.

“I don’t owe you shit. Two words: Spearmint Rhino.”

“Touché, asshole. Will you be staying?”

“Just for the night. We’re headed to Mexico. I don’t think I’m coming back this time.”

There’s a beat of silence between us. He knows I’m serious.

“Damn, you must be in some major shit. Kelli will be trés disappointed. I’m assuming you need to be off the grid so I’ll leave the garage open. Park in there.”

I hang up, send Jack the photo of Kat from my phone, and hop onto I-10, heading south toward Tucson.

I send a text to my employer.

Have to detour, other interested parties in pursuit.

A few minutes later, my phone beeps with a reply.

Let me know the new plan ASAP.

Kat peeks at me sideways. I keep my eyes on the road and avoid the conversation that waits on the tips of our tongues.

“Are we really doing this?” Kat asks while pulling her knees up and staring out of the window.

“Do you want to go to prison?”

“God, no,” she answers, shaking her head in slow motion.

“Then, yes, we’re going to try. I did a job for a guy who works at Border Patrol in Nogales. If we cross there, he may be able to help.”

I keep my eyes on the dark highway ahead and wonder how

I got here. Why am I giving up my career and my life to save this girl? The answer is simple and suddenly clear. Katherine Percle, a force so strong and sweet, hasn't changed who I am, but who I want to be.

The tension between us is palpable and it draws a solid line down the middle of the van. I sit quietly for a while, streetlights tick by like seconds. I want to tell her so many things, but I can't man up enough to say any of them. We ride in silence for an hour before Kat finally breaks.

"Who hired you, Samuel?"

I take a deep breath and let it slowly leave my lungs to clear my head. The sound of my name from her lips is enough to break me.

"Callista Brady."

"What?" Kat yells. "You're lying!"

"I'm not, Kat. Never again," I promise.

"I . . . I just . . ." Kat stutters before dropping her chin to her chest in disbelief.

"I don't know how she found me. I got a call to meet her at the San Antonio Lake Marina on a boat called *Persephone*. She hired me to find you before the authorities did. Said you had stolen something of hers, but wouldn't tell me what it was. I was supposed to bring you back to San Antonio, and once she had it, I was to get rid of you. She wanted to be there when it was done," I say, pushing those last words out like the hardest confession.

My heavy footsteps echoed on the wood as I made my way down the floating dock. I checked each boat as I passed, looking for the Persephone. *Through the grayness of twilight, I spotted a woman standing at the last boat. She wore a white pantsuit, impeccable and tailored to fit her tall, slim body. The chipped polish on her fingernails stood out against her otherwise flawless appearance. She hid behind large sunglasses, which at this time of day made her look more conspicuous. The woman looked like money and immediately I was sure this would be a big payoff. She kept her head down, her arms crossed, and tapped the toe of her designer shoe impatiently.*

"Callista?" I asked.

"Yes. Come with me," she answered.

I followed her onto the boat. It was a thirty-foot center-cockpit sailboat with great lines. Solid wood teak floorboards, a real beauty. We went below to the main salon which was just as stunning as the rest of the boat with at least six feet of standing headroom throughout.

Callista was jumpy and fidgety, although nervousness was not uncommon during these meetings. I took a seat on a bench near the door as she removed her sunglasses and poured herself a drink from a nearly empty bottle of Scotch. Without the glasses on, I could see she was older than I originally assumed. There were wrinkles in the corners of each eye and frown lines around her mouth. I could barely make out the tiny bit of gray hair growth at the roots of her dye job.

"Would you like one?" she asked.

"Yes."

She emptied the bottle into a second glass and brought it over. Sitting across from me, she swallowed down her entire glass. Her right leg bounced in place and she remained quiet for a few minutes. I sipped my drink and waited for her request. Callista shifted in her seat and recrossed her legs in the opposite direction. She combed her sleek black hair behind her ear before bringing her thumb to her mouth and chewing on the jagged fingernail. Frowning, she let out a low sigh and folded her hands on her lap. Callista's gaze appraised me unashamedly, darting from my shoes to my hands and up to my shoulders, but she never met my waiting eyes.

"You want me to find someone?" I coaxed.

"Yes."

I sighed when she didn't continue. "I'll need some information."

"Of course, I'm sorry," she said, closing her eyes and shaking her empty glass.

She stood and retrieved a photo from her bag and brought it back to me. I looked down to find a young girl smiling with her glass of wine. She was beautiful, but as with every other job, I felt no connection to her as a person. She was a target and a paycheck, nothing more.

"What do I need to know?" I asked.

"Her name is Katherine Percle. She's wanted. I need you to find her before the authorities do. She stole something from me."

"Stole what?" I asked.

Callista shrugged and placed her hands on the table between us. "What it is, is not important. But I know she'll have it on her."

"So, she's already on the run?"

"Yes. She skipped bail two days ago. Bail that I paid, the ungrateful brat!"

The woman's voice grew louder, her flattened palms balling into fists.

"Okay. I'll need you to send any information you have on her to this email address." I handed her my card with contact information on it. "Is that all you need? For me to find her and whatever she stole?"

"No," she said. She stood and went back to the empty Scotch bottle and tipped it over, coaxing the last few drops into her glass. Callista finally met my eyes, her cold stare resolute and unwavering. "I want her dead."

I looked back at the photo. I tried to imagine what this girl could have done to bring such wrath. I'd never done a hit before, but saw an opportunity for a big payout, one that could let me escape this life.

"Well, that would cost a lot more than a standard find and fetch."

"I'll pay," she said as she poured the tiny bit of alcohol into her mouth.

"Five hundred thousand dollars. Half when I find her, the other half when she's dead."

The woman slammed her glass onto the counter and stepped over to me.

"Deal," she said as we shook hands.

"My assistant will be in touch."

Tears slip from Kat's eyes and she wipes them away quickly. Her arms lay folded on each other hugging her knees. I can tell that she's fighting a complete breakdown.

"Callista is my mom," Kat answers, her voice cracking. "That was Dennis's boat you met her at."

She pulls on the chain and the key slips into her palm. She turns it over a few times, as if inspecting it for the first time.

"My own fucking mother paid someone to kill me! Not just someone. You. She paid *you* to kill me. All for this stupid key."

"Kat." She doesn't look at me, but keeps her eyes focused on the key. "I know there's nothing I can say to make you forgive me, but I need you to trust me. We're about to get into some crazy shit and for it to work, you'll have to trust me."

"I . . . I don't know," she whispers.

"At least trust that I need to do this. I need to make this right. I'll get you into Mexico and then you'll be rid of me. You don't ever have to see me again." She nods and twists her lips sideways. "We'll be in Tucson soon. My friends, Jack and Kelli, live just south of there. He'll provide us with a new identity and transportation. I'll call my contact at the border and see if he can offer any help."

"Okay," she says, reaching over and turning up the radio, ending our conversation.

My phone rings twice before we reach Jack's house. Once from Callista and the last time from Natasha. I don't know who knows about Boots or if word has gotten out that we're running, but I can't deal with any of it right now.

I pull into Jack and Kelli's garage and kill the lights. We sit in the van not talking, the only sound is the ticking of the cooling engine. Kat's eyes hold mine without faltering and she looks terrified. I don't know if she's afraid of our journey or of me. Maybe I don't want to know.

"Ready?" I ask.

She shrugs her shoulders and exits the van. Freshly showered, Jack steps into the garage wearing a T-shirt and SpongeBob pajama pants, greeting us with a hero's smile.

"Oz!" he shouts, shaking my hand and pulling me in for a one-armed hug. "Been too long, man!"

"Sexy pants, fucker. This is Kat," I say, motioning behind us.

"Kat, lovely to meet you."

"Where's your better half?"

"Cooking dinner. Come in."

Jack hits a button on the wall, closing the garage door and sealing us inside. We follow him through the dark house into the kitchen, where Kelli is busy cooking at the stove. Her black hair is curly and pinned up into a messy knot. She wears a pink apron with ruffles over a black skirt and white shirt, very June Cleaver. Her skirt is twisted, the zipper halfway between her back and hip. The wrinkled bottom of her shirt hangs out. The mail, which usually sits on the kitchen counter is on the tiled floor like litter.

"Oz?" Kat asks.

"My last name is Ozley. Everyone calls me Oz."

"Sammy!" Kelli yells, running and throwing herself at me. I grunt when her legs wrap around my sore ribs as she jumps into my arms and kisses both cheeks.

"Everyone except Kelli," I say to Kat. She finally lets go and slides down my body, landing on her high heels.

"Damn, baby, I never get that kind of greeting," Jack protests.

"Well, I see you every day," Kelli answers.

"I'm sure your greeting was just fine," I say. "I hope you bleached the counter after you had sex on it." Kelli blushes and Jack laughs, placing his hand over his heart.

Kat's wide eyes go from Kelli to Jack and then to me. I shrug and give her a half smile.

Kelli notices Kat and smiles brightly at her. "And who is this?"

"Kat," she answers before I can introduce them and gives a small wave.

"Nice to meet you, Kat. What on earth are you wearing?" Kelli points to Kat's oversized shirt from the homeless kid.

"I was going to ask you the same thing," Kat retorts, crossing her arms.

"Oh, I like her, Sammy," Kelli says, squeezing my shoulder and returning her attention to the stove. "You guys make yourselves at home. Jack didn't mention that you'd be here so soon."

"I didn't know, babe," he protests.

Kat and I take a seat at the counter, while Jack fetches a beer for everyone. I take a long pull from mine and watch as Kat does the same.

"You guys look beat to shit. What happened?" Jack asks.

Kat's hand flies to her cheek and I rub at my jaw. I'm grateful they can't see the blue and purple bruises beneath my shirt.

"We've had a rough few days," I answer cryptically.

"You hungry?" Kelli asks. We both nod. "The chicken will be done in a few minutes and then we can eat."

"Chicken?" I ask. "The last time you cooked chicken I almost died."

Kelli marches over and slaps my shoulder with her wooden spoon before pointing it at my face. "That was not my cooking, Sam. That was because you and Beavis drank an entire bottle of tequila," she says before turning back to the stove.

"Felt like salmonella poisoning to me."

She gives me a lethal glare, then turns to Kat and points over her shoulder.

"Don't listen to him," Kelli says. "He rarely tells the truth."

"That much, I know," Kat answers while picking at her bottle label.

It's a jab she deserves, but that doesn't make it hurt any less. I avoid her eyes and finish my beer. Jack darts around the kitchen, gathering ingredients and throwing them in a big bowl of salad. The couple works side by side in the kitchen, always instinctually aware of the other.

I hear Kat humph and look over.

"What?" I ask.

"This is just all so domestic. Not what I pictured."

I lean closer, my lips next to her ear.

"You figured friends of mine had to be dark and twisted individuals who keep children chained up in the basement and torture small animals?" Kat shakes her head nervously. I lean back and hold her gaze.

"Jack, you got the papers done?" I ask.

"Yeah, just finished them before you got here."

Jack leaves the kitchen and returns a few minutes later with a thick envelope. I empty the contents and sift through all the papers, IDs, passports, and two gold rings. I check the photos and names, grimacing when I compare the two.

"What the fuck, Jack?"

He leans against the counter, grinning innocently. "What?" he asks.

"Why do we have the same last name?"

Kat grabs her passport from my hand and inspects it. "Elizabeth Turner," she says. "Who are you?"

"Lucas Turner."

"Why do I have red hair in this picture?" Kat asks.

"Ta daaaaaa," Kelli says, appearing with a box of hair dye. "Clairol Natural Instincts Raspberry Créme! I was going to go red, but now it's all yours."

"I thought you'd have more luck posing as a vacationing married couple. Those are your rings," Jack says, pointing to the simple gold bands from the envelope. "Congratulations, you two!" He raises his beer and clinks it against Kat's. "To the happy couple!"

I glare at him for a long moment before Kelli steps between us announcing dinner is ready. We all sit around their kitchen table eating and drinking like tomorrow is not a do-or-die situation.

"So, Kat, where are you from?" Kelli asks.

"San Antonio," she answers between bites.

"How old are you? You look really young."

"Kelli!" Jack says. "Can the poor girl eat without you interrogating her?"

"It's just a question," Kelli insists, pointing her fork at him.

"It's not a problem, really. I'm twenty-three," Kat answers.

"So, how did you meet our Sammy?"

"Kelli," I warn. "Can we not do this?" I drum my fingers on the tabletop.

"What?" she asks innocently. "You've never brought a girl home. I'm excited. And it's my duty, as the only permanent woman in your life, to conduct thorough assessments."

"She's been watching too much CSI," Jack says.

I turn to Kat. "You don't have to answer any questions."

She raises an eyebrow in my direction.

"You always have a choice," Jack, Kelli, and I say in unison.

Kelli giggles as Jack shakes his head and continues eating.

"Okay, that was creepy," Kat says, her fork hovering halfway between her plate and mouth.

"Surely, you've heard that before tonight," Jack insists.

"Oh yeah," Kat answers. "Been there, heard that, even saw the visual aid."

"Well that's interesting," Jack sings. "You've seen the tattoo? How did she see *that* tattoo, Oz?"

"Drop it," I say. "Unless you want to discuss tattoos in general, Jack?"

Jack drops his fork and it clatters to the ground. He mumbles profanities as he stands and grabs a new one from the kitchen. Kelli silently laughs, her shoulders shaking as she looks away.

"What?" Kat asks. "Am I missing something?"

When Jack returns he spins his back to the table and pulls the side of his pants down. On his left ass cheek is a tattoo of a cartoon pirate with the word "Booty" in a banner beneath it.

"Oh my God!" Kat shouts.

Kelli can no longer hold in her giggling. She throws her head into her hands and lets it go. Kat is somewhere between flustered and amused. She laughs so hard her face turns pink. Jack ignores us, sits down and finishes his dinner like nothing happened.

When she can finally catch her breath, Kat asks, "Why on earth would you do that?"

Jack shakes his head and drinks down his beer.

"That was the same night they finished the tequila," Kelli answers, smiling at Jack's pouting face. "I was so pissed off that I'd have to look at that thing the rest of my life. Now it's just hilarious."

After a few minutes, we've all calmed down and refocus on our meal.

"So, Sammy. Going on a vacation?" Kelli asks as she spears a piece of chicken.

I shoot Jack a glance, pissed that he hasn't prepared her.

"You know I've always wanted to stay down there."

"You're not coming back?" she asks. I shake my head and take a bite. I figure if my mouth's full, she won't have any more questions for me. I should have known better. "You're leaving the business? Done? Kaput?"

I nod, keeping my eyes on my plate. Kelli squeals, jumps out of her seat, and runs over. She wraps her arms around my neck and squeezes tight. This was not the reaction I expected, but I'll take it over an inquisition.

She leans into my ear and whispers, "She's good for you, Sammy. Hold on to her."

I don't respond. Kelli doesn't understand. Since we were teenagers, she's always pressured me to find a girl and settle down. Like that would be the answer to all my problems. She wants me to have what she and Jack have. It's not something I can imagine for myself. I notice that Jack stays quiet and I'm thankful for it. It's not often he gives me a free pass.

"Kat, I've got some clothes that will fit you. Sammy, you can take some of Jack's," Kelli says after taking her seat again. "I've packed a full suitcase for you guys, in case you get stopped. You need to actually look like a vacationing couple."

"Thanks," Kat mumbles. "Do you think this will work?"

"I haven't heard any word about either of you on the inside lines. Hopefully, you'll be gone before anyone notices you're missing," Jack offers.

"It'll work," I assure her, though I'm not even convinced myself.

When we're done eating, Jack and I do the dishes while the girls pick up the food.

"I never thought I'd see the day," Jack says without looking at me.

"What day is that?"

"Samuel Ozley, giving up the career. I figured you'd be in it for life, ya know? Or death."

"Yeah, me too," I answer.

The girls leave the kitchen and I'm left alone with Jack and his knowing smirk.

"So why now?"

He turns to me and wipes his soapy hands on a towel. I finally look at him, his eyes appraise me in absolute wonder. He wants me to say it out loud. He wants me to confess. So, I do.

"Kat."

16: her

I help Kelli put away the leftover food and can't help but sneak glances at Samuel. Jack is washing and rinsing dishes while Samuel dries. That man, who sometimes seems to be made of lead and concrete, looks unexplainably sexy holding that dish towel.

He's different here, a little more relaxed in the presence of people he trusts. I steal another glance to find him watching me, his expression pokerfaced while Jack says something low enough for only them to hear. I stand at the refrigerator, door wide open, and forget what I'm doing there.

"Kat?" Kelli says.

I snap out of my daze and slam the door closed. The sound of Kelli's laughter follows me out of the room.

I grab new panties from my bag and retreat to the bathroom, where I start the water for my shower. For a few minutes, I sit and stare at my reflection in the large mirror. I don't recognize the girl who stares back. She's a criminal and a liar. She seduces men meant to kill her. I turn to the side and look again. She's kind of badass.

I catch the new light in my eyes just before the steam erases that girl completely from view. There's a knock on the door and I jump, feeling like I've been caught.

"Kat? It's just me," Kelli says.

"Come in."

"Ready to be a redhead?" she asks holding up the box of hair dye. "I brought you something to sleep in too."

"Oh, yeah. I forgot."

I shrug my shoulders and take a seat on the closed toilet lid.

"Don't worry, I dye my own hair all the time. I'm a pro."

"Okay."

Kelli turns the shower off and starts preparing the dye. I watch in fascination as she methodically places the supplied gloves over her hands and combines the solutions. She shakes it and the mixture turns into a bloodred color in the bottle.

The air is thick with steam and silence. I feel choked by it.

"Can we crack the door?" I ask.

"Sure thing." She opens the door before approaching, bottle in hand. "Now, don't worry. This won't hurt a bit. Normally, I'd drape a towel around your shoulders in case it drips, but I don't think this shirt needs protecting."

I close my eyes as she applies the solution and massages it through my hair. The feeling is calming and reminds me of when my mom would braid my hair before school. It takes a few minutes for Kelli to saturate all of my hair. When she's done, she carefully rinses her hands in the sink and removes the gloves. She sets a timer on her phone and hops up onto the counter.

"So," she says. Her eyes appraise me carefully.

"So," I repeat, a little fearful of where this conversation may go.

"You guys heading to Sammy's house in Cabo?"

"Yeah, that's the plan."

"No one's ever been to the house in Cabo. He must trust you."

I look down at my fidgeting hands and back up. "I think he feels like he owes me."

"Ah. Guilt. The biggest weapon in a woman's arsenal," she says. "Can't say I've ever seen Sammy affected by it though. There must be something else."

I shrug my shoulders. "I don't know."

"How long have you known him?" she asks.

"Three days."

Kelli's mouth drops open before her shoulders push up, making her neck disappear. There's a small squealing sound that escapes her lips. I don't know how to interpret that, so I say nothing.

"You're a special girl, Kat. I'll let you in on a little secret." She hops off of the counter and walks over to me, taking a seat on the tub. Our knees touch as she leans into me. "Samuel is damaged."

I blow out a breath and look at her. "That's not a secret."

"No, the secret is he's not who he appears to be. I've known him for a long time. It's like he walks around playing this part, this tough guy with no emotions. It's not him, Kat. Inside that man is a world of hurt and pain. But there's also kindness and fierce loyalty. He's super protective of women, and will never forgive himself for his mother's death. Sammy has been wearing this persona so long, he thinks it's who he is. You could help him find himself again."

I shake my head. "I can't. There are things about me you don't know, about how we met and my past."

Kelli places a hand on my knee, her shiny red nails in sharp contrast with my dirty jeans. "None of it matters. He's different with you. This is a Sammy I haven't seen since we were kids. Please don't give up on him."

Kelli opens a small closet and digs around, pulling out towels for me. So many thoughts spin around my head. I barely know Samuel, but I can see all the things Kelli says are true. I know that he longs for redemption, even if he doesn't feel like he deserves it. I know beneath his thick skin and dark nightmares is a man who needs to be reclaimed by humanity.

The timer sounds, jarring me out of my inner musings. Kelli turns it off and starts the shower for me again.

"I don't want to pressure you into anything," she says. "It's just amazing to see a change in him. And I know it has everything to do with you."

I nod and she exits the bathroom. Alone again, I sit there for another few minutes piecing together the Samuel I know with the Samuel she does. I can't imagine that I could change anyone in three days.

I peel off my clothes and hop into the shower. The pink water splashes around my feet as I wash the dye out. I try to keep the worry from my mind, but it seeps back in. I don't know what tomorrow will bring. All I know is that I'm scared and Samuel needs me to be strong.

As I dry off and slip into the sleep shorts and tank top Kelli left for me, I wonder if I can be Mrs. Turner for him. Can I act the part and play a role? I comb out my new red hair and find the strength to try.

An hour later, the house is quiet and I sit on a bed in the guest room. My mind races with the possibilities and probabilities of tomorrow. The pep talk I had with myself just sixty minutes ago is long forgotten. A knock sounds on the door and I ignore it. Another knock and then the door cracks open. Samuel sticks his head through. His hair is wet and some of the shorter pieces stick to his forehead.

"Hey," he says.

I don't know what to say, so I continue to stare at the blank television. I feel his gaze on me before he crosses the room and takes a seat on the bed.

"Kat," Samuel says again. He reaches out and slides a piece of hair between his fingers. "Wow. The red really suits you."

My eyes finally meet his and I find an intensity that stirs confusion and longing inside me. I know he sees all my fear and desperation.

"Samuel, I'm really scared."

"Did you study your I.D. and passport?"

I nod and look away again.

"Jack and Kelli are your friends, right? You trust them?" I ask.

"Yes."

"How do you know they won't call the police when we leave?"

"Kat, they are the only people in the world who are important to me. They would never," he insists.

"How do you know each other?"

"After my father killed my mother, I was put into foster care. I was moved from house to house, until I finally ended up in the same place as Jack. We looked out for each other, vowing to always have each other's back. The couple that housed us didn't care about where we were or what we did, as long as we stayed out of their hair. We were both on a path headed downhill until Kelli arrived."

"She lived with you guys?"

"No. Her family moved in next door. I remember the day she showed up. She was like this ball of energy that projected sunshine onto everyone she met. We were sixteen and out of control. She walked into our lives and just like that, had us wrapped around her finger."

"I see nothing has changed."

Samuel shakes his head and gives me his dimpled grin.

"We would do anything for that girl, and we did. When I graduated high school, I left. I got involved with people who eventually led me into the life I have now. But Jack wouldn't leave. Kelli was two years younger than us, so he waited for her. When she turned eighteen, they got married."

"Wow. But, he's obviously involved in shady stuff too."

"Yeah. He's the best in the business at producing false documents and new identities. Kelli couldn't keep him out of it completely."

"They seem so great together," I say.

"Jack told me the day he met Kelli that he loved her. I never doubted it. They saved each other."

"What about you?"

"What *about* me?" he asks.

"No one saved you."

"Not yet."

I look away and frown at the closed window. *Don't ask me to save you. I'm not strong enough.*

"If we don't make it, then I'll have to run again or go straight to prison. I'm so tired of running. And I'd go crazy in prison. I would."

"Kat, we'll make it. I promise."

Those words immediately bring anger. So many people, so many promises before have failed me. My fingers claw into the mattress on each side of my hips.

"You can't do that, Samuel. You can't make promises. You were hired to kill me and here you are, comforting me like you care. I want to hate you. I want to tell you to go to hell and take your promises with you. But I can't. You're my only hope now."

He leaves me on the bed, crossing the room and opening the door to leave.

"If that's all I can be, I'll take it."

Samuel wakes me at four in the morning. With no words spoken between us, we dress in the clothes Kelli laid out, me in a turquoise sundress and Samuel in a T-shirt and jeans. He thinks I shouldn't wear the key, so I take it from around my neck and drop it into an inside pocket of the suitcase. I slip on flip-flops and a cardigan and take a seat on the bed.

This time of day always feels special to me. Just before dawn when you assume no one else in the world is awake besides you. There's the sharp contrast of sleep wanting to pull me back under while nerves work to keep me awake.

Samuel sorts through our new paperwork. He hands over my I.D. and passport and I put them in my new purse. He slides his I.D. into his wallet and pockets his passport. Everything else, but the rings, is returned to the envelope and tucked into the suitcase.

He shoves the ring on his left hand and takes my hand. Gently and without looking up at me, he slides the ring on my finger. I know he's asking me to trust him. At this moment, *I do.*

"Ready?" he asks.

"As I'll ever be."

Samuel carries our suitcase through the dark house and out the front door. We load our things into Jack's truck and take off, praying to survive what lays ahead.

When we reach Highway 19, Samuel informs me that we have about an hour until the border town of Nogales.

"Nogales means 'black walnuts' in Spanish for the trees that grow there. It's the largest border town in Arizona."

"So why are we going through there? Shouldn't we try to sneak across?"

He frowns at me and shakes his head. "No. If we're caught doing that, it will be much harder to explain."

"How do you know so much about all these cities? I get that you travel a lot, but where does all this random information come from?"

Samuel keeps his eyes on the road. I can tell whatever he's about to say is not something that he wants to share.

"I told you we didn't have a television when I was a kid. Now when I travel, I still don't have much interest in it. Instead, I have a habit of reading all the travel brochures in hotel lobbies. Honestly, it's more like an unhealthy obsession."

I laugh and continue to watch him, amazed at his never-ending ability to surprise me. If he was capable of blushing, he'd be pink by now. I kick off my shoes and sit cross-legged on the seat. I tug the oversized purse into my lap and begin digging through it. While I discover the surprises inside—granola bars, sunscreen, and condoms, among other things—Samuel checks his phone.

"You know, it's not safe for you to be on your phone while driving," I say.

He shrugs.

"Just the usual text messages. Where am I? Where are you? Threats of death and dismemberment."

"The usual," I repeat, stunned by his casual talk of death.

"And the one message from my ex."

"Natasha?"

"Yeah. She's up to something."

"Maybe she wants you back," I say.

"Maybe, but that's not happening. Especially now."

I don't know what to think about that statement and I can't ask him to explain. I won't. Every word from Samuel seems to have something hidden between the lines. Just once, I wish he'd be straight with me. Though it's a lot to ask of a thug with trust issues.

As the sun begins to rise on our left, the sky turns into a palette of mixed violets, pinks, and gold. The highway signs count down the miles to the Mexican border and with each passing one, my anxiety grows. There's a ball of nervousness that sits heavy in my stomach. It reminds me of the last time I felt this way.

The building was empty, but I knew he'd still be working. When I turned the corner, my assumption was confirmed by the bit of light shining from beneath his office door. It had been three days of stewing in shock and disbelief, while working up the nerve to confront him. I stood before his door now, the sliver of light painting the toes of my shoes in a golden glow. It felt like there were angry bees and barbed wire in my stomach. I took a deep breath and didn't bother knocking.

Dennis sat at his desk, his hands poised above his keyboard as his thick fingers pecked away. The sight of him made a nauseating kind of rage consume my body in flames. He didn't acknowledge my presence.

"I know you and your sister are embezzling money," I blurted out, standing before him.

Dennis grinned from behind his enormous oak desk. It was a smile I'd seen many times. In any other place, any other circumstance, it meant for me to shut my mouth and disappear. Not this time. Chills pebbled across my scalp and raced down my arms. He tented his fingers together and leaned toward me.

"How do you think I can afford such lavish things, you ungrateful brat? Your tuition, your car, your fancy computers. There's no money fairy that pays your AmEx bill every month, Katherine."

"I don't care about any of that stuff. I want you gone. Somewhere far away from my mom, where you can't hurt her anymore. If you leave, I won't say a word about the money. If you stay, I'll go to the cops."

My head was swimming and it seemed the calmer Dennis remained, the more frantic I became. He walked to a closet between us and opened it. Sunk into the wall was a safe with a digital keypad. I wrung my sweaty hands as he unlocked the safe and pulled a small hard drive from it.

"Blackmail, Katherine? You really underestimate me, don't you? Make no doubt, I always know what goes on in my building. I knew you found out about our side project. I moved all the proof to this."

"That's a CipherShield dual key USB encrypted hard drive." Dennis raised his eyebrows, probably shocked that I recognized the equipment. "You need two keys to access the information on there."

"That's right," he said, his fingers absently tracing a chain around his neck.

If he had one key, that probably meant Marilyn had the other. Defeat drew the breath from my lungs, but I wouldn't let him win so easily.

"You're crooks," I said lunging toward him for the hard drive.

He held it high above my head, and pushed me back with a hard smack to the middle of my chest. The pain radiated out to my shoulders as I stumbled into his desk. I grabbed onto the edge to keep from falling over.

"Crooks are pickpockets and low life burglars," he answered. "I'm a hero for the common man, simply redistributing wealth from those who won't even miss it," Dennis said. "You were stupid to confront me, Katherine. You don't think things through, just like your mother. Now, you've got no proof and no job. You're fired." He placed the hard drive back into the safe and I peeked inside seeing he had a couple of thick folders, a small metal box, and a gun.

"You put my mom in the hospital again, you son of a bitch! I'm going to tell her about this. She'll finally leave you!"

Dennis charged me. His skin turned red and a bulging vein divided his forehead. My blood pumped harder, thundering in my ears. He was terrifying and my body trembled in anticipation of what would come.

"She will never leave me!" he shouted. Spittle flew from his mouth and landed on my cheek.

I flinched backward over his desk and knocked pens and papers to the ground while the edge cut into my back. I was used to his rage, although it was usually a silent kind made of cold glares and calculated movements. This was something new to me, but something my mother knew all too well.

Like flipping a switch, his snarling face evened out and became neutral as he hovered over me. Dennis seemed to regain control of his emotions and straightened his posture. He tugged on the lapels of his jacket and brushed imaginary dust from his sleeves.

"Callista already knows."

"No." The word escaped my lips on a wheezing exhale.

"Yes, Katherine. Unlike yourself, your mother knows how to appreciate the finer things in life, no matter how she comes by them. Now get out of my office."

In that moment, hatred and betrayal consumed me. The thoughts of this poisonous man and all the ways he destroyed my mother forced any self-preservation from my brain.

"If I have to take her against her will, I'll do it. You won't have her as your punching bag anymore, you piece of shit. Don't expect to find her at home when you get there!" I shouted and turned toward the door.

I heard his heavy footsteps coming and knew I'd made a mistake. I was alone in this building and he was a violent man. I'd pushed his buttons and now I'd pay the price.

I screamed when he caught up with me. I knew there was no one to hear me.

Dennis' arm came around my middle and he threw me to the ground. I landed with an oomph, and before I could move, his leather loafer came down on my throat. Panicked, my hands clawed and pushed at his leg, but it wouldn't budge. I fought hard for air as my watery eyes begged him to stop.

"You bitches never learn," he spat.

Too many thoughts ran through my head, at the forefront was survival. My chest felt like it was caving in, my lungs burned as I abandoned his leg and searched the carpet around me for any kind of weapon. Darkness began to creep into my vision, closing in around the edges like a shutter. When my fingers landed on an ink pen, I wrapped them tight around it and stabbed the pen into his calf. Dennis screamed and fell to the ground cursing.

I sucked in deep lungfuls of air as he yanked the pen from his leg, blood spilling out over his fingers. Relief washed over me like an ice bath jolting me back to life, piece by piece. White lights danced before my eyes as I blinked the tears away.

Dennis got to his feet and limped toward the safe, his determination outweighing any pain. My head was spinning as I used the desk to pull myself up.

Dennis turned, the gun from the safe clutched in his bloody hands and pointed at me. I moved backward, tripping over a chair, my hands held up in surrender.

"Don't do anything stupid, Dennis."

"I'll say you tried to kill me," he threatened. "I'll spin it so it's self-defense."

There was a gleam in his frenzied eyes, something that told me he had no qualms about pulling the trigger and ending my life. Without thought, I lunged at him, wrapping my hands around his and pushing the gun toward the ceiling. He was so much stronger than me, I knew I needed to gain an advantage. I kicked Dennis in the crotch as hard as I could. He dropped to his knees, both of our hands still struggling with the gun. Finally, I charged him, toppling him backward and landing on top of him. The loud bang rang in my ears as the vibration rocked my chest.

I pushed away from him as blood began to seep out of his chest, staining his starched shirt. He took two more breaths before leaving this world. They were the longest two breaths of my life.

After we enter the border town, we turn onto the highway that leads to the port of entry. I reach down and grab Samuel's hand out of his lap and don't let go. His gaze briefly drops to our entwined fingers and he curls his over the back of my hand. The warmth of his skin makes me feel safe and grounded.

There are only a few vehicles in each lane at this hour. We pass under a large white arc and pull to a stop behind a rusty car.

"My contact said to stay in the far left lane, and to keep ourselves turned left as much as possible without being suspicious." I nod silently. "Put your game face on, Mrs. Turner. Once we get through this, we need a green light up there and we're home free."

I look past the guard and see a two-light system. Cars that are given a green light, proceed on and disappear into Mexico. Those given a red light are being pulled over.

"What's a red light mean?"

"The truck triggers a pressure plate as you drive through the inspection lane. If the light is green, you're good. If the light is red, you have to sit through a secondary inspection. That could be trouble for us."

We creep forward as the car in front of us shows their papers. The officer glances in their car and waves them through. They get a green light. We pull forward again, stopping and rolling down the window. I remind myself to breath as I catch a glimpse of the cameras pointed in our direction. My chest feels tight and my palm sweats against Samuel's. He gives me a little squeeze.

"Good morning," Samuel says. His demeanor is light and casual. He even pulls out that rarely seen smile, punctuated by dimples on each side.

The officer nods. He's an older man with a round, childlike face and broad shoulders. His uniform buttons pull tight across his belly.

"I need to see both of your passports."

"Sure," Samuel says. "Honey?"

He stares in my direction awkwardly until I realize he's talking to me. I dig through my new purse and hand him my passport.

He places his on top and hands them over to the officer. I'm beginning to feel nauseated.

"What's your destination? How long will you be staying?" the officer asks while studying Samuel's passport.

"We're headed to Baja for vacation," he answers.

Something in the cool tone of Samuel's voice snaps me out of my panic. He needs me to be present and convincing. I blow out a slow breath and paste on a smile.

"It's our first vacation in three years!" I gush. The officer hands one passport over. Samuel looks to me and I shrug like there's nothing but vacation on my brain.

"We'll be staying two weeks," Samuel adds.

"Just long enough for me to spend all his money," I tease.

The officer chuckles to himself. He opens my passport and eyes my photo and information, leaning down to get a good look inside the car. Samuel looks furious at the invasion, but stays calm.

Thinking quickly, I unbuckle my seatbelt and kneel on my seat. I place both palms on Samuel's thigh and lean across him, wedging myself between his chest and the steering wheel.

"There," I say, "is that better? I know the picture is awful. Those never come out very flattering do they?"

He looks back at my passport. "No, I guess not. Though, yours is just fine."

"Well, thanks," I say, smiling and biting my bottom lip.

"What happened to your cheek?" he asks.

"That? Oh, my two year old threw a fit when I tried to wash her My Little Pony blanket."

He laughs at me again. "I know what you mean. It's Dora, the Explorer in our house. You look familiar. Are you famous or something?"

I can feel Samuel suck in a breath and hold it. I curl my fingers around his thigh.

"Oh, no. I just have one of those generic faces."

I reach one hand out, strongly suggesting he return the passport.

"Hmm," he says, "I don't think that's true, but I can't place it." He shrugs and drops the document in my empty hand. "Have a good vacation," he says.

I slide back into my seat and wave. "Thanks. We certainly will."

The officer sends us through and Samuel rolls up the window. We start to move forward, eyes glued to that light. *Please be green. Please be green.* Green!

"Yes!"

I celebrate by pumping my fist in the air and doing the "green light dance." Samuel actually laughs and the air inside the truck feels so much lighter. Just before we make it past the light, I hear a commotion of honking horns and screeching tires.

"Shit!" Samuel shouts.

I turn and see two officers sprinting in our direction, guns drawn. I look back to Samuel and can tell he's debating whether to make a run for it. Their shouts surround us and I know we're done for when he throws it in park and lifts his hands in surrender.

17. HIM

We're both placed in handcuffs and dragged inside, through dimly lit hallways, past countless rooms, until we reach a set of large double doors. Inside is a metal table, two chairs on each side. One wall is mirrored and I know that it's two-way glass. The windowless room's cinderblock walls are painted a muddy gray with white ceiling tiles and concrete floors, perfect for washing away evidence of previous interrogations. There's a large clock above the mirror and a tiny camera in the corner. The smell of bleach burns the back of my throat. Kat and I are placed next to each other on one side of the table and left alone.

I hear Kat sniffle next to me, but can't bring myself to look at her.

"I'm sorry," I whisper.

"I know. Sa–"

"Don't say anything, Liz, they can hear us," I warn.

I see tears create a dotted pattern on the lap of her dress. I want to comfort her and tell her it's okay. But I won't lie to her anymore. We sit for six minutes with only the ticking wall clock as company.

The lock clicks on the door and a uniformed guard comes in with another man in a cheap suit. He's got black hair, gray at the temples, and a nose that's too large for his face. There's a coffee stain on his tie, and the crease in his imitation leather belt shows that he's gained weight recently, having to move to the next hole. His walk is meant to be intimidating, but it looks practiced and stilted. He carries a single sheet of paper with a mugshot and two words printed largely across the top, Katherine Percle.

"Miss Percle, so glad to see you're alive and well." The man sneers from across the table.

"I don't know what you're talking about. My name is Elizabeth Turner."

"I see," he says, spinning the mug shot of Kat to face us. "So, this is not you?"

"Of course not," she answers innocently. I'm surprised at her convincing performance.

"This is ridiculous," I say calmly. "Don't we get a lawyer?"

"Are you guilty of something?" He humphs and tugs at his collar.

I suppress the urge to jump from my chair and break his nose with my forehead. As if sensing my hostility, the man straightens up, runs his skinny fingers down his necktie, and removes the smirk from his lips.

"My name is Mr. Foreman. I am Operating Director of the DeConcini Port of Entry. This photo has been distributed to every border crossing since you skipped bail. I've had it on the wall in my office for five weeks now. I've seen it day in and day out, memorizing everything there is to know about it." He slaps his hand over the paper, keeping his eyes on Kat. "Katherine Percle, wanted for the murder of Dennis Brady. Vanished January 29. Brown hair, blue eyes, five feet three inches tall, one hundred twenty-six pounds. You expect me to believe that this," he points to the photo again, "is not you?"

"Yes, because it's the truth. That's not me. I can see the resemblance, but that girl is what, twenty? I'm thirty next month. I'm flattered, but you're mistaken."

Foreman frowns and shakes his head.

"Who are you?" he asks me.

"Lucas Turner."

"I know what your passport says, but who are you really?"

"Lucas Turner," I answer again.

He pinches the bridge of his nose and squeezes his eyes shut. The graying hair at his temples juts out like feathers on a bird.

"Our entire network was shut down this morning for an upgrade and our I.T. department is working on expediting that. I'm sure we'll get all the answers we need once our system gets back up and running."

"Sir, you've made a terrible mistake. We're just going on vacation," Kat pleads.

"Fine!" Foreman yells, slamming his hand onto the table. "You want to play games? You want to keep up this little charade you've got going? We'll see how you do once I separate you." He motions for the guard to come forward. "Bring her to holding room three. I'll keep Mr. Turner here with me."

I see Kat stiffen next to me and hear a tiny whimper escape her lips. I finally meet her eyes and cringe at what I find there—

desperation, hopelessness. The guard pulls Kat through the door and when it closes I feel suffocated and exposed, a wriggling worm on a big fucking hook. I know he's toying with us, trying to catch us in a lie.

"You know, you'll go to prison for aiding and abetting," Foreman says.

"I know you think my wife is that girl, but you're wrong."

"We'll see," he says sneering. "I'm going to ask you some questions. Then, I'll go ask your wife," he emphasizes the word wife by using those obnoxious air quotes, "the same questions. If your answers match, I may be more inclined to believe you."

"Great, let's get started," I say.

Foreman pulls a ballpoint pen from his inner jacket pocket and begins his questioning.

"Do you have children?"

"Yes."

"What are their names?" he asks, tilting his head and waiting for my answer.

"Jake Ryan and Samantha."

He nods and writes on the back of the mug shot paper.

"Where did you meet?"

"The seafood department at Whole Foods."

"How charming . . ." Foreman scoffs as he writes again. "Who was her last boyfriend before you?"

"Paul," I answer rolling my eyes in mock annoyance.

"Do you have any siblings?"

"Jack and Kelli," I answer nodding.

"Who said 'I love you' first?"

There is no easy or right answer. Whatever I say, Kat has a fifty-fifty chance of getting it right. I twist the gold band around my finger, the metal cuffs biting into my wrists.

"I did," I say. I give him a giant benign smile. I toy with my expression, because I'm unconvinced that I look like a man in love trying to prove his wife's innocence. Instead, I feel like he can see straight through the roles we're playing.

Foreman stands, the metal chair scrapes across the linoleum like a game show buzzer. Our round of questioning is over.

"I'll be back after I have a visit with your sweet little wife," Foreman says with too much enthusiasm. My legs twitch and my fists shake in my lap.

I sit in the cold room alone. I wonder where my contact is and if he abandoned us when we got caught. I try to work out a new plan. The only answer is an outright battle that will cause violent bloodshed and my imminent end. I convince myself that if it comes to that, I'll do it without hesitation. Anything to get Kat to safety.

I watch the minutes sweep by on the large clock. Each one feels like another nail in my coffin. After twelve minutes, I'm a combustible mass of nervous energy. I want to scream and break things, mainly someone's face. I have got to get out of here.

The door swings open and bangs against the wall behind it. I watch as Kat shuffles in, looking apprehensive. She frowns and shrugs a shoulder at me. Foreman joins us again, taking a seat on the other side of the table. I glare at him, though he ignores me completely. His eyes never leave Kat.

"Well, it seems you may know each other better than I thought," Foreman spits.

Kat nudges my foot with hers. I smirk at the floor.

"That doesn't mean I trust you are who you say you are. It simply means that I will allow you to be more comfortable until we know for sure." He motions to the guard who approaches and removes our handcuffs. "I.T. says our system connections will be up and running within the next half hour, so you won't have to wait long."

A shrill ring cuts through the room. Foreman quickly retrieves a phone from his jacket pocket. He stands and takes the call, pacing in front of the mirror. I jump when I feel Kat place her hand on my thigh.

"What are you guys doing over there? Get it fixed now!" Foreman yells into the phone.

"Jake Ryan and Samantha?" she whispers.

I nod. "Whole Foods?" I ask.

"Yep," she mouths so quietly I barely make out what she says. "Thirty minutes."

I place my hand on top of hers and squeeze.

"Fine! Screw protocol! Call the authorities directly and let me know," Foreman growls, ending the call.

"We're contacting San Antonio to find out the status of Katherine Percle. We should have our answer in a few minutes. We'll see what you both have to say then."

I see Kat shudder as her fingers squeeze into my leg. She's blinking rapidly and I know she's fighting to keep the tears away. The quick rise and fall of her chest is apparent, her breaths coming faster each second. I can't sit idly by and wait for the inevitable. Kat's life is on the line. I know it's now or never.

"Can I get some water?" I ask. "It's hot in here."

Kat's head whips toward me. She knows. She remembers the story of me and my partner. Foreman motions to the guard who leaves the room. He reenters a minute later with a paper cup. As he approaches the table, Kat flips her hand over and holds mine, tugging hard.

"No," I hear her whisper. I shake my head, knowing this is the only way. "Don't," she pleads again.

I stare at the daunting cup of water as the guard places it on the table. This is it. For everyone I ever wronged, for failing to protect my mother, for my only two friends, and for Kat's freedom, I raise the cup in a silent toast and drink it down.

I begin coughing and spewing water everywhere. My face turns red and my eyes tear up, blurring my vision. Kat withdraws her hand from mine when the guard begins his approach. Even through my charade of distress I can easily see his gun and the snap that holds it in place.

The guard reaches my side as I slump over the table, still choking. I can feel his hand pounding me on the back and know that his gun is inches from my shoulder. Just as I reach for it, the door crashes open and Kat gasps. I freeze, my choking forgotten.

A large man barrels in. He's the size of a linebacker, his oxford shirt pulled around his biceps. He towers over the other men in the room.

"Foreman, we heard back from San Antonio!"

18: her

Foreman jumps from his chair and meets the large man at the door. Meanwhile, the guard next to Samuel returns to his post. Samuel wears his disappointment plainly. He's lost his opportunity and I'm thankful for it.

The man at the door is tall and extremely muscled. He doesn't seem to be a guard, more of a business type. He glances in our direction as they whisper furiously back and forth.

"That can't be right," Foreman says scrubbing his face.

"I confirmed it myself," the man says.

"Fine, take care of them. You," Foreman shouts to the guard, "come with me."

We watch as the guard and Foreman leave the room without a backward glance. We can hear his curses and heavy footsteps as he hurries down the hall.

The new guy comes forward, extending his hand to Samuel. "Mr. and Mrs. Turner, we are truly sorry for the mix-up. You are free to go." Samuel shakes the man's hand as I look on in disbelief. "Now, if you'll come with me I'll show you the way out."

We rise, both of us in a daze of disbelief, and follow him from the room. I grab Samuel's hand, needing something to keep me upright. We exchange cautious looks until we reach the large metal exit door. There's a thin window there. On the other side, the sun is shining and people walk about as if our lives aren't at stake.

"Follow the sidewalk to the left and you'll find your truck parked there with the keys already inside. Again, we apologize for the confusion and hope you enjoy your trip."

Samuel and I stand rooted to the shiny linoleum floor.

"How?" The question slips out and I cover my mouth a second too late.

"According to my phone call, Katherine Percle was captured and returned to San Antonio authorities two days ago. She is currently awaiting arraignment."

"Jason Wharton?" Samuel asks.

"That's me," the man answers, patting himself on the back.

"The network connection?"

"That was me, too." He laughs, proudly.

"Did you shut down individual networks and disable network bridging?" I ask.

Jason looks surprised, and shakes his head with a grin. "No, I unplugged the main router and the backup and cut power to the voIP phones in the control room. Too easy."

"Nice," I say.

"Thanks, man," Samuel says.

"Now, go."

Samuel ushers me through the exit and down the sidewalk. The heavy door slams shut behind us and I resist the urge to run. When we reach the truck, we throw ourselves inside and buckle up. He tears out of the parking lot, takes a left, and floors it. A thousand thoughts, emotions, and ideas hit me as we settle into the crowded streets of Mexico.

"Holy shit!" I yell. "I can't believe that just happened! I mean, I thought we were done for!"

"Me too," Samuel answers.

My breath catches in my throat. Laughter and tears seem to mix into one mess of a reaction and burst free from me. I place a hand on my chest, willing my heart to calm down.

"And the questions, I can't believe we got past that!" I say. "Then when you said you needed water, I almost had a fucking heart attack, Samuel! Goonies never say die!" I pump my fist in the air, celebrating.

Samuel pulls over onto a side street and parks. "We're safe now. You're safe." He looks relieved and still a bit stunned.

"How do you know that guy?" I ask.

"He was the contact I told you about. I found the guy who raped his wife when the police couldn't. We never met in person, but he did tell me if I ever needed anything, to let him know. I called in my favor."

I bounce in my seat and clap my hands together. "I can't believe it! I just can't!"

Without thinking, I reach over, grab his face between my palms and plant a kiss on his lips. He sucks in a breath before his lips respond, kissing me back. Flashes of our night together appear behind my eyes and create a burning need inside my belly. Before we get lost in this high, I sit back and take a few deep breaths. His eyes meet mine and there is a hunger there, a demanding desire that he's fighting.

"What now?" I ask.

"I'll get us to Cabo, get you settled at my house and be on my way." I cross my arms as he starts up the truck and pulls back onto the main road. My smile fades as I realize he intends on parting ways.

"Oh, okay." I'm quiet a moment before realization hits me. "Wait! You're giving me your house?"

"Yes," he answers.

"Absolutely not, Samuel. I do not accept."

"You don't have the option to decline, Kat. Unless you'd like to be broke and homeless in Mexico."

"I can pay you rent or something. I'll get a job," I insist.

"We'll talk about it later," he says, frustrated.

Samuel types our destination into the GPS system and follows its directions until we reach the highway. I pull the large purse into my lap and dig through it. I take out a bottle of hand sanitizer, use it, and throw it into one of the truck's cup holders. Then, I find a granola bar. My stomach growls in anticipation as I quickly unwrap the treat and take a bite.

"Mmmmm," I hum.

"I'm starving. Do you have another one of those?" Samuel asks.

I shrug. "Maybe."

"Come on, Kat."

"Are you going to let me pay you rent?"

"No," he answers firmly.

"Then, I think I'm all out of granola bars."

"Seriously?" he asks.

"Seriously," I say, feigning innocence. I take another bite, rolling my eyes and chewing exaggeratedly. "God, it's sooooo good. This could possibly be the best fucking granola bar in the history of granola bars and you'll never know its salubrious greatness because you're so stubborn. I mean, look up tasty in the dictionary and I guarantee there's a photo of this very granola bar."

"Salubrious? Fine, Kat, you can pay me rent. Now, give me one."

I giggle at his weakness, dig out another bar, and unwrap it. "So, another road trip, huh?" I ask as I hand it over.

"Yep," he answers, shoving half of it in his mouth at once.

"How long will this one be?"

"About five and a half hours until we get to Guaymas, then we'll take a plane across the Gulf to Cabo."

"Wow," I say.

"What?"

"You've always got all the answers. Are you ever unprepared, taken by surprise? Ever do anything without planning it first?"

"You," he says staring out at the highway.

"Me?"

"Yeah, you. I sure as hell never planned on you."

I blush so hard my ears burn. He shakes his head slightly and taps out a rhythm on the steering wheel.

We ride for another hour, until we can't take the growling of our stomachs anymore. Samuel pulls off into a town in search of nourishment. As we drive through, I search each building, looking for recognizable words. Growing up in the Southwest, I learned the basics of Spanish from being surrounded by people who spoke the language. And, of course, all the bad words.

"I guess I'll need to learn Spanish, huh?" I say, mostly to myself.

"It would be helpful," Samuel says.

I spot a modern looking building with the word restaurant on the sign. "Elba," I read aloud. "Oh, can we stop there?"

Samuel pulls in to the parking lot and we both hop out. There are a few people inside, who stare like we're the sideshow at a circus. I smooth down the back of my dress to make sure it's not tucked into my panties and swipe at my nose for snot.

"*Hola. Buenos días,*" Samuel says. The middle-aged woman behind the counter returns his greeting. Of course he's fluent in Spanish.

"What do you want?" he asks me.

"Umm, whatever you're having, I guess."

I don't pay attention as they continue to converse. Instead, I wander over to the large front window and take a seat in a booth there. The sun lights up the space and heats my skin. I catch the reflection of my red hair and it seems to glow. Samuel joins me and hands over a soda while he drinks coffee.

"This place seems popular," I say, awkwardly searching for conversation.

Samuel only nods as he stares out the window. He seems distracted but I'm too chicken to ask about it. Instead, I leave him to his thoughts and carefully lay my paper napkin across my lap.

After our food is delivered, we both eat in silence. Once again, his handsome expression is a mask, telling me nothing. The sun lights up the side of his face, casting deep shadows on the other. One blue eye is beach glass while the other is cobalt. His wavy hair curls around his ears and neck leading my eye to that sharp masculine jaw covered in two-day stubble. An uneven white scar cuts through the left side of his chin and I take another bite of my burrito to keep from reaching out to trace it.

I wonder if he is as confused as I am. I have all these feelings swirling around and nothing seems to surface long enough to hold on to. The thought of trusting him seems foreign, and yet, so does the thought of being without him.

I finish my lunch and head to the bathroom. When I join Samuel again, he's on his phone, his back leaning on the front glass. He's speaking in Spanish again, so I stand next to him and wait. I watch a tumbleweed blow along the lane as if obeying traffic laws. Across the street, an elderly woman sits on a crate, drinking from a flask and talking to herself. Three kids pile into the flatbed of an old truck and take off down the road, laughing and singing to the music blaring from the speakers.

Suddenly, the elderly woman's head snaps left and she stands, shading her eyes from the sun. I turn to see a black Mercedes with dark-tinted windows making its way down the street. In this town of dusty air and earthy colors, it sticks out even more than we do. I follow the car until it drives out of sight and try to shake the uneasy feeling it puts in my stomach.

"Ready?" Samuel asks, breaking me out of my daze.

"Yep."

Back on the road, he finds some music on the satellite radio while I sit braiding a strand of my hair over and over. I'm not sure if it's the bright sun or the full belly, but my eyes can't seem to stay open. Soon, I give up the battle.

I'm jarred from my nap as the truck suddenly jerks.

"What the hell?" I say. One hand slaps against the window and the other rubs at my eyes.

"Sorry," Samuel offers. "There was a lizard in the road."

He shrugs and looks out at the horizon.

"You're a liar," I say. "You woke me up on purpose."

"Me? Never," Samuel says.

I stare at his profile and wonder if I spent three weeks or three years with him, would I ever really know the man beneath all those layers.

"You're quite an enigma, you know that, Samuel?"

"Okay," he says.

"Thank you."

"For what?"

"For everything," I say. "For helping me, for saving me, for keeping me out of prison."

"Kat, I–"

"No, stop. I know what your original intentions were and I can't hold that against you. You didn't know me. You were hired to do a job, I understand that." He nods. "You don't owe me anything, Samuel."

"Kat, I'm not helping you out of guilt," he insists.

"It's just, well, I don't have anyone left. I could use a friend, ya know? Are we friends, Samuel?"

"I guess so," he says, though he seems reluctant.

"Good. So can I call you Oz?"

"I like that you call me Samuel. My mom was the last one to do that."

"Samuel it is," I say. "Friends look out for each other, right?"

"Uh huh," he answers, suspicious of my questions.

"Well, as your friend, I should tell you that you have a big glob of sour cream on your face."

"What?"

He leans into the mirror and wipes the mess from his cheek. I burst into laughter unable to contain it any longer.

"How long were you going to let me wear that?" he asks.

I simply shake my head and cover my mouth, unable to answer through my laughter. When I'm finally able to catch my breath I offer my apology.

"I'm sorry, I'm sorry," I say still wearing a huge grin.

"Yeah, you look sorry," he says.

"I am. I really am."

"Uh huh."

I turn my face toward the window to hide, because I know I'm not convincing.

"Kat?"

"Huh?"

"Payback is a bitch."

I turn to find Samuel pointing the bottle of hand sanitizer at me. His arm flexes as he squeezes with all his might. The clear gel flies all over me as I scream and throw my hands up, trying to block it.

"Samuel! Stop!" I scream.

He stops when the bottle is empty and I'm covered in the quick-drying goo.

I press my hands to my face. "It's in my eyes! It burns! Owww!" I cry.

I feel the truck veer to the side of the road and come to a stop. Samuel unbuckles his seatbelt and leans over.

"I'm sorry, Kat. I'm sorry."

I drop my hands and wink at him.

"Gotcha."

For a few seconds, his face is blank. Then, like a storm rolling in over clear skies, I see a furious change in his eyes. Samuel flies out of the truck. He kicks at the dirt and throws a fist into the hood of the truck, cursing and stomping off into the desert. There's a dent in the hood and I know he must be hurting. I'm confused and regretful as I hop out of the truck and follow.

Samuel is facing away from me. His fingers comb through his hair and lace together behind his neck. I see his stiff shoulders rise and fall.

"Samuel?" I call out. He doesn't respond, just stares off into the distance. "Samuel, I'm fine. It was just a joke."

I shade my eyes from the harsh sun and wait. He turns toward me, but doesn't say a word.

"I just need a minute," he says, rubbing the back of his neck and looking down into the dirt.

"Okay. I didn't mean to upset you. I'm sorry."

"When I thought I hurt you . . ." He stops and meets my squinting eyes. "I don't want to be the cause of any more pain for you."

I don't respond. I've got nothing to say to this beautiful and complicated man.

"Come on, let's go," he says walking past me.

The tension in the truck is thick. Once we're back on the road, it seems to grow and consume us.

"Kat, I'm going to get you to Cabo and set you up in my house. Your house. I'll give you some money to get on your feet and when I'm sure you're safe, I'll be on my way." I fidget with the hem of my dress. "And, I think we're better off *not* being friends."

19. HIM

After an hour of silence, Kat falls asleep again. The rest of the journey, just like the desert landscape, flies by. Being left alone with my thoughts and the open road is just what I need to get back into the right frame of mind. No matter how right this girl feels, I'm no good for her. I'll only bring darkness and hurt to her. It's followed me like a shadow my whole life. How can I believe that she would be any different?

As soon as we enter the city, Kat wakes up. She blinks a few times and I can't help but grin at her warm, droopy-lidded expression. There are crowds of people everywhere. Colorful banners and paper decorations stream from homes and businesses. Every block seems to carry its own brand of music. Kids and adults wear costumes, ranging from simple masks to elaborate sequined outfits. Even the family dogs are wrapped in flowers and shiny material.

"What's going on?" she asks.

"What day is it?"

Kat picks up my cell phone and checks it. "Tuesday," she answers. I glance at her and back at the crowded street. "March 4."

"Damn, it's Carnaval."

"It's fantastic," she says in awe.

Kat presses her nose to the window and stares out with child-like amazement. She waves at all the people milling about. A man in costume blows her a kiss and she mimes catching it. Before I can stop her, Kat rolls down the window and hangs herself out, waving and blowing kisses to everyone.

"Samuel! This is great! Look!"

She points down the street where a parade is crossing our path. A marching band walks by and the crowd comes to life dancing in the street. Kat squeals, opens the door and hops out of the truck.

"Kat!"

"Come on," she yells over her shoulder.

"Get back here!"

I jump out of the truck and take her hand. Soon, we're moving through a crowd of faces as she pulls me along. Somehow we make our way to the front of the mass of people. She spins in place and dances to the beat of the passing drums. Watching her is like my own personal fantasy come true. Kat's hips move and shake, and her arms stretch over her head as her feet continuously move. In this moment, she is clear of all her burdens, beautiful in that freedom.

A large decorated float comes through and everyone's hands go up. I'm afraid I'll lose her in the bustle, but Kat grabs my hand again and gives me a reassuring squeeze. She looks back at me with a smile, and I am rendered helpless by this wild girl.

As the parade wraps up, I step on toes, bump into kids, and

get two beers spilled on my shoes as we make our way out of the crowd. The music pumps from a nearby house and people are still in party mode. Streamers and confetti float through the air. Kat stops and raises her face to the sky, a childlike smile on her lips. She turns to me and time seems to slow as we stand in our bubble surrounded by the lively chaos.

Kat laughs when paper confetti lands in my hair. She reaches up and runs her fingers through it, pushing the confetti free. The moment is so intimate, so intense, that I see nothing but her. Fingers slide down my scalp and wrap behind my neck. When she pulls me forward, I go willingly.

There is no urgency to this kiss. Her lips press against mine. My tongue slides out to taste her and the hum of satisfaction rocks us both. My hands slide to her waist and I pull Kat against me. This sparks something stronger, more primal. Kat's fingers scrape against my neck as she pulls me closer. We consume each other, lips and teeth and tongue, with no regard to the world around us.

Someone bumps into me and we almost tumble to the ground. Our kiss is broken up, but her taste and the memory of the feel of her lips has me dizzy.

"Wow," she says. "I could get used to that."

Her words kill the last of this moment and anger instantly overwhelms me. I have no claim to Katherine Percle even though she seems to have claim to me. I have no right wanting her. I have no intention of keeping her. All I know is the sight of her flirty smile sent me into a faltering tailspin.

Silently, I drag her back to the truck and we climb inside. I can feel her confusion at my mood change, but can't bring myself to offer any kind of explanation. Once we arrive at the airport, I park at the main building and grab the suitcase from the truck. Kat hops out and smooths down the front of her dress.

She follows me inside and leans against the counter while we wait for help. I feel her gaze on me, but don't acknowledge her staring. I know, with one more word or simple gesture, she'd crash right through the wall I'd spent the last two hours building.

"*Hola,*" says a young girl who appears behind the counter. Heavy eye makeup is smeared beneath her bottom lashes. She smells like cigarettes.

"Hi," Kat answers, smiling.

"American?" We both nod. "What can I do for you today?" she asks. Her accent makes the simple question sound lively.

"We need to get to Cabo. Is Jorge available?" I ask.

"No, I'm sorry. He's not flying back in until tonight. It's Carnaval, you know?"

"Yeah, I know," I say.

"You want to book him tomorrow or use someone else?"

The girl looks at me, waiting impatiently for an answer. She smacks her gum and huffs. I don't want to wait, but I know and trust Jorge. I chance a look at Kat, who is also awaiting my answer.

"We'll wait. Ask him to be ready to fly out at noon." The girl nods, takes my information, and pops her gum.

I spin around and stomp my way back to the truck. This means more time with Kat, which by the hour seems to become personally more dangerous and hard to navigate. But I know not to underestimate the value of trustworthy people. I've known Jorge for years. He's middle-aged and unattached. He doesn't ask questions, and doesn't answer them either.

I pull into the Hotel Playa de Cortes and park the truck. I doubt there will be anything available with Carnaval happening, but I'm hopeful because it's the last day. Kat follows me inside, where we're in luck with one room available. I pay cash for the room and register us as Mr. and Mrs. Turner.

Kat raises a questioning eyebrow, but I just shrug it off. Even though we are deep into Mexico, it's always smart to play it safe.

"Welcome to Guaymas, Mr. and Mrs. Turner. Today is the last day of Carnaval, so you'd better get all your sins out before midnight," the clerk says to us. "Sadly, you just missed the last parade."

"We didn't miss it at all," Kat sings.

We retrieve our things from the truck and enter the hotel room. Even with the patio doors open and the cool breeze blowing through, the air around us feels dense. We haven't discussed my breakdown in the desert, and I'm thankful for that. It's easier to keep my head focused and my plan in place without the distractions Kat offers.

The walls are painted a soft neutral color, the floor is stained concrete. One large bed sits against the wall, a scrolling wooden semicircle as its headboard. There are nightstands and lamps on each side, a television in the corner and two chairs separated by a small table. The furniture is wicker, and all the fabrics are bright pops of color. I set our suitcase on the bed and watch as Kat wraps her arms around herself, stepping to the patio. She parts the curtains and throws them open. The breeze gusts in now, whipping her hair around her face, billowing her dress away from her thighs.

"It's lovely," she whispers.

Before I can stop myself, I answer.

"Yes, it is." She spins to face me, a thousand questions etched into her face. I know I don't want to answer any of them, so I change the subject quickly. "I'm tired. I'm going to take a nap."

"Well, I slept the whole way here, so I'm good. I want to see Carnaval and then the beach. A few days ago, I thought I was going to be in prison for the rest of my life. This feels like one big amazing dream."

I don't want to let her go by herself, but I'm just too tired to argue. I nod at her, kick off my shoes, and tuck my gun between the mattresses.

"Don't drink the water and don't get arrested," I warn before crawling onto the bed.

Kat unzips the suitcase and rifles through it before disappearing into the bathroom.

20: her

I step out into the city and for the first time in a while, I truly feel free. I make a note of the name of the hotel so I can ask for directions later, and set off down the street. The cool breeze smells of citrus and salt, it leads me away from the coast and farther into Carnaval.

Almost every home I pass is filled to capacity, sometimes overflowing to the front porches and yards. Men stand at charcoal grills while kids prance around in costumes and dogs give chase. The people here are welcoming and friendly. They wave and offer genuine smiles when I return the gesture. I think I'll like it in Mexico.

I follow the foot traffic and the sound of music to an open plaza with a band perched on a wide stage. Although the members are dressed like cowboys, with shiny belt buckles and oversized hats, the music doesn't sound country at all. The heavy beat and blasting trumpets make me want to move my hips.

I step into the crowd and fall in line with other dancers. Men, women, and children all take turns giving me lessons and twirling me around. One song blends into the next and my feet never stop moving. When I need a break, I walk over to a street vendor and buy a margarita on the rocks. The boy behind the counter swaps a drink for five American dollars and gives an enthusiastic thumbs up.

"Gracias," I say, holding up my cup.

I turn and gulp down most of the drink at once. It cools my insides nicely. I realize halfway through that the ice is just frozen Mexican water, but I rationalize this by assuming the alcohol will kill off whatever harmful bacteria lurk in there. Spotting some shade, I lean against a tree and watch the dancing continue. The pulse of the music fills the crowd, the whole lot of them move in peaks and valleys like the sea. Everyone's celebratory shouts and laughter float through the air. Their high spirits and happiness are contagious. I finish my margarita and head back into the crowd.

As the music lures me in, so do the men. They're very welcoming and all want to take a turn dancing. There seems to be no commitment between dance partners, everyone out to simply have a good time. I shake and move my hips, cutting through the people, making my way to the stage.

When the song ends, I gather my hair and twist it off my neck. The light air washes over my sweaty skin giving me goose bumps. I hear a loud whistle from beside me and turn to find a woman perched on the shoulders of a swaying man. Her hair is dark brown, but it's her fair skin that stands out in this crowd.

"Wahoo! Yeah!" she screams as the song ends. "I love Carnaval!" I laugh at her obvious elation and watch as she wiggles on the man's shoulders. He tilts his head up, all smiles and she says something to him in Spanish. After he sets her down gracefully, she pulls him in for a tight hug and gives him a kiss on the cheek. "Gracias," she says before sauntering away.

Without thought, my feet are in motion following her through the crowd.

"Hey!" I shout. "Hey," I say again, this time closer. She turns and stares at me, waiting. "You're American, right?" I ask.

"Yeah."

"I'm Liz," I say, holding out my hand. "I haven't come across anyone who speaks English in a while."

She laughs. She has one of those perfect faces and perfect smiles, the kind of beauty where it's impossible to tell how old she is. "Well, Liz, I'm Piper. Welcome to Carnaval!" She shakes my hand and twirls me in place as another song starts. "I'm so hot. Let's get some drinks," she shouts over the music.

Piper doesn't wait for an answer. She takes off toward the vendors and I follow. While the crowd seems to part for her, I have to dodge and squeeze between people to keep up.

"I just love the strawberry margaritas here," she yells over her shoulder. She steps up and orders two drinks, delivering one to me.

"Thanks," I say, taking a sip. "I already ran out of money."

"No problem," she answers, nodding. "I understand how that can happen here. There's so many temptations."

"You got that right." We tap our plastic cups together in a silent toast.

She leads me to a spot of grass and takes a seat. I lean back and look up at the swaying palm tree fronds, feeling so content in this moment.

"So, where you from, Liz?"

"San Antonio. You?"

"Denver," she answers. "But I spend some time here, especially during Carnaval."

I sit up and stretch my legs out in front of me wiggling my toes. "I can see why. It's great."

"After this, I'll meet my boyfriend in Cabo. He's going to be working there for at least three months, but I only get to stay for two. It's always so depressing going back home. Ugh," she grunts and rolls her eyes.

"I'll be in Cabo too. Maybe we could hang out. I won't know anyone else there," I say, finishing my drink.

"That sounds great! I love showing people around. I'm an old pro." Piper stands and dusts off the seat of her shorts. "Now, let's dance!"

I let her pull me up and follow her into the sea of people. We dance with each other and anyone else who passes by. Piper is a great dancer and as attractive as she is, garners lots of attention. After an hour, I'm sweaty and so ready for the beach.

"I'm going to go. I want to hit the beach before dark," I yell over the music.

"Aww, I was going to go buy us another round," Piper says. "We're just getting started."

Two attractive guys pass by and whistle. She blows them a kiss before looking back to me.

"I really shouldn't. I need to get back."

She sticks out her bottom lip and says, "Oh, alright. When you get to Cabo, find me. We're staying at the Villa Del Palmar. The room will be under Piper Dawson."

"Will do," I say giving her a hug. "It was great meeting you!"

"The pleasure's all mine, darling." Piper waves at me right before the crowd closes in around her, making her disappear from view.

I retrace my path back to the hotel, easily navigating the city. When I get there, Samuel is still sleeping. I slip into a bikini, throw my dress back on, grab a towel, and follow the gulls to the water.

When I hit the beach, I claim my own little spot in the sand. I stretch out on a towel and revel in the last couple of hours of sunlight. There are still people out celebrating, gathered around fires or kicking soccer balls. The sound of laughter and more music surrounds me as I drift off to sleep.

I wake to find Samuel taking a seat next to me in the sand. We don't say a word to each other, we simply sit and watch the sun disappear. When all that's left is a sliver of pink across the top of the water, I turn to him. His profile is solemn.

"Did you have a good nap?" I ask. He silently nods and looks down the beach. "The city's still really crowded. We were lucky to get a room." Still no response.

"Samuel, I can't stand this disconnected silent treatment. I'm sorry that you feel guilty. I know that somewhere in there," I say, poking his chest, "is a guy who just wants to drop this brooding act, relax, and have fun." He stares blankly at me, not wanting to admit anything. "I bet there are parts of you buried so deep you wouldn't even recognize them. Your pain, the things you've seen, all the things you've done . . . you've got to let them go."

Turning his head back to the sea, he watches the pounding of the waves against the shore. I scoot in front of him and get to my knees, so that we are eye to eye.

"Samuel, you are not the evil person you make yourself out to be. I understand why you did what you did. You have more than made it up to me. I hate the guilt that you are carrying because of me. And frankly, you're starting to piss me off. I forgive you."

"Kat, I—" I slide my hands along his jaw and press my thumb to his lips.

"I forgive you," I say. He closes his eyes and frowns. I lean in closer, inches from his pouting lips and repeat myself. "I forgive you."

Samuel tries to argue, but my thumb presses harder against his lips.

A cool gust of air blows between us, with it the smell of salt and beach fire smoke. I feel him relax and let his anger and fears slip away on the breeze. I remove my thumb and place my lips softly above his.

"I forgive you," I say one last time against his mouth.

I finally close the tiny gap between us, kissing him. I slide my hand around his neck and lean into his hard body. Samuel sucks my bottom lip into his mouth and lets it drag through his teeth. He moans when I lick his parted lips.

"You taste like tequila and strawberry," he says as we lay back in the sand.

We stay there, making out like teenagers, until the air turns cooler and stars dot the night sky. It's a cycle of lust and need that builds into frantic kisses and rough hands, but then slows down again. As I lay there, I try to identify the overwhelming feeling radiating through my body. It's unrestrained and so unfamiliar.

"You hungry?"

"Starving," Samuel answers.

"Good, let's go get some grub. I need a shower."

"You sure do," he says, making a face.

"Fuck you very much, Mr. Turner."

"Frankly, I'm appalled by your foul language, Mrs. Turner."

I giggle before throwing on my dress and shaking out the towel. We slowly make our way back to the hotel. I watch Samuel closely. He's more relaxed now, even more than he was in Jack and Kelli's kitchen. It's so refreshing.

"Samuel?"

"Huh?"

"Will you teach me to speak Spanish?"

"I'm not sure I have the patience for that. I'll just hire you a tutor once we get to Cabo."

"Well, okay then, Mr. Moneybags." He smirks at me and keeps walking. "Samuel?"

"What?"

"Exactly how much money do you have?" I ask.

"Enough."

"Again with the vague answers? That is so annoying."

"I've taken it on as a personal mission, Kat."

"Taken what on?"

"Annoying you."

"You're very good at it. But don't forget who the master of annoyance is. I wear that crown like a queen." I punch him in the arm. Samuel feigns pain as we stumble into our room laughing.

I let the warm shower water wash over me and take away the sweat, sand, and saltwater. I feel light and giddy and I know it has everything to do with the gorgeous, somewhat difficult fugitive recovery agent slash hired thug in the next room.

Apart, we were lost and tumbling through life. We were only surviving, getting by. Together we're a mess—a beautiful, promising mess. While I want to let loose and celebrate our escape, I don't want to scare him away. Samuel is a complex man, and I haven't quite figured out which buttons to press and which to avoid.

I dry my hair and slip into a purple wrap dress. It hugs my curves and after weeks of dirty jeans and Converse sneakers, these new clothes make me feel like a woman again. I exit the bathroom to find Samuel watching a Mexican game show on television.

His smile is genuine and his gaze paints me with desire. I spin for him and it seems to crumble his hard veneer even more.

"You look amazing," he says while I slip into some strappy sandals.

"Thanks," I say. "You clean up well, yourself, Sexy Fugitive Recovery Agent."

"That's not my life anymore," he says, his eyes somber below a heavy brow.

"So what is your life now, Samuel?"

He glances down at his hands for a long moment, and when he looks back up at me, his eyes are filled with uncertainty.

"You're still a work in progress," I say as I head for the door. "Me too."

The hotel restaurant isn't crowded and we're seated right away. I cross my legs beneath the table, my foot bouncing up and down. I can't seem to concentrate on the menu. Samuel orders a margarita for each of us. There's a strange air between us in this new territory. Nothing is defined.

"I think I want seafood," I say.

He nods and continues to browse the menu. When the waiter returns Samuel orders for both of us and hands the menus over. An attractive girl, with a flower tucked into her hair, delivers our drinks from the bar. She says something in Spanish and he replies. She blushes and hurries off. Immediately, I want to scratch her eyeballs out.

"Wow, this is strong," I say after taking a sip.

"Good." He looks up at me through his lashes, one dimple appears next to his devious grin.

"Are you trying to get me drunk?"

"Do I need to?" he asks. He already knows the answer.

My cheeks burn and I answer quickly. "No."

Samuel swallows down his drink and holds my eyes. I'm not sure if it's a challenge or if he's looking for something.

"So, this is like a date," I say.

"Is it?" He shifts in his seat while his fingers tap against the tabletop.

"Well, yeah. I thought . . . I shaved my legs and wore this dress. You ordered for both of us." Samuel watches me flounder for a while. He doesn't say a word while I talk myself around the elephant in the room. "I mean, you flirted with the bar girl. But then I pretty much promised you sex, soooo. . . . there's that."

He leans over the table, so that his blue eyes are lit by the candle's dancing flame.

"I did not flirt with her," he says. His stern expression keeps me quiet. "She asked if my wife was happy with our room."

I lean forward, meeting him over the table. "What did you say?"

"I said the room is perfect, but the bed hasn't been tested yet."

"You did not," I gush, averting my eyes and taking a sip from my drink.

Samuel nods and leans back in his chair. The sexually charged smirk he wears makes me want to vault over this table and drag him off to play. First, I need nourishment.

We don't say much else as we wait for our food. There is a sense of liberation and intense need radiating from each of us. Even the waiter seems to keep his distance.

After two more margaritas and our dinners are finished we go back to the room to change into our swimsuits. I'm determined to go swimming and frankly, need to work off some of this nervous energy.

I change into my bikini and make a promise to send Kelli a thank-you for her impeccable taste and preparedness. I stand in front of the mirror and pull my hair up into a messy knot. Samuel slides in behind me, wrapping his arms around my waist. It's a colorful band of inked images across my blank skin. It feels natural and at the same time electrifying. His fingers ghost along my ribs, and he pulls me back against his bare chest. His eyes meet mine in the mirror and I can't help but return his smile before turning to face him.

"We've spent too long looking at each other through mirrors," I say.

I place a kiss on the underside of his chin, grab a towel, and take off running. "Last one to the pool has a single-core processor!"

"What does that even mean?" he yells out as he chases me toward the pool.

It's late and I'm happy to find the pool empty. I kick out of my shoes, throw down the towel, and jump into the warm water. I surface just in time to watch Samuel descend the steps.

It amuses me how our approach to the pool reflects so much about ourselves. He scanned the area, determined the steps were the safest way in and slowly immersed himself. I, however, ran and jumped into the water with no hesitation.

I dive beneath the surface and swim over to him. Wrapping my hands around his calves, I yank hard and pull him under. We come up for air at the same time, wearing matching grins. Samuel charges at me. His arms hold me tight as I struggle futilely.

"Remember what I said about payback, Kat?"

His fingers tighten around my waist, while his pinkies slide down and trace the top of my bikini bottoms.

"Umm, it's a useless notion reserved for petty people?"

"Wrong," he says before standing and throwing me to the other side of the pool.

I squeal and splash him, vowing revenge, but he doesn't look worried. We race each other a few times, until we're both out of breath.

"Shit, I need to start working out again," Samuel says leaning against the edge of the pool.

His hair is a mess, sticking up in all different directions. It makes him look childlike. But the way his arms rest on the edge of the pool, creating a line of lean muscled temptation, is all man. I swim over to him, place my hands on his shoulders and wrap my legs around his waist.

"I run an excellent cardio and endurance program if you're interested," I whisper against his wet skin.

I bite down on his neck and drag my tongue up to his jaw where

I let my teeth scrape across his stubble. It's then that I remember I'm ingesting tiny drops of Mexican water, but his satisfying hum makes me continue.

"Let's go back to the room," he says.

I need no further persuasion other than the sound of his raspy, desperate voice. I unwrap myself from Samuel and hop out of the pool. My body pulsates with excitement, the tension between us palpable. The night air feels cool against my wet skin and offers a bit of relief.

We practically run back to our room, barely making it inside the door before attacking each other. He pushes me against the wall and rips the towel away. The way his ravenous eyes rake over me destroys every bit of my self-control. I attack his mouth, tasting those perfect lips. I moan when he presses his body to mine. It's hot skin and cold, wet patches of material between us.

"You're so damn beautiful," he whispers. "You make me forget who I am."

His hands touch me everywhere and still it's not enough. He reaches up and pulls the elastic from my hair, but it gets stuck. His frustration makes me laugh and I reach up to finish sliding it out. The long wet tendrils stick to my shoulders as Samuel slides his hand around the back of my neck. His fingers weave through my hair and it feels like he's afraid to let go. His chest swells with a deep breath as he pauses.

"Samuel," I exhale. He places rough kisses along my shoulder, a trail to my ear.

"I'll never get tired of the sound of my name on your lips," he says against my skin.

"Samuel," I plead again.

My fingers slide down his chest and stomach, resting at the waistband of his board shorts. Without looking, I pull the draw-string free from its knot. I'd like to say the material fell away, revealing his gorgeous body to me, but wet clothes do not work that way. Samuel pushes them down and they land around his feet with a heavy slopping sound.

I grab his hand and pull him to the bed, sitting him on the edge. I stand between his knees and run my fingers through his hair. As much as my body begs me to speed things up, I can't deny taking it slow. This time I want to see all of him. I want to cherish every touch, every kiss. I want to live in this moment.

I pull on the knots behind my neck and back. The red strings hang from two triangles clinging to my breasts. Samuel palms each one and pulls them away. He wets his lips before placing soft kisses there.

"Enough teasing," I groan.

He smirks at me and pulls the strings at each hip before yanking my bottoms off. The force makes me fall forward and we tumble onto the bed together. His hands never leave my body. His lips place hard kisses in soft places and make me shiver when his hot breath fans over my skin.

"Please," I breathe out, not sure what I'm begging for. I only know I need more.

Samuel covers my body with his own, and I love the weight of him holding me down. As I writhe beneath him, he continues his torturous path across my skin. He dots my inner thighs with kisses and gentle nibbles as I slide my hand into his hair.

When his lips and tongue taste me there I let out a cry. My fingers tighten in his hair, as my hips rock up to meet him. My body is quickly overwhelmed in the divine chaos, swirling heat, and prickling skin. Our bodies instinctually work together, seeking a common goal of breathless satisfaction. My thighs twitch, an involuntary reaction to his talents, and when I look down to find his eyes on mine, I'm lost.

"Samuel! Oh God!"

My body tenses, every muscle tight with pulsing pleasure and the release I need. After a minute, I let go of his hair and melt into the mattress. A cool breeze comes through the open patio doors and lays across us like satin sheets. I feel him crawl up and lie next to me on the bed, though I can't move a muscle. I want to thank him or worship him or sing hallelujah praises. All I can do is exhale.

"No wonder Natasha wants you back," I say.

I crack one eye open to find him frowning at me. He cages me in his arms and presses his lips to my ear.

"There is no conversation about my ex during sex."

I smile and lift my hips to meet his. "Technically, we aren't having sex right now."

Samuel's eyes become tiny slits. "That should be rectified immediately," he says.

"There are condoms in my purse."

"Kelli is a fucking genius," he growls against my neck.

I slide out of his grip and dig through my bag on the floor. I toss one foil packet to Samuel and watch as he rolls it on. The look on his face is feral, it makes my insides hum. All I can do is nod dumbly when he presses against me.

Samuel fills me and it's as if we've never been apart. Sweat-covered bodies collide again and again, composing a heavy rhythm that only we can create. He takes me roughly and unapologetically and I wouldn't have it any other way. I beg him for it, whispering profanities and prayers as he brings me higher.

He lifts one of my legs, resting it on his shoulder. The warmth and tightness inside me intensifies with the new position. Each time his hips meet mine, it's pure bliss, a connected circuit sending fire through my veins.

Slowly and surely, my climax crawls up my body. I can feel it like a pulse through my limbs. It pools in my gut until pleasure explodes. I cry out and pull Samuel closer. I don't let him go until he moans through his own release and falls on the bed beside me.

I cling to him as if my life depends on it and as I drift off to sleep, I remember that at one time, it did.

21. HIM

Light and shadows filter in through waving curtains, stirring me from the best sleep I've had in years. Kat lays draped across my body, her flaming red hair fanned over my chest. The blanket lays in a heap at the foot of the bed, a jumbled pattern of teal, yellow, and red. The stark white sheet rests across both of us, gently rising and falling as if it were breathing on its own. Every point of contact between our bodies seems to burn in the most pleasurable way.

My mind races with questions of how I got here or what I'm doing, but I ignore them for now. I just want to stay wrapped up in this girl that I can't seem to let go of.

If I could control time, I'd go back and forth between last night and this morning. I want to only exist inside her and waking up to her. Kat stirs and her hand drifts down to below my navel. The feather-light touch of her fingertips on my skin lights a fire inside me.

I roll her over and lay on my side. Kat is stunning wrapped in white sheets and nothing else. I lean in and kiss where her neck meets her shoulder, trailing down between her breasts. Kat hums and squirms beneath me.

"Mmm, five more minutes," she begs. "Sleep."

I laugh at her and pull the sheet up to her shoulders as she falls back asleep.

I'm hungry and in desperate need of coffee, so I decide to get up and go in search of breakfast. I take a quick shower and walk over to the hotel's restaurant. I sit at the bar and order chorizo, potato and egg breakfast tacos, and coffee for each of us.

While I wait for my order, I place a call to my assistant.

"Boss," he says into the phone before yawning loudly. "Sorry."

"Brad, I'm letting you know that I'm out of the game. Off the grid."

"What? Why?" he shrieks.

"Don't worry, you can still work with Jack. He'll set you up with something new."

"Do you need me to pack your stuff and send it somewhere?"

"No. You can take what you want and sell the rest," I answer.

There's nothing but silence on the other end of the line. I pull the phone away to make sure it's still connected and place it back to my ear.

"Brad?"

"Give me a sec. I'm in shock."

I chuckle. "I'll transfer your last payment and then we're done. It was great working with you."

"It was an honor, Oz. Will I ever see you again?" he asks.

"I doubt it. Take care."

I end the call and place my phone on the bar. Even though

that phone call signifies the end of my career, I don't feel dismal about it. I thought that when I retired, a part of me would mourn that life and everything I left behind, but I don't feel one ounce of regret. I'm right where I should be, at a new beginning. Whether that beginning includes Kat or not, I'm still not sure.

The waitress brings my order and I pay her, handing over a generous tip. When I get back to the room, I let myself in quietly in case Kat's still sleeping. The bed is empty and the bathroom door closed. I let go of the door and a gust of wind slams it closed.

"Sam?" I hear her yell.

"Yeah, it's me."

Kat sticks her head out of the bathroom.

"I didn't know where you went. I thought you . . ."

I wait for her to finish, but she doesn't. Kat just looks down at the tile floor.

"You thought I left?" I ask.

She nods without looking at me. I put our food down and walk over to her. I lift her chin with my fingers and force her to see me.

"I told you I would get you to Cabo and make sure you were safe."

"Okay," she says. "I'll be out in a minute."

She closes the door between us as I retrieve my needed coffee.

"I got us breakfast," I shout.

I open the boxes of food and set them out on the table, along with plastic forks and small containers of hot sauce. Kat emerges and sits down on the opposite side of the table.

"Thanks," she says, holding up her coffee before sipping it.

We eat breakfast in silence. Both of us steal insecure glances across the table as if we don't intimately know each other's secrets.

"What time is our flight?" Kat asks.

"Noon."

"So, we've got plenty of time."

I quirk an eyebrow at her. "Time for what?"

She scoots forward in her chair and meets my eyes. "Come back to bed with me," she says. "Just to talk. It seems to be the only place you're comfortable talking."

I don't answer her. I don't want to talk. I want to explore her body and forget about everything else.

Kat stands and grabs my hand resting on the table. She tugs on it until I follow her back to bed. She curls up on her side, facing me, while I lie on my back.

The room is quiet except for the static noise of waves hitting the shore. It's a soothing tempo that puts me at ease.

"I met a girl yesterday," she says. "Her name is Piper. She's from Denver. Says she always comes down for Carnaval." I stay quiet as Kat sighs, blowing her bangs from her eyes. "I forgot what it was like to have girlfriends, you know?" I nod and keep my eyes on the shadows of palm trees that dance across the ceiling. "Anyway, she's going to Cabo, too. So hopefully we can hang out."

"Sounds good," I say.

"Kelli said no one has ever been to your house in Cabo."

"That's true."

"So, why me?" she asks.

I close my eyes and curse Kelli and her mouth. I knew she would make this a big deal. Because it *is* a big deal. I feel the bed shift and then Kat's hand runs through my hair. I open my eyes and turn to look at her. Those bottomless blue eyes are begging me to open up, but not pushing.

"I don't know why. That's the truth," I say. "My house is my sanctuary. For some reason, I want to share it with you." She ducks her head onto my shoulder and I feel her smile against my chest. I'm confused and encouraged by her reaction. "My mom used to tell me that your home was supposed to be the one place you were safe and loved. She said she was sorry that ours wasn't like that. She apologized over and over for it. But she would never leave him."

Kat rests her head on my shoulder and scoots closer. She throws one leg over mine, anchoring us together.

"What makes them stay?" she asks. "I'll never understand it."

"Me either."

"Tell me something happy from your childhood. There had to be something good," she says.

I think back to a time that I've forced myself to forget. Of course there were happy moments. But they are so intertwined with the bad ones, it was easier to wipe them all away. A particular day from fourth grade sticks out.

"One day I bombed a pop quiz at school and was so upset about it. I walked home, went straight to my room, and started throwing things around, breaking stuff. My mom came in and held me for a while and then said we needed to turn the day around. She tickled me until I couldn't breathe. Then she put on one of her favorite records and we danced in the living room. She made French toast for dinner and let me stay up late."

Kat squeezes my shoulder. "That sounds great," she says.

I hold all these memories, each piece of my mom, inside because I always thought if I shared them then they would become less mine. I don't feel that way at all. Reliving those good times keeps her alive and proves that she did exist.

"Samuel?"

"Hmm?"

"When we get to Cabo, are you really going to walk away from me? From us?"

I blow out a breath and squeeze my eyes shut again. The lock and chain around my pounding heart pulls tight and groans from the strain. It thumps against my chest like a wild animal rattling its cage.

"We should start packing," I say.

"Samuel."

I sit up and slide out from under her. I busy myself by grabbing everything from around the room and throwing it into the suitcase. I can feel Kat watching me.

"If we leave now, we can avoid most of the traffic as people leave town."

I make a pass around the room, picking up clothes as I go, and returning them to the suitcase.

"Samuel," Kat says again.

"Maybe Jorge will be ready to go before noon. We should try to—"

"Samuel!" she shouts. I stop and spin to face her. "Come here." I don't move. "Come. Here," she says with authority. My feet shuffle slowly to the foot of the bed. Kat reaches for me and pulls me down to sit. She crawls into my lap and straddles me, crossing her ankles behind my back. "You don't have to answer the question."

I meet her eyes and see sincerity and apology there. I pull Kat closer and press my lips to hers. She tastes like coffee and everything Kat. Her body fits against mine so perfectly that I don't want to let her go. I don't know if I can.

"I'm going to take a shower and then we can head to the airport. Okay?" she whispers against my neck before placing a kiss there and hopping off my lap.

I watch her grab some clothes and retreat into the bathroom. I stare at the closed door for a while, dazed. How can I have faced such evil, terrible people in my life and never fear them like I do that beautiful girl?

I throw the last few items into the suitcase and step out onto the patio. The cloudless sky is reflected in the blue water.

Seagulls call out as the breeze blasts against my skin. It's peaceful and quiet here, a welcome change from what's going on in my head.

I take a seat in one of the lounge chairs and lean back. I hear Kat exit the bathroom and finish packing up. She steps to the door letting the wind whip around her. She wears a strapless dress in yellow; the color is warm and welcoming against her tan skin. The material looks soft and everywhere it touches her body, it molds around her curves. It's long, all the way to her feet, and she's breathtaking.

"I'm ready," she says, looking out over the water.

I nod and follow her to the door. Kat grabs her purse and I pick up the suitcase. Before the door closes behind us, I take one last look at the room. With its floors and pale walls, it looks generic and unimpressive. It'll never reveal what was done here or what was said. For now, our secrets are safe.

As I throw the suitcase into the truck, I notice Kat staring across the parking lot.

"What's wrong?" She doesn't answer. "Kat?"

"Huh?" She turns to look at me and then back in the other direction. "Oh, nothing I guess." I walk over to where she stands and look around for anything out of the ordinary. "I just . . . Well, that car looks just like one I saw when we stopped to eat yesterday. I guess it could be a coincidence."

"Which one?"

"The black Mercedes," she answers, pointing out the car.

I study it closely. It has illegal tint and California plates. The black paint fades into a red brown mess where dirt and road dust have covered the bottom. I memorize the license plate and make a mental note to check it before we take off.

"Probably a coincidence," I agree though something tells me there's more.

22: her

Samuel lets Jorge know we're ready to take off and buckles up. I grip the seat so tightly my fingers ache. Samuel is busy typing away on his phone, looking relaxed.

"What are you doing?" I ask.

"Checking on that Mercedes. It's registered to a Troy Middleton of Palo Alto, California. I don't recognize the name. You?"

I shake my head and grip onto the armrest. We taxi to the runway and within minutes we're in the air. I feel nauseated and dizzy before I remind myself to breathe. I inhale deeply through my nose and wipe my palms on my lap.

"Are you scared of flying?" he asks.

"A little," I admit. "Why are we flying anyway?"

"Because it's a fifteen-hour drive including a four-hour ferry ride. This is faster."

I nod and look out the window. Samuel digs his phone out of his pocket and hands it over.

"Hold that for a sec," he says.

He reaches over and unlatches the plane door. The sound of air rushing around us makes me nervous.

"What are you doing?" I yell, pressing myself against the opposite wall.

"*Señor?*" Jorge asks from the front of the plane, but the sound is lost to Samuel.

He holds his hand out and motions for his phone. I hand it over. Samuel flips it out of the door and closes the hatch, locking it back. I straighten in my seat and smooth out the skirt of my dress.

"That was a bit dramatic," I say after a few moments.

"But necessary," he answers. "I can't have any ties to my previous life."

Suddenly, the plane dips and my stomach jumps into my throat.

"Oh shit!" I say. I loop my arm through his and squeeze tightly. "Distract me."

Samuel leans in and places a kiss on my bare shoulder. "My house in Cabo is a three-bedroom bungalow on a private beach," he tells me. "It has white stucco with blue shutters." He moves to my neck and nibbles softly. "The entire back of the house opens up to the beach and when the breeze blows through, you can feel it in every corner." He presses his tongue against my pulse point and slides up to my ear. The scruff from his chin rakes along my skin. "There are palm trees and flowers all around the property." His hand rests on my knee, drawing circles with his thumb on my inner thigh. "It's the only place on earth that holds anything personal of mine."

"It sounds great," I gasp as Samuel scrapes his teeth along my earlobe.

The plane bumps again and a whimper slips from my lips before I slap my hand over my mouth.

"Kat, it's fine. Relax."

"Relax? Now you've got me all worked up," I whisper, keeping my eyes on Jorge. Samuel laughs as I pout. I place my hand on his thigh and I lean over, whispering, "You should *feel* how worked up I am."

His entire body stiffens, blood rushing south. Samuel runs his fingers up my thigh, but I slap his hand away.

"What?" he asks. "I'm just following instructions."

I shake a finger at him and cross my legs, effectively cutting him off. "Now we're even," I say, grinning triumphantly.

We don't talk for a while, just look out over the clouds caught between blue sky and fluffy white. Every few minutes I catch a glimpse of the water below until finally I see land again.

We arrive at Samuel's house in a cab. He pays the driver and retrieves our suitcase from the trunk while I stand near the front door. The house is just as he described, a perfect little place with a stunning view. It sits at the end of a long narrow street, far from any neighbor. The palm trees and flowering hedges surround it like it's a part of some secret oasis. I could definitely get used to living here.

Samuel punches a code into a numbered keypad and swings the door open.

"Welcome home, Mrs. Turner," he says.

"Shouldn't you carry me over the threshold or something?"

"Don't push your luck."

I step inside and instantly feel welcomed. The floors are a rich terra cotta tile and the walls a buttery yellow. There are a few colorful paintings scattered throughout the room and bold print curtains on the windows.

"This certainly doesn't look like a bachelor pad," I say spinning in a circle.

"I hired help for the decor." He sets the suitcase down and motions for me to come with him. "Let me give you a quick tour."

I follow Samuel down the hall where he points out a small office, a bathroom, a guest bedroom, and finally the master suite. The bed is on a low platform and is enormous. It's covered in white linens and turquoise accent pillows. There's a large sunset photo framed over the bed.

The entire back wall of the room is glass. When he slides the curtains aside, I gasp at the sight there. Beyond the glass wall is a small wooden patio, then nothing but white sand all the way to the water. It's breathtaking.

"Wow," I say pressing my nose to the glass.

Samuel chuckles and stands beside me. "Yeah, that's what I said. Come on, let's finish the tour."

He shows me the huge master bathroom, complete with tub and stone shower and then leads me back out to the main room. The kitchen sits at the back of the house and another wall of glass lets light in to the space.

I set my purse down on the counter and lean against the cabinets. Though his home is welcoming, it's hard to feel at ease here. I don't exactly know where I belong. Samuel stands at the back door looking out at the beach and I sense that he's just as unsure as I am. I fidget with a drawer pull and wait for something. After a few minutes, I can't stand the silence.

"Samuel?" He turns to me. "When's the last time you were here?"

"Six months ago, but I called ahead and had my housekeeper air the place out and stock the kitchen. She also changed the sheets and bought bathroom stuff."

I grab a bottle of water and close the fridge. "Bathroom stuff?"

He rubs at the back of his neck and looks at the floor. "You know, whatever you girls need for . . . you know."

I let out a laugh. "Yeah, I know. But it's hilarious to watch you squirm."

There's a long beat of silence before he blows out a breath and looks to the suitcase. "Should I put that in your room?" he asks.

"My room? You're not staying with me?"

He looks out at the beach again and back to me. "I think it'll be better for me to stay in the guest room."

I step toward him. "Because you're leaving?" I ask. He nods and I step closer. "Don't you think we're past separate sleeping quarters?"

I can feel the internal battle raging inside him. He doesn't want to walk away, but thinks he needs to. How are we here when less than twenty-four hours ago, we were ravaging each other? This game of hot and cold is wearing on me, but I'm not defeated. I want to beg him to stay, to give us a chance, but that would only push him in the wrong direction. He'll have to come to the decision on his own terms.

Samuel shakes his head and walks off, leaving me standing there alone. He grabs the suitcase and disappears down the hall. There's a tight pain in my chest, a hint of what's to come. It doesn't feel like he's in the next room. It feels like he's already gone.

In the morning, I unpack the rest of the clothes and make a list of what I'll need. Samuel has lent me some money until I can figure out a way to earn a living here. I insist on paying him back and he insists on denying me.

He was already in the water by the time I woke up. I watch Samuel from inside the house for a while. He looks so at home out there sitting on that board. The waves lift him up and down before he paddles hard and catches one. The way his body moves, swishing back and forth, looks like an erotic dance done just for me. After a few rides, I decide to stop being a creeper and focus on something else.

I research upgrades for the current alarm system and install a program to monitor the motion sensors and keypad from his laptop. When I'm done with that, I find a few shelves of books and pick one with an interesting cover. I change into a bikini, grab a towel, and head outside to read. Deciding on some shade, I ungracefully climb into a hammock tied between two trees. I almost fall out twice, but finally get settled with my ankles crossed and the book on my stomach. I check on Samuel and though I can't see his eyes, I feel them on me.

An hour later, he emerges from the water. For me, it's a slow motion *Baywatch* moment when he shakes the water from his hair and digs his board into the sand. Water droplets carve paths down his inked body bringing my gaze with them. The muscles of his arms and chest flex as he stretches. By the time he reaches me, I'm fanning myself with my book.

"Hot?" he asks.

"Uh huh."

"I'm getting a beer. You want?" I stare at him dumbly. "Kat?"

"Oh! Umm, I'll come in."

Samuel nods and continues to the house. I watch him go for a few seconds before pouring myself out of the hammock and following.

We meet at the kitchen island where he's already opened a beer for me.

"Thanks," I say taking a long pull from the bottle.

"You're welcome."

"I could make us some lunch," I offer.

"Yeah. Sure."

Whatever magic we found in Guaymas was lost once we entered this house. It feels like an awkward dance of avoidance, like he doesn't want me here in his space. I have no idea how to fix it.

"I was thinking of going shopping tomorrow. Maybe looking up Piper."

Samuel nods and eats his sandwich. I'm only three bites in to my lunch when he hops up and mumbles his thanks. He tips his beer in my direction and walks away. Samuel stays in his room for the rest of the day. I approach his door a few times, but I don't knock. I don't know what to say. Instead, I lean my forehead against the wood door and silently beg him to open up.

23. HIM

I sit on my board in the water and look back at the house. It's quiet and empty like it always has been. By the time I worked up the nerve to leave my room this morning, Kat was gone. I'm ashamed that I've become a coward here. Avoidance is never the solution to any problem. I know that, and just like a petulant child, I ignore it.

It's so hard being around her. She has me confused, my head spinning. Inwardly I wrestle with my attraction to her, my desire to protect her, and my feelings of inadequacy. Physically, Kat's body calls to me with that familiar lure. I've been inside her, tasted her, and it taunts me until I'm a muted teenage boy with a crush. Somehow I find the strength to deny her. But it's not just physical anymore. I want to be near her, to decipher her random eighties references and learn everything about her.

It's hard finding the middle ground between the man I am and the man she makes me want to be.

Yet, as much as I'd like to fall into a relationship with Kat, it's in her best interest that I don't. It would be wild, but eventually the darkness that has followed me my entire life would descend upon us. I can't do that to her. Not after everything she's already been through. It's my chicken-shit way of protecting her. I'll be the bad guy and she'll be better off.

It's best to just cut our losses now and when she's comfortable here, say our good-byes. I transferred the money I earned capturing her into a bank account for her this morning, found her a Spanish tutor, and started looking for a place for me—somewhere far away from here.

Fed up with the lack of waves, I head inside and shower. Hours later, I've done a load of laundry, reorganized the furniture in the guest room, and have tired of watching Internet porn. I'm parked in front of the laptop looking at real estate in South America when I hear the front door open.

There's a loud clatter, a thump, and then giggling.

"Kat?" I say stretching my neck to get a better view. "Is that you?"

"Yep," she answers, popping the *p*.

I push the computer from my lap and walk to the front of the house. The door is wide open and Kat is lying face down, her arms spread out on each side. A low, tinkling laughter echoes off the tile floor where her face presently rests. Her feet are tangled in the bottom of her pink dress.

"It's comfy here. I think I'll stay," she says.

"Are you okay?"

She laughs and rolls over, her head now between my feet. Her wet hair sticks to her face and chest like red stripes on a zebra. Her eyes are glossy and they stare at the ceiling as if it's more interesting than my face. I can smell the tequila she's consumed.

"Immakay," she slurs. "Just fell over that thingy." Her hand wildly gestures to the doorway where there is no thingy to be found.

"You're drunk."

"Uh huh. Me and Piper had the drinks," she says, hissing the *s* sounds.

I walk around, grab both of her hands, and pull her up. She stumbles and leans into me wrapping her arms around my waist.

"Mmm, this is good."

"Come on. Let's get you to bed," I say.

Kat looks up at me finally, her mouth forming a perfect *O* shape. "Well, Mr. Turner. I thought you'd never ask."

Her wobbly feet keep tripping me, so I pick her up and carry her down the hall to her room. I set her down on the bed where she immediately starts stripping out of her clothes.

"I'll go get you some water," I say turning and running for the door.

"Samuel!"

I stop and turn to face her. She's standing at the edge of the bed, teetering a bit. The thick white loops of the rug seem to curl around her feet and keep her in place. All she wears is a pink strapless bikini. Suddenly, I feel drunk, too.

"Kat," I beg. *Please let me go.*

"Why don't you want me? Huh?" Kat asks. She saunters toward me and I'm surprised that she doesn't waver. She places her hands on my shoulders, the heat from her palms burn through my thin shirt. I can tell she's working hard to keep her words and thoughts clear. "I want you, Samuel. All of you. Everything. The good, the bad, and the worst parts of you. And not just tonight. Because everything in me says that we belong together. Yes, the universe had a fucked-up way of making that happen. But I don't care. Stop fighting us."

One hand skates up my neck, her fingers weave into my hair.

"I can't," I whisper, my throat dry.

"One day I'm good enough, the next, I'm not."

"It's not you, Kat."

"Spare me the bullshit." She pulls close now, pressing her tight little body to mine. I close my eyes and think of anything but the feel of her skin against mine and the truthful words she speaks. "How can you deny what we have?"

Kat launches herself at me. She pulls me down, her lips wrestle mine into submission. All my fight vanishes. I kiss her back because I need it. I need her. My arms wrap around her and she hops up crossing her ankles behind my back. I walk forward and when my knees hit the bed, I let us fall together.

"Whoa," she says when our tangled bodies bounce on the mattress. "That wasn't a good idea. I think I'm gonna throw up." She closes her eyes and slaps her palms flat against the sheets beneath us. "Nope. I'm good."

I snap out of my lustful haze and remove my lips from her skin. I can't do this while she's drunk. I swore I'd never do it at all.

"I'm going to go. You need to sleep."

I stand and run my hands through my hair, smoothing it down where she's been tugging. I hurry to the door and try to make a quick escape.

"No," she calls softly. "Don't leave. Please."

Her words, laced with desperation stop me mid-step. I scrub my face with my hands and exhale slowly. I walk back to her and it feels like foreshadowing for the rest of my life. She's a beautiful girl who's asking nothing of me, but to stay.

I reach behind my head and pull my shirt off. Kat raises her arms as I slide it onto her. She struggles to remove her bikini and when it's finally off, she scoots back and lays against her pillow.

No words are spoken between us as I crawl next to her. She wraps herself around me and falls into an alcohol-induced sleep. One arm curls around her back while the other hand slides to her thigh. I'm awake for hours.

The next morning, I wake to an empty bed. I sit up and look outside to find Kat sipping coffee. She's wrapped in a knitted blanket and staring out at the water.

After using the bathroom, I head to the kitchen and fix myself a cup of coffee. I slide two pieces of bread into the toaster and wait as the coils begin to glow red orange. When Kat walks in, she gives me a sheepish smile and sits at the island. Her fingers trace an invisible pattern on the granite countertop. She refuses to look me in the eye.

"I'm sorry about last night," she offers.

"It's okay."

"No. It's not. I promised myself I wouldn't push you. The moment my inhibitions were lowered, that's exactly what I did."

I turn and face the toaster when it pops up, not able to choose the right words. With my back to the room, I hear her bare feet on the tile floor as she approaches.

"I'm really sorry, Samuel." I turn to face her now. There are dark circles of leftover makeup under her eyes. Her thin brows crinkle and she looks so sad. It kills me. "You should know something though."

"What's that?" I ask.

"I meant everything I said last night. I just didn't have the courage to say it before."

There's no movement from either of us. The air is still, our breaths locked inside our chests. There is only room for truth between us.

"Then, I'll stay," I say.

"Yeah?"

"Yeah. I don't belong anywhere else."

Kat squeals and wraps her arms around me. A heaviness lifts off my shoulders, a long time-carried weight gone, the moment I give in to Katherine Percle.

Kat sleeps most of the day, recovering from her night of cheap drinks. I make us a simple dinner of chicken quesadillas. She practically inhales her first piece before slowing down to chew.

"These are great. I'm starved," she says with a mouth full of food.

"I see that." She returns her attention to the meal. "So, how'd you get home last night?"

Kat looks up at the ceiling, no doubt trying to recount last night's events. "It's a little blurry, but I think Piper brought me back on the scooter and her boyfriend followed us."

I nod and drink down half of my beer.

"So, I guess you two had fun?"

"Too much. I'm a wild girl, but I couldn't keep up with her," Kat says laughing. "Obviously."

"Out partied by a tourist. The locals would be horrified."

"Am I a local already? This gringo needs time to acclimate."

"No time. It's instant," I tease.

She smiles and shakes her head at me.

"Oh! I invited Piper and her boyfriend to dinner here for Easter. It'll be their last weekend before she heads home."

I stop chewing and look at her. "Really?" I ask. The thought of strangers in my house makes me instantly uncomfortable, but I know it's my personal issue and push it aside.

"I hope that's okay."

"Uh, I guess that's fine," I say scratching the back of my neck.

"I'll cook," Kat offers.

"I hope so. This is the only thing I make that's edible."

After dinner we wash the dishes together and lock up the house. Kat meets me in the hall. "Will you move into my room?" she asks. "Our room."

I nod and follow her to bed, deciding we'll move my things tomorrow.

Soon we're wrapped up in cool sheets and each other. Kat slides her hand over my chest, down my stomach and traces the lines of my compass tattoo. Every touch from this girl drives me wild.

"If you're feeling better tomorrow, I'll take you out and show you *my* Cabo."

Kat yawns and her fingers splay out along my ribs.

"That sounds great."

Kat enters the kitchen, her bag over one shoulder. She looks much better than the day before. I throw the contents of her bag in my backpack, along with four bottles of water.

"Ready?" she asks.

"Let's go."

We take my car and drive over an hour to Santiago. We're out all day, hiking to the waterfalls and swimming in the clear water. I laugh more than I can ever remember doing so. Not only am I discovering Kat, but I am rediscovering myself.

The ride home is quiet, but comfortable. My hand rests on

her thigh while Kat leans out the window and watches the scenery fly by. When we arrive back at the house, I park the car but neither of us move. It's as if we both fear we'll lose all the progress made today if we step back into reality.

"What do we do now?" I ask, tapping my thumbs against the steering wheel.

"Now, we just live one day at a time. I want to experience everything here and I want you to be the one to show me."

Her freckled, sun-kissed face is all smiles.

"We'll drink expensive tequila until we pass out in the hammock behind the house. I'll take you to have steak dinners and lobster tacos. We'll hang out at beach bars, listen to live music, and make fun of tourists."

"And dancing? Can we go dancing?" Kat asks.

"Uh, I don't dance."

"I'm sure I could persuade you."

I shrug. "I doubt I have the strength to deny you."

"You never did," she teases.

My mouth drops open and I sit motionless for a few seconds. Kat jumps from the car and takes off running for the front door giggling. I'm right behind her, but when Kat reaches the house, she stops. I slam into the back of her, wrapping my arms around her waist to keep her from falling over.

"What's wrong?" I ask.

"The door's open."

"What?" I look up and see the door cracked open a few inches. There's no sign of forced entry and the alarm is disabled. "How?" I look back to Kat. "Didn't you come back in for your sunglasses?"

"Yeah."

"So, did you close it behind you?"

"I. . . . I . . ."

I grab her shoulders and turn her away from the house. "Kat, did you lock and close the door?"

"I thought I did. But maybe not. I . . . I can't remember."

"Shit! Stay here. Do not fucking move from this spot. Do you understand?"

She nods her head, her worried eyes searching mine for assurance. I give her shoulder a squeeze and slip in through the door, leaving it open behind me. Scanning the space, I don't find anything out of place. In the kitchen, I run my hand behind the fridge and grab the pistol stored there. I hear Kat gasp, probably unaware of such safety precautions throughout the house. I check the clip and slide it back into place.

I don't think about how or why someone would break in. Instead, I keep my mind focused on the task at hand, checking every closet and pantry as Kat watches from the front door. I move down the hall, investigating every room before clearing it and moving on to the next. My pulse is quick, but I stay calm and in control.

"Samuel?" Kat calls from outside. "Samuel?" she calls again, her voice wavering.

I step from the hall and run into her searching the main room. "Shit, Samuel! I think I peed a little."

I laugh at her and close the front door. "I told you to stay outside."

"I got worried," she protests.

"The house is clear. You probably just didn't pull the door closed all the way."

Kat takes a seat on the sofa and puts her face in her hands. She stares at the gun for a few seconds and turns to me.

"How many of those do you have tucked around here?"

"A few."

"I hope we never need them."

"Me too," I answer.

I enter the six-digit code on the keypad and wait for the green light to appear. When it does, I turn the handle and pull open the door to the safe. Inside sit a few stacks of cash, my favorite gun, and the only photo of my mother in existence.

"Kat," I call. "Can you get me the key?"

I know it was our fault the door was open, but still there's a nagging feeling that I'm missing something. I'll feel better with it locked away along with my valuables.

"Sure," she says. She enters the bathroom and comes out with it dangling from her fist. "Here." She watches me put it in the safe and stands on her tiptoes to see inside. "What else do you have in there? Your porn stash?"

I remove the photo of my mom and hold it up in the light from the window. It's a bit faded now, but the diminished colors could do nothing to lessen the image. She's wearing a simple white dress and smiling brightly at the camera. The four-year-old version of me sits on her lap caught in mid-laugh. My mouth is open showing off tiny straight teeth. Fat cheeks raise up so high my eyes are slits. I search that kid's face and wonder if the darkness had started to creep in yet. Were these two seemingly happy people already on the downward spiral that would eventually destroy them?

"You have her eyes," Kat says. "And smile." I nod silently. "I forget what that looks like, your smile."

She wraps her arms around me and pulls her body to mine. I put my mother's photo back into the safe, close and lock it, and slide the framed art back in place.

24: her

Over the next few weeks, Samuel keeps me occupied on all kinds of escapades. He introduces me to his favorite places in and around Los Cabos. He's into extreme sports and anything dangerous, though I guess that shouldn't surprise me. We hike to waterfalls, go kayaking, he tries to teach me to surf, and we ride dune buggies in the desert. The rock climbing was my least favorite. I had a hard time trusting my life to a tiny nylon rope and a hook. But, as with everything else, Samuel kept me safe.

On top of all that, his appetite for me hasn't diminished one bit. I love how he loses control, how I can push and tease him until he's practically purring from my touch. The attraction is not one-sided, though. He knows how to push my buttons, so to speak. With one look, a fiery glance, or dimpled smirk, I'm absolute putty in his hands. And what capable hands they are. Samuel has claimed me on every surface of this house and every one outside as well. We've had sex in the water, in his car, and almost in the hammock—I've still got the scar on my elbow.

It's one grand adventure after another and frankly, I'm ready for some relaxation. I call up Piper at her hotel and we make plans to spend the day together, just lounging on the beach.

When I pass through the main room, Samuel is in the kitchen wearing athletic shorts, tennis shoes, and no shirt. He's sweaty, just back from his morning run, and stands in front of the open fridge gulping down a bottle of water. That sight, first thing in the morning, makes it a lot more difficult to leave.

"Now would be a great time to try pouring the water bottle over your head thing," I suggest.

He shakes his head and finishes the water. "That's only for guys who need hotness points." He flexes his arm and casually leans against the counter. "I'm good."

I laugh and roll my eyes. "And so humble, too. I'm going to hang out with Piper for the day." Samuel lifts one eyebrow at me. "No tequila this time."

"Have fun," he says. He pulls open a drawer and removes two cell phones, holding one out to me. "I got this for you yesterday." I take it from him and slide my thumb over the screen. "My number is the only one in there. Call me if you need anything."

As much as I once missed my tech devices, I feel no joy now. It was kind of nice being detached from the rest of the world. Though I do still follow my favorite blogs online using Samuel's computer. I'm newly self-aware, not a hermit.

I drop the phone into my bag and reach up on my tiptoes to kiss his lips. He tastes like sweat and Samuel, so delicious. "Thanks. I'll see you later."

He yanks me back and pins me against the steel refrigerator door.

"Gross," I say, breathless and dishonest. "You're all sweaty."

Samuel leans down, his warm breath on my neck. Chills race down my arms.

"Be safe," he says, before kissing my shoulder and heading for the shower.

"Oh! Look at this," I say, picking up a wooden bracelet from a nearby table.

The market is crowded today with locals and tourists shopping for handmade goods, flowers, fruit, and seafood. I slip the bracelet on my wrist and hold my arm out to Samuel. He barely looks at it before his eyes search up and down the street.

That's how it's been for the past three weeks. He's always on alert, always watching and waiting for something to happen. Some nights I don't think he sleeps at all. Samuel says he's just being cautious, that we got too comfortable here. I think he's being overly cautious. I thought we were safe, so I'm not sure what he's afraid of.

I twist my arm back and forth, looking at the intricate design carved into the bracelet.

"Samuel, don't you like it?" I ask.

"Of course."

"Do you think it looks good on me?"

"Of course," he answers again.

"Did you know if I turn it around three times and say SHIZAM it makes me time travel?"

"Yeah."

"Oz!" His shoulders jump and he finally looks at me. "You're not even listening to me."

He shrugs and walks closer, placing a soft kiss where my neck meets my shoulder. It's become habit for him to do this when he wants to distract me, shut me up. I know I won't win this battle, so I slide the bracelet from my arm and place it back on the table.

"Why's it so crowded today?" I ask.

"I don't know. Maybe spring breakers."

"Oh! When's Easter?"

"On the twentieth."

"Really? Wow. I didn't even realize. I should start planning the menu for Easter dinner now!"

"Yeah, you only have two and a half weeks to get it ready," Samuel says vacantly.

"Shut it. This is a big moment for you—it'll be the first time you'll be opening up your house to new friends."

"Our house," he says. "Opening up *our* house."

When our arms are full, we head back home. It's still odd to think of this place as my home too. For a month now, we wake each morning to colorful sunrises that paint the sky in hues of orange and lavender. Each night the ocean waves lull us to sleep. It's more than I ever dreamed of.

When we reach the front door, Samuel enters the code and holds it open. We set the bags down and I start to unload them while he stands at the back of the house staring at the ocean. He's so disconnected from me lately, always close but so far away. He reminds me of the tide, pulling in close and retreating again. It's frustrating, but I try to be patient.

I put the last of the food in the refrigerator and join him at the glass door. The surf looks great today and I wonder if he'll take me out on his board.

"Something wrong?" I ask. His blue eyes are lit up by the afternoon sun as they avoid mine. "Samuel, please don't shut me out."

He reaches into his pocket and pulls out the wooden bracelet I admired earlier. He takes my hand and slides it onto my wrist. I beam up at him, knowing that his actions mean so much more than his absent words. I stand on my tiptoes and pull him down for a kiss.

"I love you," I say.

Samuel straightens up and gawks at me. I suck in a breath and seal my lips closed. My whole body trembles with my admission. I've been thinking it for a few days, but to let it slip out now is a huge mistake. He's not ready. I try to make it easier to swallow.

"I don't know how you feel about me, Samuel. I don't know what I mean to you. But, I need you to know that every time I look at you, I'm positive that I want to be with you. I do love you."

Both of his hands reach for me. They hold my face and pull me forward with such desperation, such force. He kisses me until I feel lightheaded. When he breaks free, Samuel leans his forehead against mine. "I love you too," he says fiercely.

25. HIM

I stand at the sink washing my hands so I can help Kat prepare dinner for her friends. Before I know it, I've been staring at the running water for a few minutes. Kat steps over, turns the faucet off, and wraps her arms around me. She squeezes tight, pressing her body against mine in my favorite way.

"What's been going on with you?" Kat asks with her cheek resting on my chest. "You seem so distracted lately. And this isn't you. What's been happening in that pretty head of yours?"

I return her hug, running my hands up and down her back. "In the business I was in, I always had to rely on my gut. My instincts were good and usually never steered me wrong. I keep having this feeling that something isn't right. My gut is trying to warn me."

"Maybe it's the tacos we had last night? My gut wasn't happy at all."

I ease her away from me so I can look into her eyes. "I'm serious, Kat."

"I know," she says, giving me an apologetic look. "Deflective humor."

Kat leans against the counter across from me.

"As much as I tried to leave that life behind, I feel like I need to stay vigilant. We never figured out how Boots kept finding us. Maybe he wasn't working alone. Now that he's dead, Dragon could send another goon in to finish the job. There are just too many unknowns."

"Life is full of unknowns, Samuel. Nothing is guaranteed. But we can't live the rest of our lives in fear, just waiting for the other shoe to drop. I know you. I know you hate feeling helpless. Is this just about Boots or is it about me?"

"What does that mean?" I ask.

"This," she says, waving her hand between us, "is so new to both of us. Whether you want to admit it or not, I know you're afraid of what we have. You don't hold all the power. You can't control the universe, Samuel."

"You ever think about where you'd be if you had made it to Canada?" I ask.

"No matter what happens." I open my mouth to interrupt her, but she shakes her head. "No matter what our future holds, know that I'm glad you found me in Tacoma, Samuel Ozley. And again in Los Angeles. I'm glad that I'm here with you. We're both in uncharted territory here. We might make mistakes. We might stumble. But, we're doing it together. Kat and Oz. Liz and Lucas. Whoever we are, we are together."

I grin and take the few steps to stand in front of her. Maybe I am afraid of this new relationship and what it could mean for Kat to see the real me. Maybe this feeling in my gut has nothing to do with unanswered questions from our past and everything to do with the mystery of our future.

"You're right," I say, placing a hand on the counter on each side, trapping her. "I don't hold all the power. I don't hold any of it. You rule my life now. As much as you belong to me, I belong to you. And that scares the shit out of me."

She smiles up at me. "While I hate that you're scared, I kind of like seeing you vulnerable like this."

"You make me vulnerable, Kat, not some kitchen confession. Your cute laugh, how your lips slide sideways when you're nervous, your love of shitty music, your ability to see through everything I am. It's all you."

Her smile widens, splitting her face in half and she reaches up on her toes to kiss me. It's slow and fiery, creating a buzzing beneath my skin. When she finally pulls away, she rests her forehead on my chest and inhales deeply.

"That is the sweetest thing you've ever said to me."

"You mean, 'My name's Oz and I'm here to kill you' didn't do it for you?"

"Samuel, I don't think those particular words ever came out of your mouth."

"I was paraphrasing."

She laughs, but the look in her eyes is mischievous. "What time is it?"

I glance at the clock across the room. "A little after five."

"Good. We have time."

Kat drops to her knees, her hands working on the button fly of my jeans.

"Kat," I whisper in a halfhearted protest.

She shakes her head and warns me with her eyes to keep quiet. I nod and watch as she wraps her small hands and then her lips around me. There are images that stay with you for a lifetime—some good, most bad—this is one that I will never forget. It's not a cheap act between strangers or a drunken seduction. It's an appreciation, a physical manifestation of the love between two people, the two most unlikely souls to ever belong together.

The sensation of Kat's warm mouth on me makes my knees weak. I lock them and place each hand on the edge of the counter to stay upright. She moves her hand to add to my pleasure and I know I won't last much longer.

My breaths come out in short, gasping puffs of air now and her name leaves my lips over and over. I fight to keep my eyes open, to witness this beautiful woman and everything that she offers. I feel the familiar tightness in my gut. It's like a cord winding every muscle and tendon in my body.

"I'm going to . . ."

I lose my words when her pace increases and she swallows around me. Kat wraps her hands around my thighs and holds my body tight so I can't escape, not that I want to. My head is spinning and when I finally let go, she takes all that I give her.

I collapse onto my forearms on the counter, Kat trapped between my body and the cabinets. She cleans me up and tucks me back inside my jeans before refastening all the buttons. Kat then stands, forcing me upright while I wrap her in my arms.

"If I would have known that would happen, I would have told you how I feel a long time ago." I squeeze her tight and kiss just below her ear. She lets out a loud chuckle and slaps my shoulder.

"Asshole," she says. "I'm going brush my teeth before our guests arrive."

Kat ducks under my arm and heads toward the bathroom.

"But an asshole you love, right?"

She spins and gives me a bright smile. "Absolutely."

When she returns, Kat gets right back to work in the kitchen.

"Piper is so much fun. I'm sure her boyfriend is cool, too. I haven't met him yet. They should be here soon." I nod at her and eat another carrot. She slaps the back of my hand. "Stop eating that! Can you go light the tiki torches on the back patio? I'm thinking it'll be nice enough to eat outside."

I grab the lighter from the kitchen drawer and head outside. I work my way around the perimeter of the patio, lighting the oil torches along the way. When I'm halfway through, I hear a knock at the door.

"They're here!" Kat yells.

26: her

"Oh! There you are," I say when Samuel steps inside. "This is my friend Piper. Piper, this is my husband Lucas."

He stands in the doorway stiffly, his eyes on Piper. Samuel mumbles something but I don't make it out.

"Hello, Oz. Good to see you, darling."

I turn to Piper to find her smiling sweetly.

"How do you know he goes by Oz? Have you guys met before?" I ask. I'm confused as I watch the staring match between these two.

Samuel lunges into the kitchen and runs his hand behind the fridge. He pulls his empty hand out and kicks the side of the appliance.

"Looking for this?" Piper asks, raising a gun and pointing it at him.

"Piper?" I ask, confused and terrified.

"That's Natasha," Samuel says.

I look at him and back to my friend. She laughs. It's a maniacal laugh that chills my blood.

"*The* Natasha?" I screech.

She hops up from her chair, gun still pointed at Samuel and walks closer.

"The one and only. Both of you on the couch." Neither one of us move. I slide the kitchen knife off the counter and into my pocket. "Now!"

I let out a whimper as Samuel drags me over to the sofa. We both sit as Natasha paces in front of us.

"Why are you here?" Samuel asks, trying to remain cool. "Did Dragon send you?"

"Ha. Dragon doesn't give a shit about you or Boots. Don't flatter yourself, Oz," she says gesturing with her hands. The gun flails around like a forgotten limb. Natasha stops in front of Samuel. She looks down on him with simmering rage. I tuck my trembling hands beneath my thighs. "Let's start with the key."

"The key?" I ask.

My brain works to piece together everything that's happening and who she is. I can't seem to work out her motivation.

"Yes, Kitty Kat. I need the key," she says slowly as if talking to a toddler. "Oz didn't complete the job, so Callista hired me to clean up his mess. She wants the key and both of you dead."

I fume, struck again with the hurt of my mother's betrayal. Natasha sits on the coffee table facing us. I reach for Samuel's hand and squeeze it tight. Natasha's eyes flicker down to our joined hands and a devilish grin appears. She steps forward and straddles Samuel's lap. I scoot away, flinching from her nearness.

"Have you been mixing business with pleasure, darling?" Natasha whispers in his ear.

The gun presses into Samuel's back as she slides her hands around his neck and licks at his lips. He turns away, immediately causing Natasha to scowl and hop up.

"What's wrong? I'm not good enough for you anymore?" Natasha walks to the patio and slides the door shut, thoroughly sealing us in. "You never complained before," she sneers with her back to us.

"I can match what she's paying you," Samuel says.

Her steps are quick as she runs back and hits him across the face. Samuel's eyes water from the pain and I turn to comfort him.

"It's not just about the money!" Natasha shouts. Her breathing quickens, her tearful eyes set on Samuel. "You killed Boots."

"Boots?" I ask.

"I loved him. For the first time in my life, I wanted someone who wanted me back. He showed me that I was worthy of love. I turned straight for him. Quit doing shady jobs and stuck to the legit business." Natasha wipes the tears from her eyes. Her face turns dark and serious. "A lot of good that did me, right? You took him from me, Oz. Now, I get to have my revenge and get paid to do it. It's a win-win situation."

"So, that's why you've been trying to get in touch with me? That's why you wanted in on the job. You were helping Boots."

"You were using Samuel's cell phone to track us, weren't you?" I ask. "Triangulating the signal?"

Her face snaps into a smile, like putting a mask on. Natasha spins away from us, pacing again. "Boots taught me many things you didn't, Oz. He was twice the man you are."

I nudge Samuel and show him the knife in my pocket. He quickly slides it out and hides it beneath his leg. I watch him carefully as he mouths the word "run." I want to shake my head and deny him, but the pleading in his eyes tells me I better not argue.

"I brought your favorite toy, Samuel." She pulls a pair of handcuffs from her back pocket and dangles them in front of his face.

"Put those on him," Natasha barks at me. I follow her instructions, but keep them loose.

"I'm not an idiot," she says, placing the gun to Samuel's chest and reaching down to tighten the metal cuffs around his wrists.

"Natasha, enough with the dramatics. Tell me what you want," he says calmly.

"So impatient." Natasha stands in front of us again. She moves the end of the pistol to my temple. "How do you put up with him?"

Tears stream down my face now, but I hold her gaze. "My mother hired you to kill us, but you don't get paid without that key, right?"

"That's true, Kitty Kat. So where is it?" she says nudging the gun against my head with each word.

Samuel stands and Natasha points the gun back at him. "You know, you could just take out the girl. Then, you and I could stay here, like you always wanted to," he says.

I whip my head around to face Samuel. I know he's only creating a diversion, but those words sting like the truth.

"Ah, there's the Oz I know! A selfish bastard till the very end. Just stop your lying!" she yells. "Where is the fucking key?"

"I'm not lying. With her out of the picture, you and I can pick up where we left off," he says, stepping closer. Natasha faces him. I can see the knife in one of his cuffed hands, hidden along his forearm. I slowly scoot to the end of the sofa, so I have a straight shot to the door.

"You don't mean it," Natasha whispers.

"I do."

I can see her wavering, a glimmer of hope in her eyes and I know that he's got her. When the back of her knees hit the coffee table, she raises the gun higher.

"Stop. Just give me the key and this will be over," Natasha threatens.

"You don't mean it," Samuel says, using her words against her while looking into the barrel of his own gun.

He leans forward until the pistol presses into his chest. I watch it all unfold like a nightmare. Blood and adrenaline pump through my body and I ready myself. Suddenly, Natasha's arm drops to her side and she throws herself at Samuel, attacking his lips. I should be running now, but my feet won't move. I think Samuel is just as surprised.

I see him raise the knife. Natasha must sense something because when he moves to plunge it into her side, her hand shoots out to stop him. She's not successful, but the wound is not lethal. She screams and falls backward. The gun flies from her hand and slides across the floor toward the front door. I take off running, then trip over my own feet and tumble over a chair. Without looking back, I crawl to the door, get up on my feet, and swing it open.

"I'll kill him!" Natasha screams.

I spin to find her kneeling over Samuel, the knife at his throat. In my effort to get to the door, I've missed their scuffle and have no idea how she got the upper hand. There's a blotch of blood on her shirt that's spreading like spilled ink.

"No, you won't. You still love him," I say. I curse the trembling in my voice and the lack of oxygen in my lungs.

"I don't think so, darling. You've spoiled him for me. You made him soft. And it's too bad, because the old Oz was so much fun." A gust of wind blows through the door and I try to clear my head. "Give me the key or he dies," Natasha says.

I meet Samuel's tired eyes and he shakes his head. "Don't give her anything," he says. His gaze darts to the gun near me. I don't know if I can reach it before she kills him.

"Even if I give you the key, he still dies," I shout.

She grins and nods her head. "You're a smart Kitty. You have ten seconds," Natasha says. "Nine, eight, seven."

"Stop!" I yell. Samuel struggles to buck Natasha off of him, but he can't get the leverage he needs.

"Five, four, three," she counts smiling sweetly down at Samuel. She raises the knife over him and grips it with two hands. "Say hello to your mother, darling."

"Okay, okay! I'll give you the key!"

"Do your worst, you crazy bitch," Samuel spits at her. "Kat, don't give her anything. Once she has the key, you're dead."

He's pleading with me now, his voice strong and demanding. But I can't stand here and watch her kill him.

"I bet it's in that safe behind the painting right? Now go fetch it while me and lover boy wait here." Natasha slides the knife to his chest and presses down. Blood spills out as she drags it a few inches. Samuel doesn't even flinch. "Move!" she yells at me.

I squeak and run to the bedroom, slide the painting over, and punch in the code. I open the safe and know that I'll find the key and Samuel's favorite antique gun inside. Only, it's not there. The cash, the photo of his mother, and my necklace with the key are all there. No gun.

"Shit!" I whisper slapping my hand to my forehead.

Samuel probably has it hidden somewhere in the house. That does us no good now! Every bit of hope flees my body and I'm left with nothing.

"Hurry up, Kitty Kat! He's a bleeder!" Natasha yells.

I grab the key and run back to the room. She has placed one of the kitchen chairs over his body now and is sitting in it. The footrest bar presses against his throat and I can tell he's struggling for air. Red ribbons of blood pour from cuts all over. I gasp and cover my mouth to keep the sob inside.

"Do you know how long it takes to bleed someone out? Or how

to slide a knife into someone's flesh in places just short of major organs?" Natasha jumps up, waving the bloody knife in my direction. She snatches the key from my hand. "You think he'd ever love you? He's heartless. Lovely to look at, but dead inside," she says. Her voice wavers, her eyes look crazed. "Now," Natasha says, tucking a piece of hair behind her ear and smoothing down her bloodied shirt.

Samuel gasps, his eyes flutter open, and he lifts his cuffed hands enough to push the chair off of him. Natasha raises her foot and kicks him in the stomach.

"He's losing a lot of blood, Kitty Kat. I bet he's feeling cold right about now, too weak to fight back. Soon he'll go into shock and lose consciousness. No more Oz."

She pushes me onto the sofa and takes a seat on the table in front of me, legs splayed, her elbows resting on her knees. The knife hangs down, forgotten as she inspects the key.

"All of this work for this little thing," she says. "All the searching and pretending to be your friend. Bypassing your alarm system wasn't difficult. I was here when you were out honeymooning," she spits. "I left the door open on purpose, knowing it would drive Oz crazy. Getting you drunk, weeks of waiting were all part of the plan. It was like a lovely vacation on your mother's dime. You gave a good effort. But you're no match for me. After all, I was trained by the best."

Natasha stands and pockets the key before placing the knife to my throat. I can feel the blade against my skin and her hot breath on my face.

"Don't worry, it won't hurt much, Kitty Kat," Natasha says smiling.

There's a loud thwack as the front door slams against the wall.

"Her name is Katherine, you bitch!"

We look over to find a trembling gun pointed at us.

27. HIM

My head is pounding and I'm freezing. There's blood everywhere. I can smell it all around me. I hear a strange voice come from the front door and slide my eyes that way.

There's a woman in the doorway holding the forgotten gun. She looks exhausted but determined. There's a fierceness in her expression that's familiar.

"Who the hell are you?" Natasha shouts.

"Mom?" Kat shouts.

"That's not Callista," Natasha says.

I want to tell Kat that I don't recognize this woman either, but the words refuse to form.

"Drop the knife," the woman shouts.

Natasha grunts and holds her stance. "I don't care who you are," she spits. "They both have to die."

Two shots ring out. Silence. Then Natasha's lifeless body drops beside me. Between the blood loss and hitting my head in the struggle, I fight to keep my eyes open, to make sure Natasha is dead and Kat's okay, but I'm fading fast.

The woman drops the gun, hurdles the overturned chair, and runs to Kat.

"What are you doing here? How did you find us? I thought you—"

"I know what you thought, Katherine. I didn't do it. It wasn't me."

I wake to sunlight pouring through the bedroom's glass door. A breeze blows the curtains and they dance around the frame. I can hear the waves against the shore, a static white noise that wants to lull me back to sleep. I turn over to find Kat asleep. I raise my hand to brush hair from her face and see two bandages on my arm.

I suck in a breath and sit up. All the happenings of last night play through my head. Flashes of guns, knives, blood, and Natasha make me nauseated. I throw back the sheets and check her sleeping body for injuries. She seems to be perfectly fine. Jumping from the bed, I run down the hall and into the main room where I have to clutch the wall to stay upright. I squeeze my eyes closed and reopen them to the surreal scene before me.

The house is immaculate, every piece of furniture clean and in its place. Natasha's body is gone. There's no blood on the tile floor, no evidence that she was here—besides the trace scent of bleach and other cleaners. The biggest shock is seeing the woman from last night cooking at my stove. She looks at home here.

I approach with caution and take a seat at the bar.

"Oh, Samuel! So glad you're up. How are you feeling?" she asks. I stare with my mouth hanging open, unsure if or how to answer.

She looks like an older version of Kat, only her eyes are different. Her wavy brown hair skims the tops of her shoulders as she sways back and forth in a nervous dance.

"Who are you? Where's Natasha? Is Kat okay? What happened?" I ask, trying to clear the fog from my head.

"Oh, I'm rude. My name is Callista, the real one. I'm Katherine's mother."

"Um, it's great to meet you," I say, though it comes out like a question. "If you're Callista, who hired me?"

"My sister-in-law, Marilyn, the conniving twat."

I laugh and almost choke at the use of the word twat from a middle-aged woman standing in an apron in my kitchen.

"Yeah, I guess that makes more sense. Is Kat okay?"

"She's fine. Just exhausted. And to answer your other question, Natasha is dead and gone. Can't say I enjoyed taking another person's life, but she was going after my baby," Callista says, her voice grave.

"It was the strangest thing. Kat insisted we call the police, but I think they're crooked around here." She gives me a half-smile. "An odd man named Officer Mendez showed up, loaded the body into her black Mercedes, and drove off. But he didn't look like a police officer at all. All he said was 'Tell Oz thanks again, and he should consider my debt to him paid.'"

"Wow," I say, remembering the gratitude in his eyes when I delivered his child's kidnapper all those years ago. Now I feel the same deep sense of appreciation.

"That's what I said. Anyway, you look a little peaked." Callista sets a glass of orange juice in front of me. "You should drink that. It'll help you feel better."

I nod and drink down half the glass. "Thanks."

"Good morning, Katherine. Well, afternoon." She looks past me.

I turn to find Kat standing in the doorway. She doesn't say a word as she takes a seat beside me.

"I think she may be in shock," Callista says.

I kiss Kat's temple and nudge her shoulder. "You okay?"

She nods, but her expression remains stoic.

"You want some breakfast, sweetheart?" Callista stands in front of Kat and twists her lips sideways on her face. Like mother, like daughter. She's nervous and rightly so.

"Kat?" I ask rubbing circles on her back.

Every muscle in her body is tight, her neck is stiff, and I can feel her pulse drumming wildly.

"My mom is here, in Mexico, offering breakfast to me and my fake husband. I'm in the damn *Twilight Zone*."

I laugh and finish off my orange juice.

"And you? You feel okay?" Kat asks, searching my face.

"Yeah, I'll be fine."

"She's not the one who hired you?"

"Nope. The woman I met was really tall with black hair."

Kat spots the key and necklace sitting on the counter between us. She stands, grabs it, and holds it out to her mom.

"This is what you came for, right?" Kat accuses, her fist shaking.

"Sit down, Katherine. We need to talk," Callista demands in that tone that only a mother can possess. It transports me back to the days of lessons learned from my own mom. I put my hand on her shoulder and guide Kat back into her seat.

"Katherine, you have to listen to me. I didn't hire anyone to kill you. It was all Marilyn. She posed as me, gave him my name, met him on our boat." She points at me with her spatula. There are tears in her eyes as she begs Kat to trust her. “Sweetheart, Katherine, I would never want to kill you. You are more important to me than that stupid key. I only wanted it because Marilyn was obsessed with finding it. I knew she was desperate and I figured we could negotiate with her.”

“How did you find us, Mom? How did you know where we were?” Kat says, her voice accusatory and disbelieving. I can see her hands trembling as she folds them in her lap.

“I stopped by the office one day and overheard Marilyn on the phone with Natasha. When I realized what she had done I flew into a rage,” Callista answers. She sets down her spatula and stands across the bar from Kat. Her hands rest on the edge of the counter, fingers clawing at the granite. “I threatened to go to the police and tell them everything unless she told me where you were. She bragged about posing as me, said it was easy to play a cheap whore.”

Kat drops her chin to her chest and exhales slowly. “Why did she do it?” she asks.

“Money. It’s all about the money. That key represents over one hundred million dollars to her. And she wanted revenge for Dennis’s death. She confessed that the hit man turned on her and escaped with you to Mexico.” Callista stops and takes a deep breath. I can almost see her reliving this information bit by bit. “But then, someone else approached, offering to kill you both and get the key for the same amount of money. She took the deal without hesitating.”

“That still doesn’t explain how you found us.” Kat’s voice is just a whisper now. She’s unsure of her mother and everything else. I move my hand to her thigh and sweep my pinky back and forth across her skin. She slides her hand over and hooks her pinky around mine.

“Natasha called Marilyn with weekly updates on where you

were, what you were doing—basically, a progress report. I convinced her that I'd come here and get the key if she called off the hit. She agreed, but I knew it was a lie. I came to Cabo a week ago. I've been looking for you ever since."

"Well, your timing couldn't have been better," Kat says.

"It was easier to find Natasha, because Marilyn is paying for her hotel. I found her a couple of days ago and followed her here last night."

Kat raises her eyes now and looks at Callista. The cheerful woman who greeted us this morning has been replaced by this dejected yet hopeful mess.

"It's all hard to believe. I want to trust you, but these last few years . . . I don't even know who you are anymore."

"I know I lost my way, Katherine. I let the money and the power get to me. I let Dennis knock me around and didn't do a damn thing about it." She reaches across the counter and lays her hand on top of Kat's. "I swear on Mimi's grave, I would never hurt you, sweetheart. Never."

"You sure you can't stay, Callista?"

"I've got to get back to the States. Important business to take care of," she says, holding up the key before dropping it in her bag.

Kat stands next to me, clinging to my arm. She's still unsure of everything, but she agreed to let her mother have the key. Callista promised that she's going to deliver it to the police and hopefully that means Marilyn will go to prison.

Callista throws her arms around my neck and squeezes me tight.

"Take care of my little girl," she whispers.

I nod at her as Kat looks on.

"Katherine, I'm so glad you found your happiness. I know we haven't agreed on anything these last few years, but please know that is all I ever wanted for you. I love you so much."

She wraps her arms around her daughter and soon Kat returns the hug. The two women stand there for a few minutes exchanging sniffles. When they finally part, we wave good-bye as she jumps into the waiting cab.

Kat stands in the doorway, her arms wrapped around herself, and watches until the cab disappears around a curve. She waits for the dust to settle on the road, until there is no sign of her mother at all, before she comes inside.

The last two months have felt like a tornado, spinning and disrupting everything. I've lost my former life, everything I've ever known, my career, my freedom and anonymity. But in those two months, I've also lost my desire for any of those things without Kat.

For years, I've been fighting ghosts. My mother, my father, my past always looming over me. I never stayed anywhere long enough to belong there. I never wanted to, until now.

"Is it hammock time?" she asks.

"Yes, please."

"Not to be confused with *Hammer Time*."

I stare at her and Kat shakes her head before leading us out of the house onto the sand. We kick off our shoes and climb into the hammock.

"We've got to work on your movie and music education," she says.

I feel her lips on my neck, her hair tickles my face when the breeze blows over us. I grunt as her whole body presses down onto mine. It's the most glorious feeling, and I know I'll never grow tired of it. Her knees straddle my hips and her hands grip onto my biceps between the bandages. Kat places more kisses along my jaw, finally reaching my mouth and sucking gently on my bottom lip.

"Will you go to the doctor today?" she asks.

"If it will make you happy, Mrs. Turner."

She giggles and I open my eyes to find her smiling down at me. Her tanned skin holds a golden glow in the shade of the palm trees. Her long hair contains the last hint of red dye and now has natural highlights from the sun. The blue water and white sand beaches are her background. Even then, she's the most beautiful thing I've ever seen.

"*Me haría muy feliz,*" she says.

"Your Spanish is much better. Maybe you're spending too much time with your tutor," I tease.

"Enrique is tall, dark, and handsome. But I don't think he plays for my team."

I laugh at her. "What gave it away?"

"Well, I constantly throw myself at him, but he ignores me," she answers, smirking.

I roll my eyes and place my hands on her bare knees.

"We made it, Samuel."

"We sure did, Katherine."

She wrinkles her face up at my use of her full name. I motion for her to come closer and when she does, I kiss her.

"And you love me," she says.

"I do."

There, under the shade of those palm trees and the airy umbrella of our confessions, we consume each other unapologetically.

After lunch, we head out to find a doctor. It's hard to locate an open office, as most people are still on holiday. Soon I'm seen by an older gentleman who cleans all my wounds and stitches two of them. He doesn't ask any questions and takes the extra hundred I offer to keep it that way.

Exhausted, we head home and lie in bed together. With the back wall pushed open, a cool breeze drifts through the room and the sound of the waves crashing against the shore lulls us. I ask her about last night. Kat tells me that Callista shot and killed Natasha. She and her mother bandaged me up to make sure the bleeding stopped before dragging me to bed. After Officer Mendez took care of Natasha, they cleaned the house, erasing all evidence.

"Not bad for a computer nerd and her mom, right?" she asks.

"Not bad for anyone, Kat. You could have a new career on your hands," I tease.

She traces the inked lines down my chest and rests her hand over the compass on my hip.

"I love you, Samuel Lucas Ozley."

The newness of those words has me grinning and for once, I don't care that someone can see how vulnerable I am.

"I didn't tell you my real name just so that it could be used against me in moments of weakness." She shakes her head and licks her lips before kissing the underside of my chin. "I love you too."

Kat lies on the sofa, reading a book. Her hair is up in a messy knot, glasses perched on her nose. I sit on the end with her feet in my lap, content to just be near her. I check the clock on the wall for the time again. My knee bounces up and down, vibrating us both.

"Samuel, I can't read when it feels like I'm in the middle of an earthquake," she says looking over her book at me.

"Sorry, Cupcake."

She makes a face at my pet name and returns her attention to the book. Apparently, I still haven't found the right one.

It's been a month since our brush with Natasha. As promised, Callista returned with the key and handed it over to the police, claiming she found it in Dennis' belongings. They questioned her recent trip to Mexico, which was suspicious with a daughter on the run. Callista worked out a deal on Kat's behalf, telling them everything she knew about the stolen money. They were able to arrest Marilyn for embezzlement and a few other white-collar crimes. She's currently in prison awaiting trial because her husband refuses to bail her out. Kat's not free and clear in the eyes of the law, but they won't be spending any more time on the hunt for her.

Kat and I, finally free from fear, have settled in nicely. It's a completely different path than any I'd ever envisioned walking, but I wouldn't change a thing.

A loud knock echoes through the house. She looks to the door, then back to me.

"You expecting someone?" Kat asks.

"I don't know. You should go see."

Kat grins and hops up, skipping to the door. I watch her ass in those shorts and tamp down the beast inside me that always wants to claim her.

"Surprise!" Kelli's squealing shout fills the empty house.

"Oh my God!" Kat says, pulling Jack in for a hug. "Come in!"

Jack picks up Kat and swings her around, his left hand drifts down to the curve of her ass as he looks over her shoulder at me.

"That's enough," I say, standing to greet them.

"Jack, stop teasing Sammy," Kelli says.

He puts Kat down and she pulls in close to me.

"Oz, you need to lighten up, bitch," Jack says, smirking.

"Fuck off," I answer, giving him a hug and Kelli a kiss on the cheek.

"What are you guys doing here?" Kat finally asks.

"Sammy thought you could use some girl bonding time," Kelli answers.

Kat smiles and bounces on her toes, clapping her hands together. She leans up and kisses me.

"Thank you," she whispers.

After all greetings are out of the way, we sit ourselves around the patio table.

"I'm so glad you guys are here!" Kat squeals. "We can go shopping and get our hair braided, drink margaritas, ride jet skis, go out to Lovers Beach."

"Sounds great," Kelli says. "I definitely need to work on my tan."

The girls laugh and Jack rolls his eyes.

In that instant, I feel so relieved, so at peace. Not only am I fortunate enough to have someone to spend my future with, but I've also got the only important people from my past. I take a swig of beer and think about how I must be the luckiest asshole alive.

"So, let's have details," Jack says. "Two days after you guys left, word spread like wildfire that the best of the best had finally met his end. And at the hand of Natasha, too."

"I told you it was just a rumor! I didn't believe it for one second," Kelli chimes in.

"Of course you didn't," Jack says, swatting at her curly ponytail.

For the next hour or so, Kat and I relive the details of our trip through Mexico and our brush with Natasha. We take turns telling each part, exchanging knowing glances when we exclude intimate details.

"That's crazy," Jack says, leaning back in his chair.

"So, then, you're both staying here? Together?" Kelli asks.

I grin at Kat and nod. Even though we've always had a choice, time and time again, we chose each other. Kat returns my smile and slides her fingers between mine. Her eyes say everything I already know. In the oddest of circumstances, in the darkest of hours, I saved her life and in return, she saved me right back.